Spoiled

Spoiled

Ann Barker

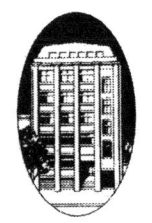

ROBERT HALE · LONDON

© Ann Barker 2010
First published in Great Britain 2010

ISBN 978-0-7090-8968-1

Robert Hale Limited
Clerkenwell House
Clerkenwell Green
London EC1R 0HT

www.halebooks.com

2 4 6 8 10 9 7 5 3 1

Typeset in 10/13pt Sabon
Printed in Great Britain by the
MPG Books Group, Bodmin and King's Lynn

Dedication

For my own Michael, without whose encouragement and support neither this book nor the others that preceded it would have seen the light of day.

Acknowledgement

Once again, my grateful thanks to Sir Richard FitzHerbert for his fine stewardship of the delightful village of Tissington and Tissington Hall.

Prologue

Christmas 1767

'Well sir? I understand that you wish to see me on some … *important* matter.' Michael, Lord Ashbourne sat easily in the chair behind his desk, rocking backwards gently. His expression as he stared at his sixteen-year-old son was completely unreadable. Most men would have looked upon such a young man with pride. He was an exceedingly handsome boy, tall and upright, his shoulders already broadening into manhood. His straight black hair was gathered into a queue, and his regular features were finely marked. In appearance, he was very like the earl had been at that age.

'I do, my lord,' Raphael replied. He had never called this man father. Such intimacy had not been encouraged. Nor had he ever approached him upon any matter if he could possibly help it. On this occasion, however, the case was urgent, and concerned his whole future happiness. He swallowed. 'I would like to inform you … that I wish to be married.'

To his surprise, his father smiled. It was not a pleasant expression. 'Excellent,' he said. 'It is what I have been planning for you myself.' He stood up. A full head taller than his son, he was very lean, and still a handsome man, although his dark hair was now grey, and there were deep lines riven upon his face. 'My negotiations with Clement Vyse have been concluded and now that I know how eager you are, your engagement to Miss Vyse can be announced immediately.'

The expression on Raphael's face changed from relief at his first words to consternation. Lord Ashbourne turned away to take a pinch of snuff. He smiled maliciously to himself. 'Is that idea to your liking?' he asked, his tone deceptively mild.

'I ... I ...' To be in his father's presence was so acutely unpleasant that for two pins, Raphael would have ended the interview there and then. He remembered in time that another person was affected. He straightened his shoulders. 'The announcement of an engagement I welcome, my lord,' he said. 'It is the identity of my bride on which we differ.'

'Indeed?' Lord Ashbourne's tone remained utterly calm. 'May one be so bold as to enquire the identity of the young lady who has caught your eye?'

'Her name is Dora Whitton,' answered Raphael.

'I see. Is she perhaps the sister of one of your fellow pupils at school? I should like to know her lineage.'

'Her family is perfectly respectable,' Raphael answered.

There was a long silence. Lord Ashbourne sighed. 'You mean that her family is quite impossible.'

'Her father is a farmer,' said Raphael hastily, then coloured.

'I see. So we are talking about a farm wench, are we? I fail to see the purpose of this conversation. If you want the wench, go and make use of her. That is what such girls are for. But pray do not confuse a roll in the hay with a suitable marriage alliance. Now take yourself off, sir. You are beginning to try my patience.'

'No, my lord.'

Very, very slowly, the earl turned his head to look at his son. On his face was an expression of icy cold rage mingled with contempt. 'What?' he whispered. Ashbourne never raised his voice. He made his anger felt in other ways.

Raphael was as white as a sheet, but he did not lower his head. 'I am pledged to Dora,' he answered. 'I love her and ... and she is carrying my child.'

The earl laughed unpleasantly. 'Then she's clearly a slut. I suppose I should be glad that you have proved your manhood; but this is where it ends. You will not see the creature again, you will not marry her, and your engagement to Laura Vyse will be announced immediately.'

'It does *not* end here,' Raphael answered. 'I *will* marry Dora with or without your permission, and Laura Vyse can go hang!' He strode out of the room, banging the door behind him.

Lord Ashbourne rang his personal bell, not the one which would summon a footman, but one which brought a burly, brutish-looking individual into his presence. 'My son needs to be taught some manners,' he said. 'Flog him within an inch of his life, but don't spoil his pretty face, or his ... ah ... equipment. We don't want his bride disappointed.'

Half an hour later, he wandered down to the stables where his son lay sprawled in one of the stalls, his clothes ripped, his back a bloody mess. 'I hope you have now learned obedience,' he said calmly, his expression quite unmoved. 'If not, I will make sure that your – Dora, was it? – gets the same treatment.'

'Bastard,' Raphael croaked.

'Perhaps; but I'm not a fool. To prevent you from making some futile, gallant gesture, I will make sure that *your* bastard is provided for; but from now on, you will do as I say.' He walked out and left his son bleeding on the ground.

Dora Whitton did not much care what happened to her after Raphael had deserted her. She had half guessed what must have happened when he failed to communicate with her as he had said he would. A short time later, a message was delivered to her father's farm by a groom in livery. It informed her that Raphael had just become engaged to be married. There would be an allowance provided for the child she was carrying until it reached the age of majority. She would not see Raphael again. She must not attempt to seek him out, or she would lose the money.

This was the first that her parents had heard of her pregnancy and they were outraged. A respectable family, they had hoped that she would enable them to move up in the world, perhaps by marrying the son of the local squire. Now, the danger was that they would all be dragged down by her disgrace. Carefully they made plans and, in a very short space of time, before the pregnancy had begun to show, Dora was sent to stay with distant relatives, with the instruction that she should be taught to behave herself. The consequence was that she found herself little better than a skivvy.

It was late one Sunday afternoon when the vicar, The Revd Paul Buckleigh came to the house to find out why the family had not attended church. Approaching from the side entrance, he found an enchantingly pretty but heavily pregnant young woman struggling with a bucketful of scraps for the pigs, and he hurried to relieve her of her burden. Kindly brown eyes met weary hazel ones and the vicar was filled with compassion. Just a few short weeks later, not long after her son had been born, Dora Whitton became Dora Buckleigh.

Chapter One

———⟨⟨◦⟩⟩———

Evangeline Granby was in disgrace and, on this occasion, she really did not think that it was her fault. She had never enjoyed visiting her uncle's family in Sheffield, because odious comparisons were always made between herself and her two cousins, Phyllida and Deidre.

'You never saw such obliging, obedient girls,' her aunt, Mrs Frean, was often heard to remark. Then she would turn to Evangeline's mother and add, in pitying tones, 'What a shame that you cannot say the same. It is your own fault, I fear. You spoiled that girl, now look at her.'

In her most honest moments, Evangeline was prepared to admit that she had been spoiled, but when such spoiling resulted in pretty dresses, outings to places of her choice, and petting and fussing, she would have been a fool to object. An only child, she had almost died in infancy and, as a consequence, had been indulged ever since. Her father called her his angel and thought that nothing was too good for her. Her mother was not strong enough to exert her will against her daughter. As for her aunt's opinion, it mattered to her not one whit.

Phyllida's engagement had brought about another set of comparisons. 'What have you been about, Matilda, to allow that girl to be so indulged? How many London seasons has she had? Two, or is it three? And not an engagement to show for it. Phyllida has secured an eligible match without even leaving Sheffield. It is time you put your foot down and insisted that she make up her mind. How old is she now? Twenty? Twenty-one? I'll not deny she's a beauty, although perhaps a little too overblown, but she'll be on the shelf before you know it.'

To such comments as these, Evangeline affected an air of carelessness, but in fact she was deeply annoyed. What business was it of Aunt

Frean's whether she was married or not? The silly woman only wanted to compare her unfavourably with her daughters.

Inevitably, the day of the wedding arrived and Evangeline, effortlessly exerting her own will as usual, contrived to appear in a stunning gown of shimmering pink silk which cast the apparel of every other lady present into the shade, including that of the bride. Even the bridegroom stared at her with his eyes nearly out on stalks. Mrs Frean's disapproval was obvious, but tempered with satisfaction, since at least she had one daughter safely married.

'And good riddance too,' Evangeline muttered to herself, as the wedding barouche carrying Mr and Mrs Vernon Battle disappeared out of sight. From now on, they would be living upon Mr Battle's estate in Wiltshire. As far as Evangeline was concerned, Cornwall, or the Outer Hebrides, would have been even better, but at least she would no longer be within easy reach for purposes of comparison.

Once the bride and bridegroom had gone, the guests settled down to further conversation, and Evangeline soon found herself being monopolized by a slim, olive-complexioned young man with a ready wit and sparkling brown eyes. They managed to disappear into a corner for a desperate flirtation, which raised Evangeline's spirits considerably. Unfortunately, the young man in question was the Honourable William Jaye, of whom Mrs Frean had had hopes concerning her younger daughter. Thanks to Evangeline's behaviour, Deidre was now in her room, crying her eyes out. What did Evangeline intend to do about it?

'I shall go out for a walk,' Evangeline replied. 'If I am not wanted here, then I shall take myself off.'

'Evangeline, dearest,' murmured her mother in harassed tones.

'You are forbidden to go,' said Mrs Frean sternly. 'Your place is here, with your family. You will apologize to Deirdre *and* to Mr Jaye, and then you will go to your room.'

Stamping her foot at Mrs Frean would not yield positive results, as Evangeline had learned from experience long ago. She was beyond that now. Instead, she executed a demure curtsy and went upstairs. She did not go to Deidre's room, however. Instead, she went to her own chamber and rang the bell for Elsie, her abigail. She was not quite sure what to do, but as she had been told to go to her room, she was determined that she should not remain there.

While she was waiting for Elsie, she picked up a book which she had been given by her friend Lady Ilam at the last wedding celebration that she had attended. This had been the party that had been held at

Ashbourne Abbey following the private wedding of Lord and Lady Ashbourne in London. Evangeline had made friends with Lady Ilam when, as Miss Eustacia Hope, she had come to stay in the village of Illingham near Evangeline's home. It was here that she had met her future husband, Lord Ilam, whose father was the Earl of Ashbourne.

At some point during the festivities, Evangeline had evaded her usual string of admirers and found a quiet place where she sat in rather wistful thought. She was younger than Lady Ashbourne by ten years, and prettier than Lady Ilam; yet they were each married to the man of their choice whilst she remained single. Would there ever be the right man for her?

Lady Ilam had interrupted her reverie by coming to sit next to her, a book in her hand. 'I've something for you,' she had said, holding it out to her friend.

Evangeline had taken it, pulling a face at the title. '*A Vindication of the Rights of Woman*. Sad stuff!'

'Scoff if you like,' Lady Ilam had replied, 'but I met and married Ilam soon after it came into my possession. Then I passed it on to Jessie, and shortly after that, she married Lord Ashbourne. She's given it back to me, so I am passing it on to you. Who knows what may happen?'

Evangeline opened it now and idly began turning the pages. Most of it seemed to be saying how silly women were on account of their upbringing. 'Sad stuff,' she said again out loud. She was about to lay it down again when her eye lit upon the following lines:

English women whose time is spent in making caps, bonnets, and the whole mischief of trimmings, not to mention shopping, bargain-hunting, &c. &c.

'Excellent!' she exclaimed, as Elsie came in. 'That book has some sensible observations to make after all. We'll go shopping.' With Elsie's help she donned the pretty bonnet and pelisse that she had been wearing earlier, and slipped out of the house with her maid in tow.

'Where're we going, miss?' Elsie asked. She had been Evangeline's maid ever since the young woman had had an abigail of her own and was her regular co-conspirator.

'Anywhere but here,' Evangeline replied. For a time she walked briskly, leaving the elegance of Paradise Square and heading for the main shopping thoroughfare. She was furious at the injustice of her aunt's accusation. She had had no idea that her cousin was interested in Mr Jaye. Had she known she would have kept away from him, for

although spoiled, she was a good-natured girl, but the alacrity with
which he had born his part in the flirtation led her to believe that the
interest was probably one sided. 'In which case, I have done her a
favour,' she said, speaking her thoughts out loud.

'Pardon, miss?' asked Elsie, a little out of breath. Evangeline was
taller than she was and had almost left her behind.

'Never mind,' Evangeline replied, slowing down. 'Let's look at the
shops, shall we? If you see a ribbon you like, then you may have it.'

Elsie smiled. People might say that Miss Evangeline was spoiled, and
perhaps they were right, but she had a kinder heart than some. She'd
been shopping with Miss Phyllida – Mrs Battle as she was now – and
Miss Deidre, and neither of them had ever thought of getting her
anything, or considering her wishes in any way.

It was not long before Evangeline realized that she was attracting
some attention. This was partly because she was still clad in her silk
dress, a gown that was not entirely suitable for shopping. It also had a
good deal to do with the fact that she was a remarkably pretty young
woman who would look attractive whatever she was wearing. She was
too used to her rather exotic good looks to find the attention disturbing.
It was while she was looking at bonnets in a milliner's window, however,
that she felt a prickling sensation in the back of her neck and, turning
round, she saw that she was being carefully observed from the other side
of the street. A tall, broad-shouldered man with ash-blond hair and
rather startling black eyebrows was watching her. He was in black coat
and breeches, his shirt open at the neck, the whole covered with a drab
grey greatcoat, and with his hat tilted rakishly to one side. As she looked
at him, he grinned, took off his hat, and bowed slightly. She had never
seen him before, yet there was something about his graceful stance that
put her in mind of the dissolute Earl of Ashbourne, with whom she had
briefly been infatuated a few years before.

Evangeline was a well-brought up girl, if over-indulged, and she
knew that for this unknown young man to acknowledge her in the street
was an impertinence which she should most certainly ignore. No doubt
she would have done so, had her mind not still been full of resentment
at the way that her aunt had assumed the worst of her. With a fleeting
thought in her mind that if she was thought to be badly behaved, she
might as well be so, she directed a smile at him from under her lashes,
looked down, then turned back to the window, to all intents and
purposes once more absorbed in the wares on display. Moments later,
he was at her elbow.

The Revd Michael Buckleigh had come away from the bishop's palace in no good mood. He had been summoned thither to explain himself, and was now obliged to kick his heels until sent for.

It had all started so well. The parish to which he had gone as curate two years before had been one to which he had been recommended by his stepfather, The Revd Paul Buckleigh. The vicar under whom he was serving had been pleasant enough, but he never seemed to be available when advice was needed. Michael could certainly have done with some help with regard to young women in the parish, who were rather prone to take a fancy to the striking young curate.

The local squire's daughter was already engaged, but, without the slightest encouragement, she had conceived a passion for the new clergyman. This had resulted in her fiancé picking a fight with him, undoubtedly expecting that he would enjoy an easy victory over his rival. Had that happened, perhaps he would have let the matter rest. Buckleigh, however, was proficient in boxing, for he had been coached by a fellow student at Oxford in return for help in learning Greek. The young lady's fiancé, therefore, had been laid out unconscious on the grass, his father had complained, and Michael had been removed by his bishop.

The second curacy had seemed to be going so much better. He had now learned how to be friendly whilst at the same time keeping a careful distance, and he had thought that his troubles were over. As time had gone by, Michael had become aware yet again that women, particularly the younger ones, were choosing to see him, the curate, rather than to see the vicar. At first, he had thought that this was simply a recurrence of what had happened before and he redoubled his efforts to be courteous, if a little distant. It was not until one of the young men had confided in him that the vicar, a married man with a family, had become over-familiar with his sweetheart, that he realized, with a sinking heart, that there was a serious problem. With considerable trepidation, Michael had attempted to approach the matter tactfully with his vicar, but had met with a cold response. Eventually, he had found the older clergyman forcing his attentions on a young woman, and he had lost his temper, going so far as to bend the vicar over his own desk, and tan his backside with a yard rule.

The consequence was almost inevitable. The bishop had sent for him and given him a good dressing-down. 'It is not for you to take the law into your own hands, Buckleigh,' the bishop had said, swelling with indignation. 'This is not proper behaviour for a clergyman. You have been very much at fault in this matter! Very much at fault! Now, it falls to me to consider what to do with you. Who will have you now, do you suppose? Very few vicars will relish the prospect of having a curate who may lay violent hands upon them. Remember that this is not the first time that you have blotted your copybook through violence. I shall have to weigh this matter very carefully. Very carefully. As for you, you had better wait at your lodgings so that I may consult with my chaplain and others. Whilst you are waiting for me to send for you, I suggest you pray that I do not have you unfrocked!'

It was with some difficulty that Michael had swallowed the hasty words that were on the tip of his tongue. Protesting his innocence would not have done anything other than make the bishop even more incensed with him. Had it just been himself in the case he would have been sorely tempted to tell his superior to go hang, but he had his stepfather and his little sister to consider.

He had never known his natural father who, he had heard somewhere, he could not remember when, was a nobleman who had deserted his mother before he was born. In order to hide her disgrace, his mother's family had sent her to distant relatives who had treated her as a servant. It had been The Revd Paul Buckleigh who had noticed the quiet, dainty, angelically fair young woman and, acting in an impulsive way that was very unlike him, had persuaded her to become his wife. He was the only father that Michael had ever known.

The Revd Paul Buckleigh had not found it easy to be a family man. Thirty years older than his bride, he had not expected to marry. He had never encouraged Michael to call him father, although he had given him his name, and his manner towards his stepson had always been that of a firm but kindly schoolmaster. There had only been one child born from the union, a girl whose birth had taken her mother's life when Michael was ten.

After her death, the bereaved husband had retreated into his study, leaving the upbringing of the children, and particularly of the new baby, to the servants. As time went by, he had gradually emerged from his isolation and had continued to tutor Michael in Greek, Latin, and mathematics, before sending him to Charterhouse to continue his education. This had been funded by money forwarded from Michael's father's family through a firm of solicitors.

Michael had always been informed that he owed his place at Charterhouse to a scholarship, which had indeed helped considerably with the cost. Having no interest in the man who had fathered him, he had not thought to ask any questions about where the money for his remaining needs had come from. When eventually he did make enquiries, he was furious to think that his education should have been partly paid for by a man for whom he had no respect. By then, however, the deed had been done, and he was realistic enough to acknowledge that a good education was essential if he was to make his own way in the world.

At Charterhouse, his good humour and generous nature had gained him some good friends, several of whom went on with him to Oxford. His stepfather had continued to coach him in the holidays. He had also encouraged him to read very widely. The texts that Michael enjoyed the most were those that were to do with foreign countries. He could not imagine how he would ever be able to afford to travel himself, unless he were to gain a position as bear-leader to some scion of a noble house. That did not stop him from reading all kinds of travel writings, and studying maps and drawings of various artefacts. The pictures of ancient ruins, statues and all kinds of pottery were the things that captured his imagination the most. This interest had been nurtured by a most unlikely friendship.

As a boy of fourteen, he had been sent to a secluded mansion with a message from his stepfather for a reclusive neighbour named James Warrener. He had been told to wait in a room that was full of statuary. When Warrener had come into the room, he had found Michael gently stroking the stone drapery which the artist had carved as a dressing for the statue of a Roman goddess.

'You like it, boy?' the man had asked gently. His heavily lined face made him seem ancient to the boy, but he could not have been much more than sixty.

'It's beautiful, sir,' Michael had replied. 'I can hardly believe that it's really stone. It has so much movement in it.' He blushed, fearing that he had said something foolish.

There were those who might have told the lad to keep his hands to himself. Warrener, however, having the wisdom to see that here was a fellow enthusiast, had shown Michael all round his collection. Henceforward, he had taught him all that he knew about pottery; had shown him how to handle it correctly and with knowledge. He had also encouraged the boy not to feel sorry for himself because of his circum-stances. 'You don't know how fortunate you are,' Warrener had said on one occasion when Michael had been inclined to bemoan his fate. 'Some of the fellows you attend school with are constrained by their position, and will one day be obliged to rule over estates whether they care to do so or not. You are free from such obligations.'

Yes, he had not been subject to those constraints; but there had been others. It had been partly to please his stepfather that he had decided to take orders, for example, and he had gone to Oxford to study for his degree. There he had kicked over the traces a little, spent some time with a wild set and frightened himself by losing a large sum of money in gaming. The following night, he had managed to recoup his losses and had resolved never to gamble again, a resolve to which he had adhered without ever having been tempted to do otherwise.

While at university, he had also discovered that he was attractive to women. He was not personally vain, but he could interpret what he saw in the mirror and had begun to realize from his late adolescence that ash-blond hair combined dramatically with black, well-arched brows, chiselled features and a fine physique together produced a package that was appealing to women. He might think his looks rather peculiar, but this did not seem to deter them; quite the contrary. For a time, as part of his rebellion after leaving home, he had made the most of his sexual appeal. Then he had discovered that the indulgence of this particular appetite broke hearts. At much the same time, he realized that to be a womanizer was not fitting behaviour for a clergyman. Thereafter he had taken great care to be moderate and discreet in satisfying his physical needs.

He had finally managed to gain a more than respectable degree and had taken up his curacy with the air of a man shouldering an unpleasant duty. To his surprise, he had found much satisfaction in visiting people, listening to their problems and having them refer to him in time of need. He had even found that the creative part of his mind gained pleasure from writing sermons! Then, not once but twice, and not entirely through his own fault, everything had come crashing down upon his head. He had no idea what he would do if the bishop declared that he must be unfrocked. His stepfather would be horrified and he himself would be denied the means of earning a livelihood which would support his sister in time to come.

Needing to shake off the constraint of behaving like a clergyman, he returned to the modest inn where he was staying and pulled off the high stock that he was wearing. Then, with the neck of his shirt raffishly open, he sauntered out into the street. Everywhere he looked he seemed to see carefree faces. Did anyone have the threat of disgrace hanging over them as did he?

Suddenly, on this dull day amid the drab stonework and serviceable walking clothes, he saw a flash of pink. An entrancingly beautiful young woman in a most unsuitable gown was walking down the street accompanied by her maid. She had lustrous fair hair and he would have been prepared to bet that her eyes were blue. Her gown and pelisse fitted her admirably, bringing out the sculptured perfection of her figure. The vivid shade of what she was wearing contrasted strongly with her surroundings. It was as if an artist, having executed a pen and ink sketch, suddenly decided to add a perfect rose in oils.

Who was she? Briefly, he wondered whether she could possibly be a street-walker. He dismissed this idea almost as soon as it came into his mind. Her maid was with her for one thing. For another, her carriage was elegant and graceful rather than bold, and her gown expensive rather than tawdry. Her very loveliness made him want to smile. Then she turned and saw him. He bowed, fixing her with a mischievous grin. What would she do? A street-walker would approach him. A well-brought-up young lady would ignore him. She did neither; but instead, directed a saucy smile at him before looking away. She was wilful, then, and probably eager for a flirtation.

This was only his third brief visit to Sheffield and he was not likely to be recognized. Thankfully forgetting about the bishop and looming disgrace, if only for the time being, he crossed the road and approached her, preparing to enjoy himself. 'A fine day, Miss...?'

'I do not know whether I should tell you, sir,' Evangeline replied coyly. 'We have not been introduced.'

'Then allow me to do the honours,' he said. 'Michael Leigh at your service, ma'am.'

'Miss Evan—' put in Elsie, horrified, but breaking off with a shriek as her mistress stamped on her toe.

'Miss Evans,' said Evangeline, taking advantage of Elsie's slip. 'Jessica Evans.'

'A charming name,' said Michael. 'May I have the honour of escorting you anywhere? Do you intend to purchase a bonnet today? I am happy to offer advice, although I cannot believe that it will be possible to find one that would become you better than that charming confection that you are wearing now.'

'Flatterer,' Evangeline replied, glancing up at him through her lashes. She liked tall men. 'I am simply looking in the windows today. To tell you the truth ...' She paused.

'Yes, ma'am?' he prompted her.

'To tell you the truth, today has been perfectly horrid so far and I am anxious for it to improve.'

He laughed. 'Why, so it has been for me as well. What has been your particular misfortune?'

She thought for a moment. It was very unlikely that she would meet him again, but she had no wish to disclose anything that might mean that he could identify her. Even mentioning a wedding could do that, for how many weddings would have taken place in Sheffield today? 'I have been blamed for something that was not my fault, and given no chance to explain myself.'

He thought about his experience with the philandering vicar and grinned ruefully. 'You might be describing my own case,' he answered. 'But let us forget about that. I little thought when the day began that it would be brightened by an encounter with a beautiful woman.'

She laughed. 'I am sure you did not, sir; for my part I could never have imagined that your day would be brightened in such a way either.'

He laughed out loud, took hold of her hand and tucked it in the crook of his arm. 'Let us stroll about a little and forget our cares. Then I'll take you somewhere to have a drink.' Elsie uttered a squawk of dismay, but could only follow in their wake as they walked together, talking and laughing.

Eventually, they came to a small inn, hidden away behind some of the shops. 'Come inside and have some wine with me,' he said, his tone one of bold invitation.

'Oh, no, miss,' said Elsie. 'Think of what your aunt would say.'

Until that moment, Evangeline had been undecided as to what to do. Conscience told her that she had already gone her length, and that to go into an inn with this young man would destroy her reputation if anyone ever found out. The mention of her aunt effectively killed the voice of conscience.

'You can wait in the hall, Elsie,' said Evangeline. 'Come in and find me if … if … well, you know.'

'A private parlour, if you please,' Michael said to the landlord, 'and bring us a bottle of claret.' The landlord showed them to a small room at the side of the inn, furnished with a table, four dining chairs, and two comfortable chairs with arms, set either side of the fireplace in which burned a cheery blaze, welcome on a March day that was not of the sunniest.

Evangeline was pleased that he had assumed she would drink wine. She was very tired of people like her aunt insisting that she must have lemonade or tea. She was nearly twenty-one, after all!

When the wine arrived, Michael poured them a glass each, and said, 'To the future. May those who misjudge us see the error of their ways.' They clinked glasses, drank, smiled at each other and drank again. Then Michael took Evangeline's glass from her, set it down on the table along with his own, and, not really to her surprise, pulled her into his arms. She gave a little gasp. He was very strong. 'Do you mind?' he asked, slanting his head, and bending towards her, his eyes on her lips.

'No,' she replied, adding daringly, 'I should mind if you didn't.' Then he kissed her, briefly and tantalizingly at first, before covering her mouth with his, and ravishing her senses with a long, passionate kiss.

Evangeline was no stranger to flirtation and this was not the first time that she had been kissed. Never had any caress been as demanding or powerful as this, however. His tongue running gently across her lips coaxed her into opening her mouth, and then he deepened his kiss, the seductive nature of his caress impelling her to wrap her arms around his neck and return his embrace. When eventually he released her they were both a little breathless.

Evangeline, realizing the enormity of her behaviour, coloured and turned her head away. He released her, then gave her back her glass, from which she took a deep gulp. He eyed her ruefully. He was aroused enough to feel a strong desire to take her upstairs to bed, but that blush, together with other aspects of their conversation, had convinced him that she was not sexually experienced. She was a young lady – perhaps rather badly behaved, and probably somewhat spoiled but a lady none the less – who was out on an adventure. He could not take advantage of her, much though he might desire to do so.

He took a sip of his wine, then waited until she was looking at him. 'Delicious,' he said, touching his lip with his tongue.

She laughed self-consciously. 'Likewise,' she replied.

She had only one more glass, leaving him the rest, and while they drank they talked idly of this and that, both of them carefully avoiding personal subjects. Eventually, she said, 'I think I must leave you, sir. Elsie will be having a fit by now and I may have been missed.'

'*I* will certainly miss you,' he replied. He took a step closer to her. 'One more?' he suggested. She slid into his arms, and they kissed, not passionately, but tenderly and almost with affection. 'You have made my day brighter,' he said. 'I will not forget you, Miss Evans.'

'Nor will I you, Mr Leigh,' Evangeline replied, before donning her bonnet and leaving the room.

Chapter Two

$\sim\!\!\infty\!\!\sim$

Michael Buckleigh stood looking out of the rain-splattered window of the taproom and silently thanked divine providence that he had reached the inn in the dry. It was a cold wet evening in March. It seemed as though the weather, conscious that winter was now over, wanted to give of its very worst one last time, as if to warn travellers that they could never hope to win. He himself was particularly vulnerable at present, since his old horse had recently expired and his income did not yet permit him to purchase another.

His encounter with the ravishingly pretty blonde had lifted his spirits, encouraging him to believe that good things could be just around the corner. He had therefore returned to the bishop's palace the following day in a spirit of optimism, on this occasion with his high stock in place, and his hair caught tidily behind his head with a black ribbon.

As he had sat waiting in an anteroom, the bishop's chaplain had walked through the room and he had sprung to his feet. The chaplain, a tall, thin, fair man – although not as fair as he was himself – had paused next to him and looked curiously into his face. Slightly resenting his scrutiny, although not knowing why, Michael had raised his brows and lifted his chin a little. An arrested expression had crossed the other clergyman's face before he had disappeared into the bishop's study.

A short time afterwards, Michael had been called back in and told that he was to be the curate of Illingham village, serving under the vicar, Henry Lusty, who also happened to be the bishop's chaplain. He had left the palace much relieved. He would perhaps have been a little more wary had he been privy to the conversation that had taken place between the bishop and Mr Lusty.

'Well, Lusty, what are we to do with the fellow?' the bishop had asked, when his chaplain had seated himself at his superior's behest. 'He cannot possibly go back to where he was. Pettigrew would not have him, I have been reliably informed.'

'I am not surprised, my lord,' Lusty had answered. 'To offer violence to one's vicar is very shocking.'

'Undoubtedly,' the bishop had agreed leaning forward, his elbows on his desk, his fingers steepled before him. 'Were it not for Paul Buckleigh, I would almost certainly have him unfrocked, especially after that last incident. However, I have a good deal of respect for Mr Buckleigh, so I must accommodate this fellow in some way, even though I would much rather be rid of him. Do you have any ideas?'

'I think so,' Mr Lusty had replied, leaning back with a little smile on his lips. 'I have a suggestion that I believe might at one stroke rid us of Mr Buckleigh, and bring Illingham into your full control.'

The bishop took a deep breath. 'Then you would indeed be a prince among chaplains, my dear Lusty.' It had for many years been a source of irritation to the bishops of Sheffield that the gift of the parish of Illingham had to be shared between the church and Lord Ashbourne. In the event of a dispute over the candidate, the earl of the day would have a second vote. Ever since a previous bishop had brought about such a state of affairs through reckless gambling, his successors had resented being obliged to take second place to the earls of Ashbourne. To be able to change this situation in the church's favour would be a coup indeed.

'Have you ever met Lord Ashbourne, my lord?' Lusty asked.

'No, I have not,' replied the bishop, 'although I have engaged in very unsatisfactory correspondence with him. I have met his son briefly. Stay, though,' he added thoughtfully. 'Was it not Ashbourne who...?' He paused delicately.

'Yes, you are right,' Lusty answered, a little tight-lipped. 'It was Lord Ashbourne who married Miss Warburton whilst she was still engaged to me. I have met him on several occasions, and I must tell you that I have a suspicion that the young man waiting outside may be intimately related to him.'

'Indeed!' exclaimed the bishop in arrested tones.

'It is only a suspicion,' Lusty repeated, raising one hand. 'The likeness is not strong, but eyebrows like his are often a feature in members of the Ashbourne clan. In height and build he is very like the earl. Not only that, but when I ventured to look at him more closely, he raised his chin in an arrogant gesture that could not but put one in mind of Lord

Ashbourne. I have an inkling that he may be one of his lordship's – hem – love children.'

'Indeed! What, then, do you suggest?' asked the bishop.

'Since I have been appointed to the parish of Illingham, I have found myself unable to carry out my duties here in the palace as well as I would like. I wonder whether he might act as my curate there?'

'As your curate,' murmured the bishop, beginning to smile. 'My dear Lusty, how very Machiavellian. If Buckleigh is indeed related to the earl, then Ashbourne, or his son who resides in Illingham, will recognize this … ah … unofficial relative, and will be anxious to hide the scandal. *I* will only agree to remove him if Ashbourne signs his vote over to the church of England in perpetuity.'

'On the other hand,' Lusty put in, 'even if I am wrong, young Buckleigh, who seems to have a tendency to blot his copybook, will no doubt entrance some other village maiden with his rather strange good looks and cause another scandal. He will have failed for a third time. Not even Paul Buckleigh will expect you to find him a fourth curacy, so you will have an excuse to be rid of him permanently.'

'Don't put it like that, Henry,' answered the bishop. 'You make it sound as if I was going to have him murdered.' They both laughed. 'I'm sure I could find some far distant, obscure diocese that would have him, or perhaps some missionary work? I hear that America needs priests. What if he succeeds, though, and proves to be the model parish priest?'

'He will be eternally grateful to both of us for giving him another chance and will be falling over himself to oblige us. We cannot lose.'

'Well then send him in, Lusty. Let's break the good news.'

Quite unaware of the scheme that had been hatched against him, Michael had left the bishop's palace with a spring in his step. From there he had travelled to tell his stepfather and sister what had happened. The Revd Paul Buckleigh was delighted. He had been invited to join a party of academics travelling to Greece to inspect some ancient sites. He intended to give up his parish and take up an academic career in Oxford on his return. Michael's sister, Theodora, could have no place in such a future, and the older clergyman had been hoping to see her settled with her brother before leaving for the Continent. Thanks to Michael's new appointment, this might now be possible. Much would depend on the accommodation that was made available for him.

Resolved to save as much money as possible in order to make a home for his sister, Michael had set out to walk to Illingham. On the first day he had had a stroke of luck when a carter had taken him up and enabled him to break the back of the journey. On the following day he had met up with an acquaintance of his stepfather who had given him a ride in his carriage. The day after that he had been obliged to walk. It had been fine to start with and he had made good progress. The weather had begun to deteriorate at about the time when he was thinking of taking shelter for the night, and he had entered The Pheasant with the first droplets of rain standing out upon his hat and the shoulders of his greatcoat.

He was feeling rather hungry but, constantly aware of the need to economize, he ordered a bowl of soup, which he decided to eat downstairs rather than alone in the room that had been prepared for him. The only company to be had was that of the landlord himself, for the evening was far too unpleasant for anyone to be out except on essential errands.

The inn was rather a small establishment, not really suitable for the entertainment of the quality, for there were not many bedrooms and no private parlour, guests who had no liking for the taproom being obliged to dine in the privacy of their chambers.

'Nasty night, Reverend,' the landlord remarked, setting down the glass of wine that the young clergyman had ordered.

'It certainly is; but we have the best of it here,' Buckleigh replied with a smile, glancing at the roaring fire.

'Far to go?'

'I am to take up a curacy in the parish of Illingham.'

'You've another ten miles, then.'

Michael sighed. He did not object to walking and had indeed accomplished the journey from Oxford to his father's parish on many occasions on foot. A ten-mile walk with a cloak bag on water-logged roads, possibly with the rain still falling, did not appeal to him very much, however. At least his trunk with his books and the rest of his belongings had been sent on ahead, so he did not need to worry about them. He was about to ask whether the landlord knew of anyone who might be going his way in the morning, when the door of the inn opened, the draught causing the fire to writhe convulsively and the candles to shudder in their brackets.

'House!' The voice was undoubtedly that of a gentleman.

Before the landlord could respond, however, a lady added imperiously, 'I doubt whether there is anyone able to provide for our needs in this shabby hovel, Papa.'

'There must be,' the gentleman replied. 'Mama cannot possibly travel on in this weather.'

The landlord hurried through wiping his hands on his apron. Michael heard him respond to his visitor's request by asking how he might be of service. He pricked up his ears, for there had been something about the voice of the young lady that had been strangely familiar.

'My name is Granby,' was the gentleman's reply. 'I was hoping to complete my journey this evening, but the weather has closed in, so I am seeking accommodation for myself and my wife and daughter.'

'And a private parlour,' the young lady added. 'It is essential that we have a private parlour.'

Michael rose to his feet, a dreadful sinking feeling in the pit of his stomach, for with this mention of a private parlour he had recalled where he had heard that voice before. It had not been so imperious in its tones, but it was undoubtedly that of Miss Evans; yet it seemed that she was now Miss Granby. What was going on here?

'I have rooms that you can use,' the landlord was saying, 'but I fear that I've no private parlour. The taproom's clean, and there's nobbut a young clergyman in there tonight.'

'Then surely he could go and sit elsewhere,' said the young lady, in the same imperious tone. 'Papa, you know that I cannot possibly sit in a common taproom, and nor can Mama.' An inaudible murmuring indicated that the other lady was making her contribution.

'I am afraid that there really is no alternative, my angel,' her father replied placatingly. 'Surely a clergyman must be quite unexceptionable company.'

'If you'll just come this way sir, ladies, I'll find you something to eat and send missus to make sure the beds are aired.'

As the visitors entered the taproom, Michael saw that Mr Granby looked very much the gentleman in a well-cut coat and breeches surmounted by a greatcoat. He was of average height and probably in his late forties, with light-brown hair and a rather thin face with well-marked features. Leaning on his arm was a lady of a similar age, well dressed and looking rather pale and tired. Their daughter was without doubt the young lady who had introduced herself to Michael as Miss Evans, and whom he had kissed in the inn in Sheffield only a short time before. She was dressed rather more practically than when Michael had seen her last, for she was now wearing a blue carriage dress and a cloak of a darker shade, and a bonnet lined with blue silk. She looked enchantingly pretty and glowing with health.

Michael had had warning of her arrival. She had not been so fortunate and, at sight of him, she paused, instantly recognizing him. Her complexion lost a little colour, and she faltered in her step.

'Evangeline, my angel,' said Mr Granby, turning to her concernedly, 'are you feeling giddy?'

'It is quite all right, Papa,' the young lady responded, glancing quickly up at Michael, then away again. 'The sudden warmth of the room has affected me, I think.'

What was he doing in here, she asked herself, horrified at this turn of events? That little adventure that she had enjoyed in Sheffield had been a thing of the moment, snatched out of time, an encounter with no past and no future. Now here was the buccaneer whom she had met, but looking somewhat tidier on this occasion. What did it mean, and where was the young clergyman to whom the landlord had referred? It could not possibly be this young man in front of her, could it? Thank goodness that Elsie had gone straight upstairs with her parents' personal servants and all their belongings. The girl was quite incapable of putting on any kind of an act.

'Good evening,' said Michael bowing politely. 'How wise of you to take shelter from this shocking weather. My name is Buckleigh – Michael Buckleigh.' He glanced quickly at Evangeline and saw her gaze narrowing.

'Good evening, Mr Buckleigh,' replied the other gentleman, bowing in turn. 'I am Robert Granby, and with me are my wife and daughter. I trust you do not mind our intruding upon your solitude, but there is no private room.'

'Really, Papa,' exclaimed Miss Granby, her tone a little breathless. 'Why should he? It is not his personal room after all.' With half an eye on Michael, she wandered over towards the window, ostensibly to look out at the rain and in so doing dropped her gloves. Buckleigh immediately bent down to pick them up and took them to her. She glanced towards the fire, where her father was absorbed in settling her mother down in a comfortable chair, and took the opportunity to hiss, 'What on earth are you doing here?'

'I might ask you the same,' he responded, also in a low tone.

'Are you following me?' she said suspiciously. 'Why are you pretending to be a clergyman?'

He was unable to answer this question because Mr Granby's attention was now turned in their direction, so instead he said more loudly, 'Have you travelled far, Miss Granby?'

Miss Granby, with her back to the room, was not aware that her father was approaching them and said, 'Don't be absurd.'

'Evangeline?' questioned her father disapprovingly.

'I beg pardon, Papa,' she said obediently, but Buckleigh could see that her eyes were blazing.

'It is not my pardon that you should be begging,' said Mr Granby.

Michael intervened quickly. 'No indeed, sir, it is not necessary. You heard Miss Granby's words, but did not see her expression. She was teasing me for forgetting that you had already told the landlord in this very room that you had come from Sheffield.'

Granby's expression lightened a little. 'Indeed. Well, that is a different matter, although the teasing of a clergyman is perhaps not quite the thing.' He frowned briefly, for he could not remember saying anything about Sheffield. In his book, however, the contradicting of a clergyman was just as unsuitable as the teasing of one, so he did not dispute the matter. Besides, they had indeed come from Sheffield, and there was no other way that Mr Buckleigh could have known this unless he, Granby, had said as much. The entrance of the landlord turned his mind to other matters.

'Rooms are ready now, sir and ladies, if you care to go up,' he said. 'Dinner can be ready in an hour if that will suit.'

Granby turned to his wife who had been sitting with her eyes closed. 'Our rooms are ready, my dear, if you would care to come upstairs and rest. Will you join us all for dinner, Mr Buckleigh?'

Michael had already resolved not to dine that evening and the presence of the bogus Miss Evans only confirmed his intention. 'Thank you, sir, but I have just enjoyed a bowl of excellent soup,' he replied courteously.

Granby smiled. 'You have a substantial frame, sir, and I doubt if a bowl of soup would fill more than a small corner of it. Give us your company, I beg.'

'Papa, Mr Leigh has just said that he does not want any dinner,' Evangeline put in, with a sideways glance at the young man. 'You must permit him to know his own mind.'

'His name is Mr Buckleigh, Evangeline,' Granby reminded her gently.

'Did I mispronounce it?' she asked, her tone all innocence. 'I wonder what made me do that?'

Granby turned to the young clergyman. 'Will you not change your mind, sir?' he said.

Had it not been for Evangeline's deliberate use of his assumed name, Michael would have stayed with his original intention, but, as she had spoken her last two speeches, there had been mischief in her eye and he was bound to retaliate. 'Since you are so pressing, I shall be glad to join you,' he said. Then, not wanting to be caught at fault, he followed father and daughter up the stairs in order to smarten himself up.

'Elsie! Disaster!' exclaimed Evangeline, as soon as she had closed the door behind her.

'Why, what is it, miss?' The little maid was just finishing setting out the clothes that her mistress was to change into for dinner. 'Can't we stay after all? Have we got to go back out in that downpour?'

'Worse!' Evangeline replied, allowing Elsie to make a start with unfastening her, then moving restlessly away before the job was done, obliging the girl to run after her.

'Well?' prompted Elsie, when her mistress said no more.

Evangeline thought for a moment. Elsie was not always the most discreet of mortals, but the need to unburden herself was great, and anyway the girl already knew half the story. 'You remember that ... that blond buccaneer which whom I had my little adventure? The one in Sheffield?'

'How could I forget, miss?' Elsie replied, taking advantage of the fact that her mistress was now standing still to finish unfastening her and help her out of her gown. 'There I was, waiting for you as you said and some saucy lad wanders over and wants to exchange the time of day.'

'Never mind that,' said Evangeline. 'He's downstairs.'

'What? Not that lad?' cried Elsie, looking delighted.

'No! Not *your* gallant! *Mine*! And masquerading as a clergyman, would you believe!'

'My life!' Elsie exclaimed, allowing the gown to fall to the floor. 'What wickedness!'

'I'm not at all sure that he can't be hanged for it,' Evangeline agreed. 'So why is he here?'

'He must have followed you, miss.'

'Why would he do such a thing?' Evangeline protested. 'I know I let him kiss me, but—'

'You *what*, miss? Shame on you!'

'Well, he is very handsome,' Evangeline answered, blushing, for she had not intended to tell Elsie about the kiss. 'Come to think of it, he can't have followed me, because he was here first. It must be one of those dreadful coincidences.'

'Lucky for you, miss, that he is pretending to be a clergyman,' Elsie responded, busying herself about her tasks now that she had recovered from her earlier shock. 'He can't tell what the two of you got up to, because if he does, you will be able to expose him for a fraud.'

'Of course,' Evangeline responded slowly. 'You're a genius, Elsie. If only I could have a word with him without Papa's being present, I could make sure that he knows that.'

'Doubtless he'll guess it,' the maid replied. 'These rogues are very quick thinking.'

'Yes, and so must you be,' Evangeline retorted. 'Elsie, if you so much as breathe a single word about what happened in Sheffield, then I will give that blue gown I promised you to ... to Cassie the housemaid.' Elsie and Cassie were fierce rivals, especially where attracting the local menfolk was concerned.

'Miss, you wouldn't!' Elsie exclaimed.

'See you keep quiet and I won't have to.'

Evangeline was in no danger of being exposed by Michael. He was far too concerned about his own position. He had thought just to have a little harmless fling before learning his fate. No one knew better than he how damaging it would be if the story of his adventure got back to the bishop. What would be seen in a young gentleman as a piece of harmless if rather desperate flirtation would be condemned in a clergyman as behaviour unsuitable to a man of the cloth, especially if that clergyman had already blotted his copybook. There would be no escape from unfrocking on another occasion. He would simply have to rely on the fact that Evangeline's reputation would suffer as much as his.

He looked at himself in the mirror, remembered the moment when his mouth had sought hers, and smiled as he thought about the intoxicating taste of her kiss. Pull yourself together, Buckleigh, he told himself severely. He stood, gave his neck-cloth a last tweak, straightened the sleeves of his best evening coat and left his room to go downstairs.

The meal, which was served by the landlord on a table which had been laid by his wife in the taproom, was plain but excellent, consisting of a roast chicken and a beef pudding with cabbage and carrots, followed by baked apples, some jam tarts and bread and cheese.

Mr Granby made his wife's apologies before they sat down. 'The journey has worn her out so she begs to be excused,' he said. 'Following your recommendation, sir, she is having a bowl of soup in her room.'

Michael expressed his regrets. 'I trust that a night's sleep will restore her,' he said politely. Both Michael and Evangeline approached the table a little warily, for despite the decisions that each had made, neither really trusted the other not to make some embarrassing disclosure. Hunger soon took over from anxiety, however, and Michael, who did indeed have as healthy an appetite as might be found in a young man of twenty-eight, did full justice to his plateful. Evangeline also enjoyed her food and, although pride demanded that she should make unflattering contrasts between the fare on offer at The Pheasant and that which graced the tables of the *ton*, she ate some of everything that was put in front of her.

For a time, the conversation ranged around general subjects such as the meal, the state of the roads, the recent weather and the Derbyshire scene. Eventually, however, Mr Granby said, 'Are you far from home, Mr Buckleigh? Do you come from this part of the world?'

'I was born some fifty miles away from here,' he replied. 'My stepfather still lives there with my sister. What of you, sir?'

'Unlike yourself, we have a mere ten miles or so to travel to our destination,' Granby replied. 'We have been in Sheffield for a family wedding.'

'I, too, have been in Sheffield,' Michael responded.

'How strange it would have been had we caught sight of one another,' Evangeline remarked, as she picked up her glass of wine.

'But we would not have known one another's identities,' Michael pointed out. For a moment, she looked at him over the rim and he was reminded most forcibly of the few moments before he kissed her. His gaze dropped to her lips, she coloured and her glance fell away.

'Were you in Sheffield on business, Mr Buckleigh?' Granby asked.

'In a manner of speaking. I was paying a visit to my bishop, and I am now travelling to take up a new curacy in this area.'

There was a clatter as Evangeline dropped her fork on to the floor. The landlord was not in the room, so Mr Granby, waving to Michael to sit down, stood up and went to the door to ask for a clean one.

'How long are you going to keep up this masquerade?' Evangeline hissed.

'What masquerade?' Michael whispered back.

'This pretence of being a clergyman.'

'It's no pretence: I am a clergyman.'

'Then you should be ashamed of yourself,' she whispered.

'I am not in the least ashamed of being a clergyman,' Michael responded.

'What was that?' asked Mr Granby, who had just returned to the table, and had therefore heard Michael's last sentence. 'Ashamed of being a clergyman? I should think not. Whatever were you thinking of, Evangeline?'

'I was only wondering whether in some circles Mr Buckleigh might find his calling ... inconvenient.'

Michael laughed. 'Inconvenient perhaps, but real none the less,' he replied.

'Indeed,' said Granby nodding. 'And where might your appointment be?'

'I am to be the curate of Illingham,' Michael explained. 'Do you know it? My vicar is Mr Lusty. Perhaps you have heard of him?'

Evangeline dropped her spoon this time, luckily only onto her dish. 'Oh yes, we've heard of him,' she put in, her tone a little on the cynical side.

'You know, this is quite extraordinary,' exclaimed Mr Granby. 'We reside between Illingham and Ashbourne, and are members of your future congregation.'

This time, it was Michael's turn to drop his fork.

Mr Granby glanced from one to the other. 'Really you young people are exceedingly careless with your cutlery this evening,' he remarked, then looked self-conscious as he realized that he was criticizing the clergyman as well as his daughter.

'I beg your pardon,' said Michael, making a swift recovery. 'I was simply astonished at my good fortune. You will be able to tell me all about my future appointment.'

'That will probably take all of two minutes,' observed Miss Granby tartly. 'It's the dullest place you ever did see and there's nothing whatsoever to do. Although I am sure that Mr Buckleigh will find plenty to absorb him.'

'I am certain he will,' said her father.

After a little more conversation, Evangeline stood up. 'I can see you are going to be talking about Illingham for ever, so I shall retire. Good night, Papa.'

The gentlemen stood up. 'Good night, Miss Granby,' said Buckleigh, bowing.

Evangeline dropped a small curtsy and turned to go. 'Evangeline,' Granby prompted.

Michael was half expecting her to say that she had already said good night and she wasn't going to say it again. Instead she said 'Good night, Mr Buckleigh', before leaving the room, closing the door behind her.

Granby sighed. 'I must apologize for my daughter,' he said wearily, as if it was something that he had either done or thought about doing many times before.

'There is no need,' Buckleigh answered politely. Then when Granby's disbelieving gaze met his, he added, 'A person of Miss Granby's age is surely old enough to make her own apology.'

'I apologize because it is I who indulged her,' the other man admitted frankly. 'My wife has always sought to check me, but, as perhaps you can see, she has never been strong. Evangeline is our only child and, because she was rather sickly when small, she became extra precious to us. Now, with years of hindsight to aid me, I see that I allowed this circumstance to make me foolishly fond and over-indulgent.'

'I see,' Michael answered. He had become used to the fact that his position as a man of the cloth meant that many people chose to confide in him much more quickly than in any other stranger.

'You must not allow this evening's events to make you think the worst of her, however. She can be good-natured and very kind, but she has been visiting cousins, and my sister-in-law is rather apt to make unfavourable comparisons between her daughters' behaviour and that of Evangeline. It puts her out of temper I'm afraid. Now, to other matters. Let me tell you about Illingham.'

Michael was delighted to find an unexpected source of information with regard to the place where he would soon earn his living. When he looked at the clock some time later, he was amazed to see how late it was. He expressed his sincere thanks to Mr Granby who shook his head dismissively. 'Not at all, not at all. I am delighted to have been of service. May I ask how you are travelling, Mr Buckleigh?'

'On my own two feet,' answered the clergyman, trying not to sound sorry for himself.

'Then you must travel with us on the morrow,' Granby declared. 'I fear you would have a muddy walk otherwise.'

'Thank you, sir,' replied Buckleigh. 'I admit that I was not looking forward to it.'

Soon after this last exchange, the two men retired to their rooms. Michael did not prepare for bed immediately, but stood looking out into the darkness of the inn yard. On the one hand, he could not help being delighted that he had met and been befriended by a prominent member of his congregation. On the other, he had no way of knowing how discreet Evangeline might be. If she chose to reveal what had happened between them in Sheffield, then the consequences could be disastrous, especially if she chose to give the impression that he had somehow forced her to go into a private room. His heart sank at the very thought. He told himself that he would have to behave towards her with the greatest circumspection. Even so, part of him was conscious of a surge of excitement; in anticipation of what, he hardly knew.

Chapter Three

---◦◉◦---

The following morning, mindful of his duty, Michael read the Morning Office before coming downstairs. As it was quite early, he also had time to read a chapter or two of *Tom Jones*. Even so, he found that he was still downstairs before the Granbys.

If asked to hazard a guess as to which of the family would appear first, he would probably have put his money on Mr Granby. It was Evangeline who entered the parlour before either of her parents, however.

She had been awake half the night wondering whether Mr Buckleigh would keep quiet about their encounter in Sheffield. Ironically enough, had he been the buccaneer that he had first appeared, she would have felt more secure. Such a man, after a flirtatious glance or two, or a pleading look, would probably keep such an encounter to himself. The trouble with clergymen, or so it seemed to her, was that they could display a tiresome tendency to tell the truth, however inconvenient or inappropriate. Mr Buckleigh might therefore feel bound to tell Mr and Mrs Granby about the bad behaviour of their daughter, even though it would reflect upon him personally. It might even become known locally that she, Evangeline Granby, the toast of London during two seasons, had actually permitted the curate to kiss her! How foolish would she look then? That was the kind of escapade that parlour boarders of sixteen got up to! No, something had to be done and, for this reason, she had resolved upon approaching Mr Buckleigh to make sure that he kept quiet.

Glancing round rapidly, she said, 'I am glad that I have found you alone, Mr Buckleigh, for I feel that there is something that I must make clear to you.'

'I am at your service,' the clergyman replied. He had risen at her entrance, and now he pulled a chair out for her.

'We must not waste time, sir, for I fear that Mama and Papa will be coming down soon. In short, I would like to know whether you have any plans to disclose what passed between the two of us.'

'What passed between the two of us when, Miss Granby?' he responded.

His words had been intended to act as a reassurance that he was prepared to forget about the whole matter, but Evangeline, not catching his tone, did not grasp his meaning. 'You know perfectly well to what I am referring,' she snapped. 'I mean the encounter between us in Sheffield.'

'Ah yes,' he replied. 'Very improper.' Again, she missed the teasing note in his voice.

'Improper! I should think it was,' she answered, springing to her feet. 'And you a clergyman! You have already heard that we know the vicar well. What would Mr Lusty say if he were told that you had lured a young woman into an inn in order to make love to her?'

'You know perfectly well that the luring came just as much from you,' Michael responded, her aggressive approach removing at one and the same time any desire either to tease or to reassure. 'When I think how you looked at me from across the street, your every glance conveying "come hither".'

'I had something in my eye,' Evangeline responded defensively. He gave a snort of derisive laughter. 'As if I would respond to the lures cast out by some down-at-heel ne'er-do-well.'

'Liar,' he said softly. She had been pacing up and down the room. Now, when she turned, she found that she was standing very near to him, almost as close as when they had been together in that little inn in Sheffield, just before he had taken her in his arms. Really, he was far too preposterously handsome for a clergyman! It should not be allowed! Briefly, tension crackled between them.

She gave a little gasp. 'If you dare to kiss me again, I shall slap you hard, and tell Papa that you forced your attentions upon me,' she said.

He stepped back as if stung. 'I would not dream of touching you, ma'am,' he told her coldly. 'Don't disturb yourself; I will keep the Sheffield episode to myself; but I shall be watching you for any signs of impropriety, you may be sure.'

'And I you,' she retorted, as the sound of footsteps on the stairs warned them that Mr and Mrs Granby were descending. 'One wrong step and I shall report you to the bishop, mark my words.'

Mr and Mrs Granby greeted their daughter with affection and Mr Buckleigh with courtesy. The clergyman noticed that with a night's rest, Mrs Granby had acquired more colour and looked much better as a result. He was now able to detect that it was from her that Evangeline had inherited her remarkable beauty.

After a few desultory remarks about the improved weather, they sat down to breakfast together. Like dinner the evening before, the meal was brought out and placed on a table in the taproom. There was home-cured bacon, eggs and fresh bread, as well as preserves and fruit. Ale and coffee were provided to wash breakfast down. Michael and Mr Granby both enjoyed a hearty plateful, and Michael noticed that Evangeline also had a good appetite. Mrs Granby, however, merely played with a piece of bread and jam, and drank a very weak-looking cup of coffee.

They chatted easily over the meal, Miss Granby's sunny good-humour in marked contrast to her demeanour when speaking to Michael before her parents had arrived. Clearly the young lady had a talent for dissembling. When they had finished, she held out her hand to Michael as they stood up. 'I will wish you goodbye then, Mr Buckleigh, and look forward to seeing you soon.'

'Evangeline, my angel, Mr Buckleigh will be travelling with us today,' said her father.

For an instant, an impatient look flashed across Evangeline's features before she said, 'Delightful! We shall be able to continue our conversation on the journey.'

Michael bowed and left the taproom, in order to go upstairs and gather his belongings together, and shortly afterwards, the Granbys also left the table.

Michael was determined not to force his companions to converse with him, so he took his copy of *Tom Jones* into the chaise, prepared to bury himself in his book. In the event, however, Mr Granby was very keen to talk and, as he himself had been to Oxford some years before, they had much to discuss.

'There is a scholarly man, Dr Littlejohn by name, who lives quite close to our house,' Mr Granby remarked. 'He also went to Oxford and I'm sure you'll find much in common with him. You may want to call on Lady Agatha Rayner as well. Her husband was our vicar until his death.'

'That's an extraordinary way of putting things,' Evangeline

remarked. '*Having* to call on Lady Agatha, perhaps; *needing* to do so, possibly; *putting off* doing so, frequently; but *wanting* to do so? I think not.'

Mrs Granby turned to Michael. 'You must excuse Evangeline, Mr Buckleigh. She has too many memories of having been made to feel uncomfortable by Lady Agatha.'

'Oh have done, Mama,' said Evangeline impatiently. She had intended to sound witty. Her mother's intervention has made her seem childish, uncivil and faintly pathetic.

'I shall certainly wish to call upon her and upon all my parishioners,' said Michael to Mr Granby, after casting a brief, disapproving look at Evangeline. He wished that his words did not make him sound irritatingly pious. In truth, it was not what she had said about Lady Agatha that had shocked him, but her manner towards her mother.

Evangeline gave a snort of disdain, at which her mother murmured, 'Evangeline dearest,' in protest. How often must she have felt obliged to do that, Michael wondered?

He leaned back, and took up his book, but before he could read more than a line or two, the chaise came to an abrupt halt, and muffled shouts were heard from outside.

'What have we stopped for now?' Miss Granby asked curiously.

'I don't wish to alarm any of you, but I very much fear that we may have fallen prey to highwaymen,' said Michael in calm tones.

'Highwaymen!' exclaimed Mr Granby, looking anxiously at his wife.

'Oh merciful heavens,' murmured Mrs Granby, turning as pale as she had been the previous night.

Her husband grasped her hand. 'There there, my dear,' he said reassuringly. 'We never carry valuables. We have nothing worth stealing.'

Michael glanced involuntarily at Evangeline. He had heard of highwaymen whose vileness did not stop at relieving people of their belongings. Her beauty was enough to attract the attentions of any man as he himself knew only too well. Her eyes met his. In that moment, he knew that she understood what he was thinking. He gave her a brief nod. In it, he sought to convey that he would do all that he could to protect her.

Before Mr Granby had finished speaking, they heard the cry of 'Stand and deliver!' which confirmed Buckleigh's suppositions.

'You had best pray for us,' said Miss Granby, looking perfectly calm. Inside, she was feeling very afraid, but something about the resolute demeanour of the clergyman gave her courage.

The young man smiled faintly. 'I will do my possible, never doubt it.'

Moments later, the door was flung open and a rough-looking individual in a long frieze coat, a hat pulled low, a mask over the lower part of his face and a pistol in his hand, demanded that they get down. They all did as they were asked.

Mr Granby was obliged to support his wife who was chalk white and noticeably trembling. Evangeline emerged from the coach like a queen and, after a brief glance at the pistol in the highwayman's hand, stepped without hesitation in front of her mother.

Once out of the coach, the clergyman looked around. Apart from the man who had opened the door, there appeared to be two other highwaymen. One was covering the coachman and groom with a pistol, whilst a third was beginning an examination of their belongings which were on the roof of the coach.

'I beseech you,' Michael said clearly, holding up the handsomely bound book which had lain beside him on the seat, 'take heed of what is written in this volume.'

'Garn!' the man beside them growled contemptuously.

'Then I shall have to impress its message upon you,' was the reply. Moments later, the book was flying through the air, knocking the pistol from the hand of the man on horseback. The pistol discharged, startling the horse which then threw its rider, whilst those harnessed to the stage tossed their heads in fright and moved restlessly, thus dislodging the highwayman on the roof from his perch. At the same time as this was happening, the clergyman kicked the third highwayman's legs from under him and, when he attempted to rise, rendered him unconscious with a blow to the side of his head.

Meanwhile, Granby possessed himself of the unconscious man's pistol, and commanded the man who had fallen from his horse to stay still whilst the groom tied him up. Buckleigh looked round to see what had happened to the man who had fallen off the roof and discovered that Miss Granby was carefully tying his bootlaces together whilst he was still stunned. He could not help grinning, even whilst he sought out some rope. Very soon, all three rogues were securely tied up. In the midst of everything, Mrs Granby had quietly fainted.

'I suggest that you send your groom to fetch the nearest magistrate,' said Michael to Mr Granby. 'In the meantime, why not escort the ladies home? I can easily watch over these fellows.'

'But what of you, sir?' asked Mr Granby, kneeling beside his wife and chafing her hands whilst Evangeline searched in her reticule for some smelling salts. 'It seems very unfair to offer you a ride and then go on without you.'

Buckleigh shook his head dismissively. 'We must have accomplished over half the journey,' he replied. 'The roads are drying nicely, and the walk will be quite pleasant. If you would be so good as to take my cloak bag with you, however, I will collect it when I arrive.'

'With the greatest of pleasure,' answered Mr Granby. 'The magistrate, Sir Lyle Belton, is known to me. He lives nearby and I am sure that he will not be long. I must admit that I will be glad to assure myself that the earlier coach carrying my servants and the rest of our luggage has arrived safely.'

'Hush, Papa,' said Evangeline urgently, glancing at her mother. 'Not in front of Mama.' By this time, Mrs Granby had regained consciousness and her husband assisted her into the chaise with Evangeline's help.

Michael turned to Evangeline. 'I do trust this adventure has not discomposed you too greatly, ma'am,' he said.

She tossed her head. 'It would take a good deal more than a few incompetent highwaymen to discompose me,' she declared.

'Uppity bitch!' spat the thief who had opened the door of the chaise.

Before either Buckleigh or Granby could respond to this insolence, Miss Granby had walked over to him. 'You may say what you please, but do not forget that you are the one who is on the floor trussed like a chicken,' she said. Then she turned to her father who had got back down in order to assist her. 'Shall we go, Papa?'

'By all means, my angel,' replied Granby. He looked at Buckleigh, who was walking over to where his book had fallen. 'I do trust that it is not damaged, sir,' he said. 'Such a handsome volume.'

'No, I think not,' replied the clergyman, bending to pick it up.

'Such quick thinking on your part, Mr Buckleigh – if not entirely in keeping with your calling,' said Miss Granby. 'But then, who are we to complain when we have such a happy result?'

'Speak for yourself,' growled the highwayman who had been knocked off his feet.

'You hold your tongue,' said Granby, turning from climbing into the chaise, having just helped his daughter to her seat. 'That young man is under the protection of the Good Book. Are you not, sir?'

Buckleigh grinned, as he glanced down at the book in his hand. It had fallen open at the title page. *The History of Tom Jones: a Foundling*. It had been a gift, whose donor had written underneath the title:

From your friend James Warrener. Remember that no one owes you anything.

Then, as the chaise disappeared, he sat down with his back to a tree and the book open on his knee. If he were honest with himself, however, his mind was on the young lady who had just left rather than on the printed page. Had the incident with the highwaymen not taken place, he would simply have said that although she was very pretty, she was also high-handed, demanding, rather unscrupulous and more than a little spoiled. The robbery had revealed another side to her. He recalled how she had looked at him, understanding his unspoken message, then descended from the coach with dignity and without a trace of the fear that she must have been feeling on her lovely face. He also remembered how she had put herself between the pistol and her mother, and later hushed her father when he had said something that might have alarmed the older lady. Obviously she had hidden depths. He would have liked to discover more about her, but, as a poor curate, he must be realistic. A woman like the lovely, pampered Miss Granby could never be destined for a man in his position, however much his imagination might toy with such an outcome.

The magistrate did not keep him waiting for very long. He arrived tooling his own sporting carriage, followed by a closed wagon with four men. He greeted Michael with a beaming smile.

'This is excellent!' he declared, climbing down and holding out his hand after one of the men had run to his horses' heads. 'You are to be commended, sir. These fellows have been making a nuisance of themselves in this district for far too long. It is high time that decent people can go abroad without risking attack.'

'I am delighted to have been of use,' the clergyman replied. 'Michael Buckleigh at your service.'

'Honoured to make your acquaintance. I am Sir Lyle Belton, magistrate for this area. My men will take these felons into custody to await their trial. In the meantime, sir, I must request that you return to my home now and make a statement. I shall also need your address, since you will probably be called to testify.'

Michael held back an inward sigh. He would have preferred to have got on with his journey immediately. He could hardly object to this request, however, so, smiling politely, he said, 'Of course; although as I am new to the district, I do not know my address as yet.'

'Needless to say, I must also speak to Mr and Mrs Granby and their daughter, who were with you when the hold-up occurred. May I therefore suggest that you have some refreshment at my house and that I then drive you to Illingham to join them? This might act as some recompense for having delayed your journey.'

'Thank you. I would be much obliged.'

On the way to Sir Lyle's house, Michael soon discovered that the magistrate did not drive a sporting equipage for nothing, for he went at a rattling pace, feather-edging corners, and entering his own narrow gateway without a check in his pace. Michael was a bruising rider, but he had never had the opportunity or the means to drive more than a one-horse gig. He found himself hoping that one day he would be in a position to purchase such a carriage and pair as this.

'Here we are – The Cedars,' said Sir Lyle, as they drew up outside the front door of a handsome, square-built house that looked no more than thirty years old. Two fine trees, one on either side, showed why it had been given its name. 'This was built by my father,' he went on. 'But come in, sir, do. We'll go to the book room and you can tell me exactly what happened while my steward writes it all down. Then we'll join my wife and daughter for refreshments.'

The sunny aspect of the book room was very welcome after the previous day's rain, as was the fine red wine which was brought to them, following Sir Lyle's instructions. This courtesy was much appreciated by the recipient, for Michael had soon discovered that a curate could sometimes be treated with thinly veiled contempt and, on occasions, the poorer wine would be brought out for his consumption. He tolerated this, but sometimes wondered from where he had inherited his taste for the finer things. Wine, horses, food, even porcelain; he had to admit that he liked the best, but, much to his frustration, he could often only afford the mediocre.

Sir Lyle sat quietly listening whilst Michael described the incidents of that morning in as much detail as possible, and the steward wrote it all down. Then, when that job was done and the account had been checked through, he rose, rubbing his hands together. 'Come, sir, you have done your duty. Let's join the ladies for some refreshment, shall we?'

'Pray do not tell me, sir, that your wife and daughter have delayed their meal on my behalf,' Michael protested.

'Oh, it's of no consequence,' said Sir Lyle dismissively. 'You know what women are like. They will be anxious to meet the hero of the hour.'

Michael felt rather embarrassed at being described in such a way, but he soon discovered that at far as Lady Belton and Miss Amelia Belton were concerned, he was speaking no more than the truth. The two ladies both listened with bated breath as Sir Lyle described Michael's heroism, his accurate account bearing witness to the fact that he had been listening very carefully.

When the baronet explained how Michael had managed to subdue all three men virtually at the same time, Miss Belton gave a little gasp and breathed 'Such heroism!' Miss Belton was very like her mother, both ladies being dark and petite, with neat figures and lustrous brown eyes.

'Your father makes it sound more impressive than it really was,' said Michael frankly. 'The fact that the man on the roof was startled into falling was a piece of good luck and nothing more.'

'Mr Buckleigh, you are too modest; is he not, Mama?' said Miss Belton.

'I think he is,' her ladyship agreed.

'In any case, I cannot imagine what I would have done with them had Mr and Miss Granby not been there,' Michael told them.

'I am sure that Evangeline was very brave,' said Miss Belton admiringly. 'In her place, I would have fainted quite away and been of no use to you. I fear I do not have her bold spirit, do I Mama?'

'No, my love, you are quite unlike her,' answered Lady Belton with a satisfied smile. 'Do you have brothers or sisters, Mr Buckleigh?'

'I have one sister who is ten years younger than myself,' he replied.

'Does she have your distinctive colouring?' asked the baronet.

'No,' Michael replied. 'She is fair, but without my strange eyebrows, I'm pleased to say.'

'I think them very distinguished,' said Miss Belton, who then blushed and looked down at the tablecloth. Lady Belton smiled indulgently and changed the subject.

Michael was intrigued. His experience in houses where young ladies were present was generally that they would be kept at a safe distance from him. A curate earning less than forty pounds a year was not considered to be a good match. His striking looks tended to attract female attention, so he would often be steered towards grandparents, older brothers, and maiden aunts of at least fifty. An occasion such as today, when an only daughter was looking at him admiringly and her parents were doing nothing to prevent it, was rare indeed.

Whilst hoping that one day he might marry for love, Michael was honest enough to admit that he could see a good many advantages in having a well-dowered bride. There would be no more worries about providing for his sister Theodora for a start. Nor need he become anxious about what would happen if his stepfather's health broke down. A wealthy father-in-law would probably mean a parish of his own, too. He was well aware that men could continue as curates for many years. His own stepfather had a curate who was well into his forties. He, Michael, had hardly done anything to distinguish himself in a favourable way. He was therefore unlikely to gain a parish very quickly through his own unaided efforts.

The idea of marrying for money alone was distasteful to him, but looking at Miss Belton's blushing countenance, he knew that it would not be hard to be fond of her. It would not be the kind of roaring in his blood that he felt as he thought of Miss Granby, but he and Miss Granby had begun their acquaintance by snatching a few hours out of time. Once she had discovered who he really was, she had seemed to regard him with thinly veiled contempt. Her behaviour, too, had hardly suggested that she would make a suitable wife for a clergyman. He would do much better to set his sights upon Miss Belton. With a courteous smile, he turned to listen to what she was just saying to him.

After they had eaten, then drunk tea in the drawing room, Sir Lyle said, 'Mr Buckleigh will be anxious to view his accommodation, no doubt. Are you ready to leave now, sir?'

'Whenever you like,' Michael answered politely.

'Papa, may I come with you?' Miss Belton asked prettily. 'It is simply ages since I have seen Evangeline. I should like to hear her account of the hold-up.'

'That rather depends on whether Mama can spare you,' Sir Lyle answered.

'Mama thinks that a little fresh air would do her no harm,' replied Lady Belton indulgently. 'Go and put your bonnet on, my dear.'

Michael smiled. He was not at all averse to seeing more of pretty little Miss Belton. Her modest demeanour made a welcome change after Miss Granby's more commanding style.

They were somewhat crowded up on the seat of Sir Lyle's curricle, but nobody complained. Miss Belton apologized with engaging bashfulness for taking up so much room, but her father dismissed this comment. 'A dainty little creature like you takes only a scrap of space,' he said. 'Anyway, we are not going far. I'm sure Buckleigh doesn't mind.'

'No indeed,' Michael answered, looking down at the young lady whose thigh was touching his. Doubtless in her place Miss Granby would be insisting that he perched up behind with the groom!

'Have you preached a sermon yet, Mr Buckleigh?' Miss Belton asked. 'I should be so nervous. However can you dare to stand up and speak in church in front of a lot of people?'

'It is something to which one becomes accustomed,' Michael answered, easily. 'I have done it before, so it will not be strange to me.'

'Are you to preach on Sunday?' Amelia asked.

'So I believe.'

'Papa, may we come to Illingham to hear Mr Buckleigh?' Amelia asked. 'It is not very far away.'

'And what of Mr Wilson?' her father asked, referring to their own vicar. 'I should hate him to think that we were forsaking him.'

'We could send a message to him to say that we wanted to welcome Mr Buckleigh who is new to the area,' she suggested. 'Would it not be an appropriate gesture, given the service that he has rendered the community in ridding it of those scoundrels?'

'Yes, perhaps,' Sir Lyle agreed, 'but we must see what Mama thinks. She is very strict about church attendance, you know.'

'But we would still be attending,' his daughter pointed out.

'That will do for now, Amelia. I have said that we will ask Mama.'

'Yes, Papa,' Miss Belton answered dutifully, deciding that she would be able to twist Mama around her little finger later.

Michael smiled approvingly at this demonstration of filial obedience, and thought of how agreeable it would be to have Miss Belton and her parents watching as he conducted his first service. Then he remembered his vestments, packed inside his luggage, and hoped that he would be able to find some obliging woman to press them. He would hate to appear for the first time in creased robes, particularly if these new friends were going to make a special effort to see him conduct worship!

Granby Park was a fine-looking building, which could be admired from several angles owing to the long, elegantly curved drive. It was larger than The Cedars and the brickwork was more mellow, leading Michael to think that it was probably a little older. Sir Lyle steered his curricle through the gateway without checking, and negotiated the curves in the drive at a smart trot.

'You seem to be a capital whip, sir,' said the clergyman admiringly.

'I enjoy driving more than riding, I must confess,' the other man replied.

'Papa is teaching me to drive,' said Miss Belton, 'but he does not often have very much free time. I don't suppose you would teach me, Mr Buckleigh?'

Michael laughed ruefully. 'Willingly, Miss Belton, but I fear that I drive very little myself. I would be much more likely to ask *you* to give *me* lessons.'

She looked a little disappointed at this revelation, but by the end of his speech she had regained her sparkle. 'Be sure that I shall do so, just as soon as Papa says I may,' she promised.

'My dear, you have only just started to learn,' said her father with a laugh. 'It will be years before you are proficient enough to teach others.'

Glancing down, Michael observed a flash of temper cross her face before her features composed themselves into their usual obedient lines, and she murmured, 'Yes, Papa.'

Mr and Miss Granby were both in the drawing room, and they rose to greet their visitors. Miss Granby and Miss Belton embraced with unconvincing cries of mutual affection, whilst Mr Granby and Sir Lyle greeted one another in a more restrained style.

'Evangeline, my dear, it has been far too long!' Miss Belton exclaimed. 'I do declare, you have grown taller.'

'That is not what my dressmaker tells me,' Evangeline answered. A little over the average for a woman, she was somewhat sensitive on the subject of her height. 'You, on the other hand, my dear Amelia, are blooming; positively blooming! What a good colour you have.'

'This is not a social call, as I am sure you must have guessed,' said Sir Lyle. 'I need you both to make statements of what happened this morning.'

'Yes, of course,' Mr Granby agreed. 'Fortunately, my agent is on the premises. He may act as secretary.' He rang the bell. 'I am afraid that my wife has retired to bed after her ordeal. I do hope that you will not want her statement. In any case, she fainted during the hold-up and would not be able to give a full account.'

Sir Lyle agreed that it would not be necessary to disturb her at present. 'If the facts of what occurred are disputed by the villains, then she may need to tell what she remembers of the affair at a later date,' he added. Michael did not say anything. He very much wanted to inspect his lodgings, but knew that these legal matters must come first.

Mr Granby's agent soon came in, and readily agreed to act as scribe, with Sir Lyle sitting in as before, to make sure that all was conducted as it should be. 'You must go first, my angel,' said Mr Granby. 'In the meantime, I will take Mr Buckleigh to his accommodation.' Michael's cloak bag had been placed ready for him in the hall.

'May I go too, Papa?' Miss Belton asked. 'Then I can assure Mama that Mr Buckleigh is comfortably settled. There is nothing I can do here, after all.'

Evangeline was on the point of leaving the room in front of the agent. She paused briefly, directing a narrowed stare at the other young woman. 'I hope that you can manage the journey,' she said in solicitous tones.

'You forget that I am still a country girl, unaffected by London ways,' Amelia responded, smiling sweetly. Evangeline left with what might almost have been a sniff.

'Yes, by all means,' Sir Lyle responded, answering his daughter's question. 'As long as Granby is willing to take you.'

'Certainly,' Mr Granby responded. 'I will send for my coat.'

Whilst he was doing this, Amelia walked over to Michael's side. 'I would so like to be able to picture where you are living,' she murmured. 'I hope that I will not be dreadfully in the way.'

'No, not at all,' Michael responded politely.

'Are we all ready, then?' asked Mr Granby, as the footman helped him on with his coat. 'It's only a short walk.'

'We are *walking*?' Miss Belton exclaimed involuntarily, her tone one of consternation.

'Why yes,' replied Mr Granby. 'You are very welcome to stay here, if you think it will be too far. The cottage that has been set aside for Mr Buckleigh's use is just outside Illingham on this side. I suppose the walk there will be a little under two miles.'

Miss Belton gasped, but made a gallant recovery. 'That is not such a distance,' she said in a determinedly cheerful tone. 'Let us be off, then, gentlemen.'

In the event, Miss Belton only made it to the bottom of the drive; a fact for which each of the two men privately gave thanks, for her pace was quite irritatingly slow. Indeed, Michael was beginning to wonder whether they would actually make it to Illingham before nightfall. When they got to the gates, however, Miss Belton said brightly, 'Now I have seen you on your way, I shall wander back to the house, if you have no objection. Mr Granby may describe the cottage to me upon his return.'

'With the greatest of pleasure,' Granby assured her.

'It has been a pleasure to meet you, Miss Belton,' said Michael, bowing politely.

'I shall persuade Mama to come and hear you preach on Sunday, never fear,' she replied, giving him her hand.

'I trust that you will not be disappointed,' he remarked.

'I don't think that I could ever be disappointed in you, Mr Buckleigh,' she said, her eyes sparkling. 'I will visit you to see your lodgings another day.'

As soon as the two men had seen her off up the drive, they set out for Illingham, their strides soon matching one another easily. 'That's better,' said Mr Granby. 'I don't want to seem ungallant, but I fear we would have made slow progress.'

Michael made no reply to this, but instead began to ask questions about the land around them, and to whom it belonged.

'My own property is not extensive,' answered Granby, 'so very little beyond the park surrounding my home belongs to me. Much of what is around here is part of the Ashbourne estate.'

'You are speaking of Lord Ashbourne, I believe,' said Michael. 'I understand that the living of Illingham is partly in his gift.'

'Yes, that is so. Lord Ashbourne and the Bishop of Sheffield make the appointment between them. It's not a very comfortable arrangement, and in times past the village has sometimes even been without a priest whilst the earl and the bishop have engaged in a private quarrel. But now that Mr Lusty has been appointed, things may quieten down. However ...' He paused for a few moments in indecision, then went on, 'It is just as well that you should be aware of some of the history surrounding this place. It may prevent you from offending out of ignorance.

'You may remember I told you yesterday that Lady Agatha Rayner, Lord Ashbourne's sister, was married to the former vicar, The Revd Colin Rayner. She had as her companion a single lady named Miss Warburton. This lady became engaged to Mr Lusty, oh, it must be over a year ago now. She travelled to London to stay with Lusty's sister, but while there, she renewed her acquaintance with Lord Ashbourne. The next thing that any of us knew was that they had been married privately.'

'I have heard – perhaps mistakenly – that Lord Ashbourne is something of a rake,' said Michael a little diffidently.

'You are not mistaken,' answered Granby. 'He has indeed been a great rake in the past. He is also an exceedingly handsome man, as well as having considerable address.' He sighed. 'There was a time when Evangeline was very smitten with him. Fortunately, he did nothing to encourage her, but it was a worry. There are those who predicted that he would soon tire of Miss Warburton once married to her. I have to say that there has been no sign of it so far. They are away in Buxton at present. Lady Ashbourne is expecting a child and his lordship is overseeing her drinking the water. Have you tasted it?' Buckleigh shook his head. 'Well, don't bother: it's deucedly nasty stuff.

'The landowner you're more likely to have dealings with is Lord Ashbourne's son, Viscount Ilam. He lives in the manor house on the main street in Illingham. It is to him that you owe thanks for the cottage in which you are to live, as it belongs to the estate. Ilam's wife has recently had a child, and they are away visiting Lady Ilam's parents.'

'Has the child been baptized?' Michael asked.

Mr Granby shook his head. 'No doubt that will be one of your first duties, unless Lusty decides to step in. And here is your cottage.' He took a key out of his pocket. 'Our meeting on the road was most fortuitous, but I had been instructed to look out for your arrival and give you the key.' He handed it over. 'You may have the honour.'

As Michael took the key, he reflected that Mr Granby could not possibly have known what this meant to him. In his last two curacies, he had lodged with parishioners, once above a butcher's shop, the smell of which had risen and drifted into his room on hot days and had often been quite offensive. On the other occasion, he had had no separate room in which to study and had been obliged to sit in a cold, damp church in order to write his sermons. This cottage was the first home that he had ever had to himself. Already, he could imagine having Theodora here with him.

The inside of the cottage was plain and clean, and neatly furnished with items that seemed to Michael to be of a much better quality than might have been expected in such a dwelling.

'Lady Ilam was responsible for the furnishings,' Mr Granby explained. 'Most of them are from the Hall.'

'She has been very kind,' said Michael, looking about him at the rug in front of the fireplace flanked by two chairs, the small table next to the window, the reading desk and the bookcase standing against one of the walls. The fire was laid, he noticed, and a big basket was full of logs. There were also several candlesticks in evidence, all with new wax candles in them. 'I shall need to make arrangements for my trunk to be brought here,' he went on. 'Do you have any idea where it will have been taken?'

'Your trunk is upstairs,' said Mr Granby. 'Ilam ordered it to be brought here from the Olde Oak on its arrival. Another day, you will have to decide what to do about food. For tonight, I suggest that you unpack in the daylight, then walk back to Granby Park where you may dine with us.'

'You are very good,' said Michael, shaking the other man's hand heartily before he left. Then he ran up the stairs two at a time, impatient to see the rest of his new home.

Chapter Four

———⟨☙⟩———

After watching the two men disappear from sight, Miss Belton gave a little sigh at the pleasing vista of the new curate's retreating figure before wandering slowly back up the drive. Her aim was to get back to the house at about the same time as Evangeline emerged from giving her statement. She wanted to give the impression that she had spent more time in Mr Buckleigh's company than had really been the case.

In her own way, Miss Belton had been indulged as much as Miss Granby. She, too, was an only child of well-to-do parents, who were anxious to procure the best for their child. It might be supposed that this would mean that Sir Lyle and Lady Belton would be looking for a title for their daughter; indeed, at one time, they had had hopes of Lord Ilam. But Ilam had married Eustacia Hope and there were no other young titled single gentlemen in the district. Lady Belton's chief fear was that some gentleman would marry Amelia and whisk her off to a remote part of the country. That was why she had resisted giving her nineteen-year-old daughter a London season. Amelia had no doubt that should her fancy light upon the young clergyman, her mother in particular could be persuaded to welcome him with open arms. As she climbed the steps up to the front door of the house, she pictured Mr Buckleigh in her mind's eye and decided that her fancy definitely had lit upon him. A penniless curate was not an obviously eligible bridegroom, but he was undoubtedly a gentleman and the very poverty of his circumstances and the nature of his occupation would tie him to the area. As Sir Lyle's son-in-law, he would soon get his preferment.

The one stumbling block to her schemes, as far as she could see, was Miss Evangeline Granby. Her looks were spectacular, she had met

Mr Buckleigh first and, furthermore, she was in the same parish. It had not been possible to detect whether Miss Granby had set her sights on Mr Buckleigh, but Amelia doubted it. She was, after all, a regular participant in the London season, and probably regarded a curate as being beneath her notice. Nevertheless it would not do to take anything for granted. A little delicate questioning would not come amiss.

A servant showed her into the drawing room and took her cloak and bonnet. She sat down to leaf through a copy of *The Lady's Magazine*, and was thus engaged when Miss Granby returned to the room, having made her statement.

'I am surprised to see you here, Amelia,' said Evangeline. 'I thought that you were going to walk to the village with Papa and Mr Buckleigh.'

'I decided that the gentlemen could get on more quickly without me,' Amelia replied. 'Did you manage to remember everything about the hold-up to Papa's satisfaction?'

'I think so,' Evangeline replied carelessly. 'It's a lot of fuss about nothing, in my opinion.'

'Oh? Mr Buckleigh wasn't particularly gallant, then?'

'Quick and business-like would be a better description, I think. Shall we have some tea? You cannot go until Papa has returned and given his statement as well.'

Amelia concurred. 'Mr Buckleigh is very striking in his looks, though, don't you think?' she added, with a sideways glance at her hostess.

Evangeline had thought Michael striking from the moment that she had seen him in Sheffield. At the back of her mind, however, was a determination that no one should suspect her acquaintance with him was of longer duration than it should have been. Perhaps it was for this reason that she said, 'Striking? I should have thought that odd was a better description. That combination of pale hair and dark brows is almost freakish, don't you think?'

Amelia was saved from replying by the arrival of a servant, summoned by the bell. She was satisfied by what she had heard. Evangeline did not have her sights set upon Michael Buckleigh: the field was clear.

After the servant had left with their order for tea, Amelia drew Evangeline's attention to something in *The Lady's Magazine* and the subject of Mr Buckleigh did not arise again. But Evangeline had very far from dismissed him from her mind. She could not forget how that very morning he had told her that he would watch her for any signs of impropriety. Yet, before the day was even over, he had obviously managed to captivate Amelia Belton. How dared he lecture her!

It was only after Sir Lyle Belton and his daughter had left that Mr Granby told Evangeline that the curate was dining with them.

'Oh Papa,' Evangeline exclaimed in tones of consternation.

'Do you dislike him so much, my angel?' said Granby concernedly.

'Dislike him? No, not really. But it is tiresome to be in the presence of a clergyman and to be constantly upon one's best behaviour.'

He smiled indulgently. 'It is only right to be hospitable. After all, he has only just moved in and has no food in the house.'

'One would not want him to starve. From what I have seen, he appears to need an enormous amount of food to keep him going.'

'He has a big frame,' Mr Granby agreed. 'Lord and Lady Ilam have made the cottage very comfortable for him. I should think it will not be long before he sends for his sister.'

'I hope she's not as big as he is, or there will not be room for both of them in there,' Evangeline observed dispassionately.

However tiresome Miss Granby might have said that she found Mr Buckleigh, it did not seem to prevent her from putting forth her best efforts when dressing. The consequence was that when she came down-stairs, her appearance was more suitable for a dinner at Carlton House than for a family meal in the provinces. She was wearing a gown of ivory silk, cut very low and trimmed with pearls. Her hair was dressed high, with pearls entwined amongst her glowing blonde locks, and around her neck was a string of exceptionally fine pearls of a very unusual shade of pink. They had been a gift from her father on her come-out, and she was exceedingly proud of them, for she had never seen any like them. She allowed Elsie to drape an ivory silk shawl with a pink swirling pattern and a long fringe about her shoulders, before she left her chamber. She paused on the threshold, seized by a sudden notion. So Mr Buckleigh thought that he could keep an eye on her behaviour, did he? Would this include telling her father if she were to flirt outrageously with some man? What, though, if the man with whom she decided to flirt was Buckleigh himself? It would certainly serve him right if she used her much vaunted charms to enslave him!

She had not planned to make any kind of an entrance, but it so happened that as she was descending the staircase, Mr Buckleigh was being shown into the hall, having been relieved of his coat and hat. He stood watching her, his head thrown back. He was dressed all in black as befitted his calling, his neck-cloth plain and snowy white, his blond hair caught behind his head with a black satin bow. There was a natural grace in his stance, a slight smile played about his well-shaped lips, and those starkly contrasting dark brows were raised.

Suddenly, she was transported back to Lord and Lady Ashbourne's reception which they had held to celebrate their marriage. It had been a dazzling affair with dancing in the great ballroom, lavish refreshments, cards in one of the drawing rooms and the opportunity to stroll in the conservatory or on the terrace for those who wished to do so. Evangeline had been talking in the ballroom with her friend Lady Ilam, and Lord Ashbourne had been standing nearby, exchanging words with one of his guests. Then, as Evangeline was looking at him and reflecting that no man had the right to be so attractive, an arrested look had crossed his features. Following the direction of his gaze, she had seen the new Lady Ashbourne descending the stairs.

There were those who in the past had described Miss Jessie Warburton as plain. The woman approaching them was elegant, glowing and transparently in love with her husband. Observing Lord Ashbourne's face, Evangeline had seen that he felt exactly the same.

Now, looking down at Michael Buckleigh, she found herself thinking, why, he is just like Lord Ashbourne. Then her father entered the hall and spoke to the curate, the young man turned, the likeness was gone, and she wondered whether she had imagined it.

'My goodness, Evangeline,' said her father, seeing his daughter's splendour. 'You do us too much honour this evening.' He himself was dressed for evening with propriety, in knee breeches and coat of grey cloth and a maroon waistcoat.

Evangeline reached the bottom of the flight and looked up at Michael Buckleigh. She had forgotten how tall he was. 'I cannot see the point of having lovely clothes and not wearing them,' she said. 'To discard things that have not been used must be sinful, and I am sure that Mr Buckleigh must disapprove of sin.'

'Undoubtedly,' Michael answered, lifting her hand to his lips and directing a glance at her that only she could see. If he were honest with himself, she had taken his breath away and ignited the powerful surge of desire that she had seemed to kindle within him from the very beginning of their acquaintance.

During the course of the evening, Buckleigh wished more than once that there might have been twenty guests and a room full of people. Even the presence of Mrs Granby would have helped, but she had still felt too unwell to come downstairs. It was only with extreme difficulty that he prevented himself from leering at Miss Granby's well-displayed bosom. She had no business to be exposing herself in such a way at such an event. It was more than any red-blooded man could stand!

He had thought that he had managed to disguise his interest. When they retired to the drawing room, however, neither Michael nor Mr Granby wanting to linger over their port, he discovered how pitiful his efforts had been. Miss Granby glided over to the pianoforte and he joined her at the instrument, offering to turn over.

'Only if you agree to stop staring,' she answered in a low tone, smiling serenely as she leafed through the music. 'It is very unbecoming to a man of the cloth, you know.'

'If you were to be dressed more modestly, there would be nothing for me to stare at,' he responded swiftly.

Her smile disappeared. 'Are you accusing me of immodesty in my father's house, under his very eyes?' she asked him, remembering his words to her before breakfast.

He stared at her appalled. He could almost see this new curacy vanishing before he had even taken it up. 'That was not my intention,' he replied.

'Then your words were ill-chosen for their purpose.'

At that moment, Mr Granby's butler entered and began a low-voiced conversation with his master. This was Michael's opportunity to put things right. 'I did not say that you were not dressed becomingly, Miss Granby,' he said swiftly. 'But a lady of your undoubted charms constitutes a temptation to any man. Now a man of my calling is supposed to flee temptation, so what was I to do; run from the house when you came down the stairs? I would then have missed my dinner. You must advise me, ma'am. How must I proceed?'

Evangeline looked up at him, her expression unchanged. For a brief moment, he felt as if his fate hung in the balance. Then, with a teasing smile, she tossed her shawl completely off her shoulders and ran her fingers across the piano keys. 'Why, Mr Buckleigh, you must sing *con brio*. That should do the trick.'

After two songs, the tea tray was brought in and soon after that, Mr Buckleigh took his leave. 'It seemed to me, my dear, that you found Mr Buckleigh more congenial this evening,' Mr Granby remarked before they both retired.

'Since he is to live here and be our clergyman, it would be wrong not to make an effort to get on with him,' she answered carelessly. She smiled inwardly at the way in which she had discomposed the curate that evening; yet if she were honest with herself, she had to admit that his open admiration had discomposed her just as much.

In the clear light of day the following morning, Michael's cottage looked every bit as appealing as it had done the evening before. There were two bedrooms, both furnished with a bed, a cupboard with drawers, a chair and a fireside rug. Each room also had a corner curtained off, with hooks behind, on which clothes could be hung. The larger of the two rooms, which was at the back of the house, was the one in which Michael's trunk had been placed. There was also a small attic, which could be used as another bedroom, or for storage. Again, Michael silently thanked Lady Ilam for her forethought and, once he was back downstairs, he wrote a polite note of thanks, which he resolved to take to the Hall. He would thank her in person when he saw her, but did not want to be backward in any attention. He had been dreading spending a portion of the small amount of money that he had on furnishings and fuel. This expenditure would not now be necessary. More importantly, because he was so comfortably settled, he would be able to send for Theodora almost immediately.

He was just finishing his note when there was a knock at the door. He opened it to discover a respectable-looking girl in a crisp white apron standing on the threshold. She was holding a basket with the contents covered by a cloth. 'Mrs Davies said as I was to bring you this, sir,' she said, bobbing a curtsy.

'Mrs Davies?' he echoed, with a tiny frown.

'The housekeeper up at the Hall, sir,' she replied. 'May I bring it in?'

'Yes ... yes, of course.' He stood to one side so that she could enter with her basket. She took it through to the kitchen and removed the cloth to reveal a fresh loaf of bread, butter, milk, bacon, cheese, some eggs and a packet of tea.

'You've got the fire going, I see,' the girl said approvingly, as she took a frying pan from the kitchen dresser, put a knob of fat into it and set it over the fire.

'Yes, I heated some water for shaving,' he replied. 'Are you about to cook my breakfast?'

'That's right, Reverend,' the girl replied. 'Why don't you go and study your Bible, or some such, and I'll call you when it's ready.'

'Very well,' he answered, amused but also delighted. He had woken hungry, and had been wondering whether to go to the Olde Oak to see if they could serve him with something at this early hour. To have someone come and cook for him had been more than he had hoped for.

He had already read the Morning Office, so instead of taking the young woman's advice, he decided to unpack more of his things. He went upstairs and from his trunk he carefully removed his most prized possession. It was a fine, glossy red Roman pottery bowl, and it had been bequeathed to him by James Warrener who had died only the previous year. He could probably have sold it for a tidy sum, but he could not bear to do so. Apart from its sentimental association, it was the finest thing that he possessed. He carried it downstairs carefully, and placed it on the table in the window. His box of books stood open, but he had not put them on the shelves, so he busied himself with that task until the girl had set a place for him at the table in the window, and told him to sit down as his breakfast was ready.

'May I know to whom I am indebted?' he asked her.

'My name is Janet, sir,' she replied, watching him as he tucked into the plate of bacon and eggs which she had just cooked for him. 'But it's his lordship as has arranged for me to come and cook for you.'

He put down his knife and fork. 'You mean, you are to come regularly?'

'Oh yes, sir,' the girl answered. 'I'm to cook your breakfast, and make sure you've enough of something for midday. If you're not out anywhere for dinner, I'm to come and bring you something then, too. Oh, and Mrs Davies says I can clean for you once a week and change the sheets, but if you want cleaning done more often than that, you'll need to find someone.'

'But this is more than kind,' Michael exclaimed, thinking of his lodgings over the butcher's shop, where he had had to clean for himself, and find what food he could or starve. He felt terribly torn. It was wonderful to be looked after in this way, yet how could he afford it? Eventually, because he could do no other, he said, 'Mrs Davies must send me an account of what I owe her.'

Janet looked shocked. 'Oh no, Reverend, t'wouldn't be proper,' she said in hushed tones. 'It would be like charging the Lord Himself. Would you like a cup of tea, now, to wash it down?'

Michael agreed that would be most acceptable and, after he had eaten and drunk his fill, he left Janet to do the washing up, whilst he discarded the note that he had written and wrote another. The thanks that he had offered in his first note had been barely adequate, considering all that had been done for him.

His note written, he left the cottage, and prepared to walk into Illingham in order to deliver it to the Hall. Mr Granby had pointed out the direction in which he should go and he soon found that he was indeed only just outside the village. He met one or two people in passing as he walked and the smiles, together with the touching of forelocks, curtsies and 'Morning, Reverend,' convinced him that his arrival was indeed welcome. From what Mr Granby had said the previous day, it seemed to him to be very likely that he would see little of his vicar, Mr Lusty. This would be all to the good, for he might perhaps be able to carve out his own role, without constantly referring to another clergyman.

Illingham Hall had been described to him as being on the main street, but he had not been prepared for how close to the road the house actually was. No long, sweeping drive here, but a set of wrought-iron gates, with a short roadway behind, leading directly to a mellow-looking Elizabethan manor house. It took him less than a minute to walk up to the front door. He had intended merely to hand the note in to the butler, but in view of all the kindness that he had received, he asked if he might have a word with Mrs Davies.

The butler conducted him to the housekeeper's room where Mrs Davies, a wiry-looking woman with grey hair, stood up from dealing with her accounts in order to receive him. She seemed taken aback by his appearance, looking up at him in surprise, and saying, 'Oh! But you must be—' rather blankly, before breaking off and going on, 'of course you are the new curate. It is a pleasure to meet you, sir.'

Michael smiled. 'It is certainly a pleasure to meet *you*, Mrs Davies. I have just come from consuming an excellent breakfast cooked by Janet, and she tells me that I have you to thank, at least in part. I could not reconcile it with my conscience to walk past without requesting an interview.'

Mrs Davies's thin face coloured with pleasure. 'Well, I'm glad to help, that's certain,' she said. 'It was his lordship's idea, but he is away and he instructed me to make sure that you would be looked after when you arrived. We were many months without a priest in the village, you see, sir, so his lordship says to me, "When he does come, Mrs Davies, we must look after him. We can't expect him to tend the flock and do all his own cooking and cleaning as well".'

'That's very thoughtful of him,' Michael answered. 'I have written a letter of thanks to Lord and Lady Ilam, which I have left with the butler, but I wanted to speak to you in person, to thank you for your own kindness.'

'It was a pleasure, sir. You must tell Janet if there's anything you need. One of the men from the estate will look in to make sure you've enough logs, and Mary Scroggins, your nearest neighbour, will send her lad round first thing each morning to clear the fireplace and start a new fire; you may need to pay him a few pence to do it.'

Feeling as if he was living in the lap of luxury, Michael bade the housekeeper farewell, and set off to continue his walk.

The village was built on a slope and, as he walked on down the main street, he saw a drive leading off from the left which clearly went towards the vicarage. He stood looking at the house that would have been his had he been the vicar here and smiled ruefully. It seemed very sad that Lusty, who was entitled to live there, should choose to live in Sheffield, and this fine house should be unoccupied.

The next building of any size was the church. Michael walked up the path towards it, observing that it looked to be early English. An elderly man with gnarled hands approached him, identifying himself as a church warden, and asking whether he could be of any service. Michael introduced himself and requested a conducted tour of the church. He soon discovered that there was very little that old Samuel did not know, although most of the anecdotes with which he was familiar seemed to have a rather depressing conclusion.

'You'll not find any of the family here,' said the old man, as Michael read the words on one of the memorial plaques. It was dedicated to an incumbent who had been the vicar of Illingham for thirty years. 'All the angels of Ashbourne are buried in Ashbourne.'

'The angels?' echoed Michael, puzzled.

'All the men of his lordship's family are named after angels – like you, Reverend.'

Michael smiled. It had never occurred to him that he was named after an angel. His name had been his mother's choice. 'I shall not remember the half of what you have told me,' he said after they had completed their tour. 'You will have to tell me some of it again, I'm sure.'

'If I last that long,' said Samuel gloomily.

'Or if I do,' Michael added with a grin.

Samuel looked at him with a rheumy eye. 'I've known fellows as young and fit-looking as yourself to be carried off,' he said, nodding in agreement. 'Will you be wanting anything special for Sunday?'

They spoke for a little while about Michael's requirements for the service before they parted company for the time being.

As Michael came out of church, he saw two young ladies who were placing flowers on a grave and he walked over to speak to them. They greeted his advent with curtsies, but both appeared to be on the verge of having a fit of the giggles. 'Forgive my introducing myself,' he said with a bow. 'I am the curate, Michael Buckleigh.'

'I am Miss French and this is Miss Barclay,' said the taller lady of the two. They were both about Miss Granby's age, Michael decided.

'Miss Barclay; Miss French,' he acknowledged politely. 'Are you members of my congregation?'

'Yes indeed, Mr Buckleigh,' replied Miss French. She was as tall as Miss Granby, but dark, and with rather prominent features. 'We both live just outside the village.' She pointed in the opposite direction to his own home.

'Have you met many of your congregation so far?' Miss Barclay asked him.

'Not many. I am just getting my bearings. I met Mr and Mrs Granby and their daughter as I travelled here, and they were kind enough to take me up in their carriage.'

'They have returned from Sheffield, then,' remarked Miss French.

'They were attending a family wedding, I believe,' Michael answered.

'Yes,' Miss French agreed. 'It seems quite extraordinary to me that Evangeline should be going to weddings and yet not be wed herself. After all, she is quite the prettiest young lady around here. I dare say *you* have noticed how pretty she is, Mr Buckleigh.'

Michael could not think how to reply to this, so he was glad that Miss Barclay butted in by saying, 'Of course he has noticed! Prettiness is not everything though, is it, Mr Buckleigh?'

This time it was Miss French who did not give him a chance to speak. 'I have never pretended to be as pretty as Evangeline, but *I* am spoken for!' So saying, she peeled off her left glove and extended her hand so that Michael could see her ring.

'Charming,' he murmured. 'Will I have the pleasure of marrying you?'

Both young ladies began to giggle. 'That sounds so funny,' said Miss French. 'I expect you will. As for my friend, well, I may be spoken for, but she is not!' Yet again, they both lapsed into immoderate giggles.

Judging that there would be no sensible conversation to be had here, Michael simply inclined his head and, after saying that he hoped he would see them both in church on Sunday – which expectation they both vowed fervently to fulfil – he took his leave of them, hearing their giggles and whispers as he walked to the lych gate.

He continued his progress down the main street and put his head around the door of the Olde Oak Inn. It looked a respectable place and the landlady seemed to be pleased to meet him. He made up his mind to eat his dinner there once a week. It would be a good way of getting to know some of the villagers, as well as relieving Janet of the task of cooking for him every day.

He was leaving the Olde Oak when a sudden explosion of noise told him that the children had just been released from school. As they came running out, he entered the schoolroom on impulse, blinking a little as his eyes became accustomed to the interior after the bright spring sunshine.

'Can I help you?' said a female voice.

He took off his hat. 'Good day,' he said politely. 'I am Michael Buckleigh, the newly appointed curate. I have just been looking round and I saw the children leaving. Are you the village schoolmistress?'

'Yes, I am.' The teacher came towards him and he saw that she was a pleasant-faced woman of about his own age, simply dressed with brown hair neatly braided and brown eyes. 'I hope you are not going to ask me very much about the village or the church, however, for I am very new myself. The previous teacher, Miss August, has only just left to go and care for her widowed mother.'

'That's a disappointment,' he replied, his eyes twinkling. 'Perhaps I should leave immediately.'

'No, please don't, Mr Buckleigh,' the teacher said. 'I should introduce myself and tell you that I am Miss Leicester.'

'I'm pleased to meet you, Miss Leicester,' said Buckleigh, executing an elegant bow. 'For how long have you been a teacher? Is this your first appointment?'

'It is the first time that I have had a school to myself,' she admitted. 'My last post was with a vicar's family. As well as teaching his children, I helped his wife with the village school for one day a week. I enjoyed the work so much that when my appointment there came to an end, I resolved to look for something similar. My previous employer's wife is friendly with Miss August, and recommended me.'

'Who employs you?' he asked. 'To have a school in a village of this size is quite unusual.'

'Lord Ilam is my employer, but Lady Ilam has made the school her special concern. I wonder, Mr Buckleigh, would you be prepared to come into school from time to time? You could tell the children Bible stories, and help them to learn their catechism.'

'Yes, certainly I will come,' he replied. 'I would like to get to know the children and this would be a good way. No doubt I will see you on Sunday if not before.'

She escorted him to the door in order to say goodbye. 'I look forward to hearing you preach,' she said.

As he returned home, Michael reflected that quite a number of people were intending to hear him preach on Sunday. He only hoped that he would not be a dreadful disappointment.

Miss French and Miss Barclay had gone to the village driven by Miss French's groom in her father's gig. After they had encountered Michael, Miss French suggested that they should go and pay Evangeline a visit.

'Do we have to?' complained Miss Barclay. 'She always makes me feel so very plain.'

'Yes, we do,' Miss French replied. 'I want to show her my engagement ring, and see how green she looks when she hears that yet another of her contemporaries is engaged before her.'

'It's all very well for you,' grumbled Miss Barclay. 'At least you have a beau.'

'So will you when you come and stay with me in London after Reggie and I are married. Anyway, you can always say that Mr Buckleigh flirted with you outside the church.'

'He didn't, though.'

'That doesn't matter, does it?' replied Miss French with more than a little touch of impatience. 'If she likes him, it will make her jealous. We might also find out exactly what happened when the Granbys took him up in their carriage.'

Evangeline was at home, and professed herself to be delighted to see dear Maria Barclay and Jennifer French. As they kissed the air next to one another's scented cheeks, Evangeline suddenly felt weary of the pretence of friendship expressed by such as these young ladies. It seemed so utterly false. Had it been the encounter with danger when they had been held up that had made her suddenly aware of this? Or had it been that meeting with the rakish Mr Leigh which, despite their assumed identities, had had an earthiness about it that had stirred her blood?

Nevertheless she smiled, welcomed them in, and rang the bell for cakes and tea. After the initial polite introductory chit-chat, Jennifer said, 'I don't suppose that anyone has told you about my good news.' She took off her glove, and extended her hand as before.

Evangeline crossed to her side to examine the ring. 'It's charming,' she said, looking at the diamond surrounded by sapphires. 'Absolutely charming. Who is the lucky man?'

'Reggie Price-Matthews,' Jennifer answered, with a satisfied smile.

Evangeline smiled in polite acknowledgement, her expression giving nothing away. 'I am very pleased for you, Jennifer. When is the wedding to be?'

'The date is not set,' said Jennifer coyly. 'You will have an invitation, of course. I am so sorry to have taken your beau from you, Evangeline.'

Reggie had been one of Evangeline's court over two years before. For some months he had loitered about in Illingham, constantly bombarding her with bunches of flowers. He was a pleasant enough young man, but, at the time, Evangeline had been in the throes of her infatuation for Lord Ashbourne, and she had not given him a second glance. Obviously, he had seen the hopelessness of his cause, and transferred his interest to Jennifer.

Evangeline had no desire for Reggie's admiration. She did not want him back and, although she knew the power of her own beauty, she was too good-natured to take him away from Jennifer, even though she was sure that she could do so if she exerted herself. But it did seem a little hard that plainer girls were finding their life's partner before her. It was particularly difficult to tolerate when they stood before her with the kind of triumphant air that Jennifer was displaying at that moment.

'Please don't give it another thought,' she replied airily, pouring the tea which had just been brought in. 'It is not as though he is the only beau I have had, after all.'

'No, there was Morrison, wasn't there?' said Maria. Both the two visitors giggled. This time, Evangeline really was annoyed. Morrison had jilted Eustacia Hope, now Lady Ilam, at the altar nearly two years before. After this disgraceful behaviour, he had fled to London where he had attached himself to Evangeline, and then returned to the district as a guest of her family. As soon as she had realized that he was a jilt, she had dropped him like a live coal. Lord Ilam had seen that the fellow had left the district immediately. By no means everyone knew the whole story, however, and unfortunately there were those who had chosen to believe that Morrison had run away to escape from Evangeline.

'How sad to be so devoid of news that one feels bound to bring up something that happened years ago,' she remarked, trying not to show how irritated she was feeling.

Miss French looked annoyed at this remark, but merely said, 'You cannot expect us not to take an interest in you, Evangeline. After all, you are a local celebrity.'

'Like our new curate,' Maria put in helpfully.

'You have met Mr Buckleigh, then,' said Evangeline.

'Yes, just now in the village,' replied Maria Barclay. 'He really is exceedingly handsome, isn't he?'

'If one can tolerate the contrast between his hair and his eyebrows,' Evangeline agreed.

'You, of course, had a chance to meet him before any of us,' said Jennifer. 'He told us that you had taken him up in your carriage.'

'Yes. We met him at an inn on the way from Sheffield. We dined together then he travelled on with us in the morning.'

'You have stolen a march upon us, then,' said Miss Barclay, in rather a sulky tone.

'Oh, pooh, what is one carriage ride?' responded Jennifer. 'We have had the most charming conversation with him outside the church just now.'

'Indeed,' Evangeline responded dubiously. She had had a number of conversations with him, some of them flirtatious, some angry, some passionate, and some whispered. She could not recall any that could have been called charming.

The two other ladies must have caught something of the ambivalence in her tone, for Miss French said, 'Oh dear, Evangeline, you must be losing your touch! I showed him my engagement ring and, when he heard that Maria was not spoken for, his eyes fairly gleamed.'

'I very much doubt that,' said Evangeline, thinking only that from what she knew of Michael, she could not imagine him being so hopelessly indiscreet with such a silly young woman on such slight acquaintance.

'Well, really!' exclaimed Maria Barclay. 'Just because you are so pretty yourself, you cannot imagine any man taking an interest in another woman whilst you are about.'

'No, not at all,' Evangeline protested.

'I dare say you think that he is yours for the taking,' declared Miss French indignantly, springing to her feet.

'If that is your view, then I can't deny you the right to express it,' Evangeline replied, reaching the limit of her patience.

'Come, Maria, we will bid Evangeline farewell,' said Jennifer, seeing that they were not going to find out anything else. 'Obviously Evangeline still thinks that she can snare any man she wants. Well, she will soon find that she is mistaken, that is all.'

Chapter Five

—◦◦◦—

It was not until Friday that it occurred to Michael that he had still not found anyone to iron his vestments. Necessity had ensured that he was quite capable of ironing them himself, but he had no flat iron. He was quite certain that Janet would willingly do them for him, but so much was already being done for him by the staff of Illingham Hall that he rather shied away from asking for more. Had there been a laundry day that week, then he might have sent them with the washing, but as he had only just moved in, there was no need for anything to be washed.

After a little thought, he waited until he knew that school was over, and walked down the village street in search of Miss Leicester.

'Bring them down here,' she said, when he had explained his dilemma. 'I'll do them for you.'

'I am quite happy to do them myself,' he said. 'I am very capable and do not want to give anyone extra work.'

Miss Leicester thought for a moment. 'I have a suggestion to make,' she said. 'Two of the window frames in the schoolroom are not very secure. If you would be so good as to fasten them for me with hammer and nails, then I will iron your vestments. It will be a fair exchange.'

'An excellent idea,' Michael replied. 'I'll go and get them.'

'And I will have hammer and nails at the ready.'

In the event, Michael's task did not take as long as Miss Leicester's, so he remained in the cottage talking to her whilst she finished the ironing. 'Thank you very much, Miss Leicester,' he said, when she had finished. 'I shall be the image of the perfectly dressed clergyman.'

'Please, call me Juliana,' said the schoolmistress. 'We are very much in the same boat, are we not? Both educated people in a country village where education is a rarity; both incomers; very much the same age, if my guess is correct.'

'Very well, then; you must call me Michael,' he answered.

He had been so pleased to find friendship that it was not until he lay in bed that night that he wondered whether he had been entirely wise to encourage a spinster to call him by his Christian name so early in their acquaintance. However, the deed was done, and it would be dreadfully insulting to tell her now that she must call him Mr Buckleigh. He decided that since she was a sensible woman, she would probably be prepared to accept that they should only use Christian names in private. But then, that suggestion would imply an intimacy between them that did not exist. Really, life could be very complicated.

It was with a feeling of anticipation that was part excitement and part anxiety that Michael collected his crisply ironed vestments and his service books and set off for church on Sunday morning. Fortunately, the day was fine and bright, but the walk did give him pause for thought. Come a wet morning with muddy roads, he could easily end up looking like a drowned rat. He might keep his robes in the vestry, as long as the church was not damp. He would have to ask Samuel's advice. If there was any danger that they might become mouldy, no doubt the verger would be delighted to say so!

So well prepared was he that it was with a sense of shock that he opened the door to find Henry Lusty already there. 'Ah, Buckleigh, I'm glad you're in good time,' he said. 'You will assist me.'

Of course, Mr Lusty was the vicar and he was perfectly entitled to come and conduct the service. It seemed a little unfair, however, that he should have allowed his curate to make all the preparations without informing him that his work would be unnecessary. Michael must have looked completely taken aback, for Lusty spoke again, this time with a touch of impatience. 'I do trust that you have not forgotten that I am the vicar of this church and you are merely the curate?'

'No indeed,' Michael replied, pulling himself together. 'It's an agreeable surprise to see you here. I had not expected you today. I was feeling very nervous, I must confess.'

'It's not at all surprising,' said Lusty, his tone indulgent now that his superiority had been established. 'You will soon become accustomed. I shall turn up from time to time, you may be certain, just to ensure that you are on your toes. Come now. You may help me into my things.'

Much to his annoyance, after the service was over Michael was forced to acknowledge to himself that his greatest disappointment had been that he had been unable to do anything to impress Miss Granby. She and her father had come in just before the start of the service and had taken their places near the front. She had been dressed on this occasion in a pink gown and pelisse and a straw bonnet with pink ribbons and feather to match. He had imagined her being in the congregation whilst he captivated all present with his powerful and eloquent words. Instead, he had been obliged to wander about after Henry Lusty, holding things for him, reading what was passed to him and, in his own mind, impressing nobody at all, least of all himself. It had taken all the self-control of which he was capable to conceal his disappointment. At the close of the service, he had wanted to disappear into the vestry and never come out. He would have been quite surprised to discover that he was far from being the only disappointed person present.

When the new vicar had been selected, Lusty had been the preferred candidate of the Bishop of Sheffield. Perhaps partly out of guilt because he had robbed the clergyman of his bride, Ashbourne had confirmed the appointment. However, the villagers did not care for Mr Lusty, who had never taken very much interest in parish affairs, preferring to attend to his duties as bishop's chaplain. Michael, on the other hand, had made a favourable impression even in the few days that he had been in the village and had begun to endear himself to many. He had listened tolerantly to Samuel's ramblings, and exclaimed appreciatively about Janet's cooking. His personal call on Mrs Davies, and his willingness to taste her peapod wine had not gone amiss. He had made sure that he was up in time to thank the lad who had come to clean the grate. The landlady at the Olde Oak was partial to a handsome young man and had enjoyed her conversation with him; some of the children who attended the school had spoken to the new curate and received a cheerful reply. This had duly been reported to their parents. The congregation was a large one that day. Most of them were local to the village, but among them were Sir Lyle and Lady Belton and their daughter Amelia. Everyone had come to church hoping to see Michael in action.

Evangeline Granby had been among those who were disappointed, somewhat to her own surprise. She had come intending to look for things in the curate's conduct of worship in which she might find fault. Instead, she had had to watch Henry Lusty taking charge whilst Michael acted as his assistant. The thing was that she found herself not watching Lusty at all, but observing the other clergyman instead.

Whether performing the tasks allotted to him by the vicar, or simply standing or sitting, he played his part with enormous dignity and grace. By the end of the service she realized, to her mortification, that whereas she had absolutely no idea of what Mr Lusty had said or done, she could have described Michael's every gesture and movement in some detail.

Mr Lusty, though pleased at the numbers present, was disappointed at the restlessness of his congregation. He was also a little baffled at their behaviour afterwards, as they dutifully thanked him for his message, but spent as long, if not longer, commending the curate for his reading, his stance, and his expression.

'You must ask Mr Buckleigh to dine with us,' Amelia told her father, as they left the church.

'Very well, puss,' he answered, smiling down at her. 'No doubt you'll want us to come again so that we can hear him speak.'

'It was very disappointing, I must say,' agreed Lady Belton, unfortunately in Mr Lusty's hearing.

They were then obliged to speak to Mr Lusty who was also exchanging words with Mr Granby, for he wanted to be certain that his curate knew that he was in good standing with some of the best families. This meant that by the time the Granbys and the Beltons were free to engage Mr Buckleigh in conversation, he was already talking easily with Mr and Mrs Crossley, who were tenant farmers of Lord Ashbourne.

'We can take you up with us when we go home if you like, Reverend,' Mrs Crossley was saying comfortably. 'We have plenty of room for you and Miss Leicester, now that our Anna is married and living away.'

Mr Granby greeted the young curate warmly at this point, and commended him for his first public appearance. 'I was pleased to see that you didn't fling the Good Book today in the way that you did when we encountered the highwaymen,' he said jocularly.

The busy hubbub stilled for a moment as those who had been talking about their own concerns took in this interesting piece of information. 'What was this?' Mr Lusty asked, his face disapproving. 'I trust that Buckleigh has not been treating the scriptures carelessly.'

'Mr Buckleigh has been of great service to the community in aiding the capture of some desperate rogues,' Sir Lyle explained, his very tone a warning against further criticism of the young curate.

'Indeed,' answered Lusty. 'Remarkable.' He sounded very unimpressed.

'In fact, Mr Buckleigh, I have been meaning to ask you, are you a cricket player?' Mr Granby enquired.

'Why yes. I very much enjoyed playing at Oxford,' Michael replied.

'It is just that there is an annual match which takes place at the Illingham Hall garden party in the summer,' he went on. 'I always captain one side, and Lord Ilam captains the other. I was wondering—'

'For shame, Mr Granby, sir,' interrupted Mr Crossley in his deep rumble. 'His lordship should have an equal chance to claim a new player.'

'We'll talk about it over lunch, if you'll join us,' said Granby craftily.

'We were rather hoping that Mr Buckleigh would dine with us today,' said Sir Lyle, his words echoed by his wife and daughter.

'You are all very kind, but I have already accepted an invitation to dine with Mr and Mrs Crossley,' Michael answered. His eyes met those of Miss Granby. He thought that she looked disappointed, but he could not be sure.

There was a moment's quiet, during which a number of those present became conscious of Henry Lusty's rigid figure. 'Mr Lusty, you must join us instead, then,' said Mr Granby. The vicar thanked him and accepted, but he did not look at all pleased at being second choice. Michael would not have gone so far as to say that he had made an enemy, but he was aware that he would need to treat his superior with kid gloves. Evangeline did not look very excited at the prospect, either.

After most of the congregation had left, and Lady Belton had also accepted an invitation on behalf of her family to dine at Granby Park, the two clergymen prepared to remove their clerical robes.

'I intend to leave them in the vestry,' Michael said to Miss Leicester, who was standing nearby. 'That way, they should not become creased.'

'I will always iron them for you again if there is need,' she replied.

'Only if you have other chores for me to do in exchange,' he responded cheerfully.

Both Evangeline and Amelia eyed the schoolmistress with interest. She was dressed neatly, if not fashionably, but her figure and carriage were excellent. Many would say that a woman in such a station in life would be an excellent match for a clergyman. Amelia was not pleased at the reflection. Evangeline, though disturbed at the thought, could not have said why.

The Crossley family, together with Miss Leicester, were waiting for Michael when he returned from hanging up his vestments. He had had a brief and rather unsettling conversation with Henry Lusty in the vestry. 'Well, Buckleigh, you have certainly wasted no time in making yourself popular here.'

Michael hardly knew what to say in response to this, so he simply murmured something about people having been very kind. 'No doubt,' Lusty replied, rather thin-lipped. 'Pray do not imagine that the popularity of a clergyman can be built upon his ability to attract young women. Such allegiance is all too fleeting, believe me.'

'I have never thought, sir, that a clergyman would be wise to seek popularity in such a way,' Michael answered, lifting his chin a little.

'One would not have supposed it from past experience,' Mr Lusty retorted.

The only other occupant of the wagon, apart from Mr and Mrs Crossley themselves, was their younger son, Elijah, a boy of about 14. 'My daughter Anna is lately married to the son of a farmer on the other side of the valley,' Mrs Crossley explained. 'David is engaged to be married to Miss Welland, the doctor's daughter, so he is eating his dinner with the Wellands today.'

'Will young Mr Crossley and his bride come to live at the farm with you when they are married?' Michael asked.

'Yes, they will,' Mrs Crossley answered, 'and very pleased I will be to have another woman about the house again. I've missed our Anna, for there's no denying that apart from a skittish year or two a little while back, she's been a good help to me.'

The Crossley farm proved to be neat and immaculately kept, from the well-swept farmyard to the spotless farmhouse. 'Miss Leicester has eaten with us before, and I trust this will not be *your* last visit with us, Mr Buckleigh,' said Mrs Crossley. 'Or would you prefer me to call you "Reverend"?'

As Michael got down from the wagon, he assured his hostess that he would much prefer to be called Mr Buckleigh. He then turned and helped Miss Leicester down, and offered her his arm so that they could go into the house.

The meal was not yet ready, so Mr Crossley volunteered to show the visitors around the farmyard. Miss Leicester was sensibly shod and, moreover, disclosed that she came from a farming family, so she was happy to accompany them and demonstrated her knowledge by her comments. After this, they all went inside and Mrs Crossley invited them into the parlour, a handsome, spotlessly clean and tidy room, so that they might partake of sherry. Michael was a little surprised that a farming family should have such a beverage in stock, but Mrs Crossley explained that it had been given to them by Lord Ilam.

'I was his foster mother from when he was a baby. I do believe that he could not be more attentive if I was his real mother,' she declared. 'Indeed, sir, if I were to tell you how it all came about, you would be so shocked that ...' Her voice tailed away and, when she spoke again, it was to ask Michael about his own family.

'I am very much hoping that my sister will be coming to live with me soon,' he said, when he had explained how his stepfather wanted to go abroad. 'We are not a wealthy family and I am anxious to be able to take my turn in supporting her.'

'But surely your sister will be looking for a position as a governess or a companion,' suggested Miss Leicester, rejoining them. For the past few minutes, she had been standing with Mr Crossley allowing him to point something out to her from the window.

'My sister's health does not permit that,' Michael answered. 'It will always be my duty as well as my pleasure and privilege to look after her.' Miss Leicester raised her brows, but he did not enlarge upon his statement.

'I believe every big brother wants to look after his sister,' said Mrs Crossley comfortably. 'David was very protective of Anna when she was still living at home.'

'But women can sometimes almost be turned into children or invalids by the overprotective attitude of their menfolk,' Miss Leicester maintained. 'How many spoiled young women does one see these days? They are indulged from the very beginning of their lives, pampered, and under-educated until all they are fit for is lying about on sofas reading, and enumerating their complaints to anyone who will listen.'

'Someone has been reading Miss Wollstonecraft's writings,' Michael murmured.

'Oh, have you read *A Vindication of the Rights of Woman*?' Miss Leicester asked eagerly. 'We must discuss it together some time.'

'I would be honoured,' Michael answered. 'However, I must disabuse you of one misconception: my sister really does need looking after.'

The teacher smiled and nodded. 'As you say,' she replied, but she did not look convinced.

After the meal was over, Miss Leicester expressed an interest in seeing part of the farmyard again, and Elijah went with her and his father. Michael was going to accompany them, but received an unmistakable signal from Mrs Crossley to stay behind. 'I was telling you something about Lord Ilam,' she said. 'Normally I wouldn't disclose private things to a stranger, but you being a man of the cloth, I know that you can be trusted to be discreet.'

'Naturally I will,' Michael answered, 'but you must not feel obliged to tell me.'

'No, I will do so, because it will help you in your dealings with Lord Ilam and Lord Ashbourne if you know how things stand. The previous Lord Ashbourne was a wicked man, and he sent his grandson, the present Lord Ilam, who was then only Master Montgomery, to be brought up by us. The lad's father was not permitted to come near him most of the time. As a result, the two became estranged. It's only since the present Lord Ashbourne's second marriage that they have begun to get on better.'

'I see,' Michael responded.

'Mr Lusty would never have brought them together. Who knows, you might be the one to help father and son to become properly reconciled.'

'I?' Michael exclaimed, his brows soaring.

Mrs Crossley stared at him, lost for words. Then, as if aware that she ought to say something, she muttered a few words about his being a new clergyman to the area, with different ideas to offer. Michael was left with the feeling that that was not at all what she had really been thinking. A few moments later, the farmyard party returned; soon after that, they had tea. Once that was consumed, Mr Crossley went out to prepare the wagon, whilst Michael and Miss Leicester said goodbye to their hostess.

'It's been a pleasure,' said Mrs Crossley, as her guests thanked her; 'a real pleasure.' But it was Michael's hand that she squeezed most tightly, and it was at Michael that she directed her warmest smiles. In just such a way, he thought to himself, she might have smiled at a favourite nephew. He thought of what she had said and hoped that he would be able to help in some way.

They reached Miss Leicester's house first, and Michael got down as well, insisting that he would walk the rest of the way home. 'It's only a step and if I'm not to end up as broad as I'm long after that excellent meal, I really ought to get some exercise,' he said.

Miss Leicester invited Michael to come inside for a few moments. 'I want to apologize for the way in which I seemed to suggest that your sister ought to be earning her living,' she said frankly. 'Of course, you know her needs much better than I do. Sometimes, though, young women can be much more capable than we suppose.'

'I assure you that Theodora does as much as she can,' Michael replied briefly, for he had not been entirely pleased at the way in which Miss Leicester had been so ready to imply that his sister was just being idle.

'Perhaps she might like to help me in the school,' Miss Leicester suggested. Then she looked rueful. 'Oh dear, there I go again. I do apologize, Michael. Please say that I am forgiven!'

'Yes, of course,' he answered, a little surprised for he had forgotten that he had agreed that they should use one another's Christian names.

'"Yes, of course, *Juliana*",' she corrected him, with a laugh.

'I'll try to remember,' he replied, 'although I'm sure you understand that Christian names must only be used between us privately. And now I must be going.'

'Oh surely you could stay for tea,' she insisted. 'Otherwise I shall think that you are still annoyed with me.'

'Very well,' he agreed, not wanting to hurt her, but feeling slightly manipulated. He remained for about half an hour, talking mostly about books. As he left, he agreed to go into school the next day in order to give the older children some religious instruction, but he resolved to be alone with her as little as possible.

Chapter Six

---◦◦◦◦◦---

The following Sunday's service proved to be much more satisfactory as far as the residents of Illingham were concerned. No Mr Lusty appeared to steal the new curate's thunder; consequently Michael was able to conduct worship in his own way. The vestry proved to be an ideal place in which to store his vestments and, although Miss Leicester volunteered to iron them, there was not the least need. It did seem to Michael that the teacher looked a little disappointed about this, but as he had had experience of ironing his own robes and had not found the task to be congenial in any way, he decided that he must have been mistaken in this impression.

He was glad that as this was the third parish in which he had served, any nervousness that he might have been feeling had nothing to do with his conduct of worship. He had no fears that he would fall over his apparel, drop the chalice, or set fire to his sleeves, for instance, and, indeed, none of these disasters occurred to spoil the morning. The sermon that he had prepared late into the night made a good impression, and he tried hard not to feel gratified at the number of people who said how much better everything had been than on the previous Sunday. That would indeed have been falling prey to pride.

It would have been almost impossible not to notice the number of attentive female faces that were directed at him as he stood in the pulpit. Miss Leicester, with some of the older pupils sitting beside her, nodded seriously as he made each point, but it was Miss Granby who threatened to take his concentration away, as she listened with her head tilted slightly to one side, her beautiful face framed charmingly with a straw bonnet trimmed with pink flowers and ribbons, and lined with pink silk.

Sir Lyle and Lady Belton and Amelia were not here on this occasion, and Michael remembered that the baronet had declared that they must not be disloyal to their own parish church. Their absence at least made it possible for him to accept an invitation to dine with Mr and Mrs and Miss Granby without fearing that he would be disappointing the other family.

'You are a fine preacher, sir,' said Mr Granby when they were sitting at table. 'You pose an intelligent argument without making your premise too difficult for plain folk to understand.'

'Take care, Papa, you will be making Mr Buckleigh conceited,' said Evangeline, with a saucy look at the clergyman.

'Evangeline, dearest,' murmured Mrs Granby.

Michael darted a look at Evangeline's face, which suddenly looked a little stormy. He wondered whether perhaps Mrs Granby so much expected Evangeline to say something wilful, that she reacted as though her daughter had done so, whether in fact she had or not.

'Praise, when merited, should always be bestowed,' remarked Mr Granby.

Mrs Granby asked Michael about his sister, and seemed very pleased to hear that she might soon be coming to stay in the village. 'If you are agreeable, she might like to come and visit us here,' she suggested. 'Evangeline will be glad of the company. I think she sometimes becomes bored with only her father and myself to entertain her.'

'Nonsense, Mama,' said Evangeline dutifully. 'But, of course, your sister will be very welcome,' she went on, speaking now to Michael. 'You must know that we would be glad to meet any member of your family.' She glanced up at him through her lashes.

'I'm very glad to hear it, ma'am,' he answered, inclining his head slightly.

The day had clouded over after church and by the time they arrived at Granby Park, it had begun to rain, and continued in this depressing manner for the rest of the day. After dinner, the family withdrew to the drawing room, where a merrily blazing fire succeeded in banishing much of the gloom of the day. Mrs Granby sent for tea, and Mr Granby asked Michael if anyone had told him about the well dressing.

'I have heard of it and am eager to learn more,' Michael said.

'It's a very ancient custom and is pagan in its origins,' Mr Granby explained. 'When the Christian faith came to these parts, the custom was banned. Its revival dates back to about three hundred years ago when all the wells in the area ran dry, excepting only the wells of

Illingham. The custom of blessing the wells was revived, but this time with the agreement of the church.'

'When does this take place?'

'On Ascension Day,' Granby replied. 'It would normally be the task of the vicar to lead the procession and say the prayers of blessing at each well.' He paused, choosing his words carefully. 'I do not think it at all likely that Mr Lusty will want to perform this task. He has shown little interest in village concerns. I suspect, therefore, that the job will fall to your lot.'

'I look forward to it,' said Michael. 'What form do the decorations take?'

'Evangeline has some sketches of them, do you not, my dear?' said Mrs Granby.

To Michael's surprise, Evangeline coloured delicately, and seemed very reluctant to display her efforts. From what he had seen of her, he would have thought that she would be all too ready to do so. In fact, Mr Granby had to add his persuasions to those of his wife before Evangeline would consent to fetch her sketch book. Even then, she was careful to keep hold of the drawings herself, and only show the ones about which they had been speaking.

The pictures showed the three wells in the village, each decorated with garlands and branches. 'Everyone in and around Illingham who wishes to take part is allowed to do so,' said Mrs Granby. 'Different garlands are made by families, or by the school or by other groups. We send one from this estate, and so does Lord Ilam.' Michael studied the pictures carefully. Evangeline's drawing was no worse than that of most other young ladies, and better than some, but it was a modest talent.

'I do not think that I have seen anyone draw better than Evangeline,' said her father fondly.

'Papa!' exclaimed Evangeline self-consciously.

'It is true,' her parent replied. 'I suppose I might be allowed to believe that my angel is the best. Look, Matilda.'

He took one of the drawings to show to Mrs Granby. While he was doing so, Evangeline said to Michael 'What do *you* think of my drawing?'

'Your drawings are very pleasing,' he said eventually.

'But not the best you've ever seen.'

He paused. 'No; but I was lucky enough to see some drawings by Leonardo when I was at Oxford.'

She sighed. 'I think that even if my father saw drawings by Leonardo, he would *still* think that mine were best.'

Michael laughed. 'That's a parent's prerogative, surely.'

'All the time? People say that I am spoiled, Mr Buckleigh. Can you wonder at it? I am sure that your parents were too wise to praise you in such a way.'

'I do not remember my mother doing such a thing, and she has now passed away,' Michael replied. 'Certainly my stepfather would never think of praising me except under very unusual circumstances. So, you see, I have no one to tell me that I am best.'

'That's not fair,' she replied. Their eyes met, and for a long moment, neither of them said anything. Soon afterwards, the folder was put away and, not long after that, Michael went home in the Granbys' carriage.

The following morning, Evangeline rode into Illingham. It was not something that she did often, preferring the open country if she just wanted to ride, or Ashbourne if she needed to make any purchases. Today, however, she had decided to call on Mrs Davies to see if she had had any news about when Lord and Lady Ilam were likely to return home. She herself was as likely to have news as Mrs Davies, because of her friendship with Lady Ilam. Nevertheless, there was a chance that the housekeeper might have more recent news, and it would only be courteous to call upon her. Then, perhaps, if she had time, she might have a look and see how the new curate was settling in. He was a single gentleman, of course, and normally she would not dream of calling upon a single man, but she had her groom with her. Anyway, she told herself, a clergyman was in a different position to others of his sex.

Evangeline had a dainty little mare named Snowball, because of her colour. She was very conscious that perched on the mare's back in a riding habit of peacock blue, with a saucy hat embellished with a peacock's feather, she looked absolutely stunning. If there was anyone to dazzle in Illingham, like a certain curate for instance, then she would be ready. Followed by her groom, she rode in the direction of the village at a sedate trot.

They passed the curate's cottage, but although the groom got down to knock on the door at Evangeline's instruction – for it had occurred to her that it might be civil to inform Mr Buckleigh of her intention to call later – there was no answer.

Feeling a little disappointed, she rode on to Illingham Hall and was very politely received by Mrs Davies, who invited her into her sitting room. 'Please do come and have something to drink after your ride, Miss Granby,' said the housekeeper, eyeing the young woman a little warily. For Evangeline to call upon her personally was almost unprecedented. Furthermore, the visitor was known locally to be a somewhat over-indulged young woman, who could be haughty at times.

'Thank you,' Evangeline replied. 'That is very kind. I would be glad of some coffee.'

The housekeeper's room was warm and comfortable, with a neat sofa and two armchairs, two small tables, and a desk on which several ledgers were laid out, with an inkwell and quills bearing silent testimony to the fact that Mrs Davies was busy about her household accounts.

'Have you had any news of Lady Ilam?' Evangeline asked, as soon as they both had their coffee. 'I was wondering if you had heard when she might be returning.'

'Not for a little while yet, I think,' answered Mrs Davies. 'His lordship may come back for a while to see to the estate, then return to fetch her.'

'That sounds like him,' answered Evangeline with a smile. She had known Ilam for as long as she could remember, and he had always been committed to working the land. Until recently, Lord Ashbourne had shown no interest in his property and his son had had the whole of the Ashbourne estate to manage, which he had done very capably.

Mrs Davies smiled fondly. 'He's a fine master,' she said. 'We'll all be glad to have him back amongst us.'

A brief silence fell whilst both ladies sipped their coffee. Then, after Evangeline had considered how to raise the subject of Mr Buckleigh and failed to think of a way of doing so obliquely, she simply said, 'Do Lord and Lady Ilam know that the new curate has arrived?'

Mrs Davies shook her head. 'I've had no reason to write since he came. But I've done everything that his lordship said, such as making sure he's got someone to cook for him and that he's got food and logs enough. Mr Buckleigh came to see me in this very room and thanked me for all I'd done, which was little enough as I told him. After all, I only passed on his lordship's orders, and sent the girl to do for him.'

'Do you ... what do you think to him, Mrs Davies?'

The thin-faced housekeeper smiled. 'Such an agreeable young man,' she said. 'All the staff were disappointed not to hear him preach the first week, though he did very well yesterday, didn't he, miss? Mind you, he took me by surprise when he first arrived, for in some lights, he could almost be a relation of Lord Ashbourne.'

Evangeline listened to what the housekeeper was saying with great interest. She, too, had remarked a likeness to Lord Ashbourne in the young curate. It was interesting that someone else should have noticed what must be, after all, just a strange coincidence. 'Yes, indeed,' she agreed.

'Let's hope he stays,' said Mrs Davies. 'Mind you, from the way lots of young ladies were looking at him, I shouldn't be surprised if he does. Take Miss Leicester, for instance—'

Evangeline decided that she did not want to hear about the school-teacher. 'Yes, thank you, Mrs Davies,' she interrupted. 'I do not think that we should be speculating on the curate's romantic entanglements, should we?'

'No, miss,' replied Mrs Davies in a more subdued tone. 'More coffee, miss?'

Evangeline left soon afterwards. She was on the point of sending for her groom, when she remembered what Mrs Davies had said about Miss Leicester and decided instead to wander down to the school. The children had left, but she heard voices inside and, walking quietly in, she saw that Michael Buckleigh was in his shirt sleeves, obviously having just stepped off a ladder. Miss Leicester was offering him his coat, saying, with a smile, 'I'm sure such gallantry deserves a cup of tea.'

'Good morning,' said Evangeline. 'This looks like a scene of industry.'

'Good morning, Miss Granby,' replied Miss Leicester, not noticeably discomfited at the unexpected interruption. 'Yes indeed, Mr Buckleigh has been very industrious. He has been fastening a loose shutter at this window.'

'How commendable,' Evangeline replied, wandering about the room and looking around. 'Are you intending to teach in the school, Mr Buckleigh?'

'I am to teach the older ones their catechism,' answered the curate, who had greeted her advent with a bow, and was now allowing Miss Leicester to help him on with his coat. 'In what way may I serve you, Miss Granby?'

'In no way in particular,' responded Evangeline. 'Did you suppose that I had come to find you? By no means! I was simply wondering how well you had settled in, that was all.'

'Then you may see, if you wish to walk back with me to the cottage,' he said. 'I take it, though, that you are on horseback.'

'I am, but my groom may come from Illingham Hall to collect me if I leave word.'

Michael turned back to Miss Leicester. 'Then I will say goodbye, but see you very soon, no doubt.'

'No doubt,' she answered, smiling. 'And thank you for your help.' As he turned away, she said, 'Oh, one moment, Mich— I mean, Mr Buckleigh. There is some dust on your coat.' She stood on tiptoe and brushed something, which Evangeline was almost certain was completely non-existent, off his shoulders. 'There, that is better.'

'Thank you,' he answered, before bowing to her. 'Good day, Miss Leicester.'

'Well, this is an interesting development,' said Evangeline, after they had started to walk away from the school. A boy who had been hanging about in the street had been sent to the Hall with a message for Evangeline's groom. 'I had no idea that you were already acquainted with Miss Leicester before you came here.' Instead of walking straight up the main street, they left the village by a footpath which would bring them out very close to the curate's cottage and which cut a corner off their journey.

'I was not acquainted with Miss Leicester before,' Michael replied, rather tersely. He was a little annoyed with the teacher for treating him in such a proprietary way and letting slip his Christian name; with Evangeline for appearing at such a moment and making such assumptions; most of all with himself for agreeing to be on Christian name terms with Miss Leicester, and for allowing himself to be alone with her when he knew that it was not wise.

'Oh,' replied Evangeline innocently. 'I quite thought that you were.'

'And what gave you that impression?' he asked, his tone even.

'Well, when a lady betrays that she is on first name terms with a gentleman, then brushes fluff off his coat, it argues a close degree of acquaintance,' Evangeline replied airily.

'There is no close degree of acquaintance,' Michael insisted. 'She is a pleasant lady who works in the community, as do I. It is only sensible to be on good terms with her.'

'I see,' Evangeline replied. They fell silent for a while. She glanced up at him as he walked beside her, his strides athletic, long and easy. He really was extremely good to look at.

For his part, Michael was having very similar thoughts. He had just been working closely with Juliana Leicester, having her help him off and on with his coat, climbing a ladder while she held it, and making one or two other minor repairs to the schoolroom whilst she stood alongside him. Not once had he felt the slightest twinge of interest in her as a woman. It seemed that he only had to walk next to Evangeline Granby, not touching her but being aware of her presence, her perfume, for him to want to drag her into the nearest field and finish what they had started in that little inn in Sheffield.

Pull yourself together, Buckleigh, he said sternly to himself. You are a clergyman and this lady is a parishioner. He quickened his pace, intending to cut this time of temptation as short as possible. They walked on for a few minutes, until Miss Granby halted. 'Mr Buckleigh, this is too much,' she said. 'You forget how tall you are!'

She laid her left hand on his arm. He turned to look at her. Her voice sounded as if she was out of breath; her bosom was heaving a little, her right hand pressed to it. His body reacted before his mind sounded the alarm. Their eyes met and held. He caught hold of her right hand and pulled her round to face him, looking down at her, his own breathing a little faster, but not because he was out of breath.

He was saved from making a complete fool of himself by the sound of footsteps in the lane. He dropped Evangeline's hand as if it were red hot, and took a step backwards. Moments later, Miss Barclay and Miss French appeared from round the bend and, once they had seen the couple coming the other way, began to giggle behind their hands. They barely stopped to exchange greetings, before continuing on their way after casting a knowing look in Evangeline's direction.

'I beg your pardon, Miss Granby,' said Michael, when they were alone again. He was a little flushed, though whether because the day was warm or from mortification it would have been difficult to say. 'I will measure my pace a little better to yours.'

'I am obliged to you,' replied Evangeline. She, too was flushed, but, of course, that may have been because she had been obliged to walk too fast.

They said nothing more until they reached the curate's cottage. Evangeline's groom was already outside and he touched his forelock to them. Michael smiled, and immediately approached the horses the groom was holding, his manner of petting and speaking to them clearly showing that he was very much at ease with the animals.

'She's a beauty,' he said, as he patted Snowball. 'Is she yours, Miss Granby?'

Evangeline smiled. 'She is, and I love her dearly. Do you ride, Mr Buckleigh?'

'I do,' he answered ruefully, 'I have no horse of my own at present. I shall purchase another when I am able, but my priority must be to provide for my sister at this time. Would you like to come inside and inspect my domain, Miss Granby? We can leave the door open so that your groom may remain within sight.'

She looked up at him, wondering whether this would be wise. She knew perfectly well what had just happened on the path. He had almost kissed her and she would probably have let him. That would have been disastrous. It was one thing to flirt with the curate upon her own terms: it would be quite another to permit such intimate attentions from him, no matter how much faster he caused her heart to beat. Then she recalled that she had more to say to him with regard to Miss Leicester, so she walked past him gracefully as he held the door open for her.

She eyed the interior of the cottage with approval. The furnishings bore the stamp of Lady Ilam's handiwork, but there were a few things already set out which gave an indication of Michael's character. He was clearly a tidy person, for his books were arranged carefully on the bookcase, and the few other belongings that were visible were neatly in their places. There was a fine pottery bowl on the table in the window.

'Do you hope to have your sister to stay very soon?' she asked him.

'Thanks to the kindness of Lord and Lady Ilam, I see no reason why she should not come almost immediately.'

'That might be as well,' said Evangeline. 'If I had the mistaken notion that you and Miss Leicester were already acquainted, then others might think the same.'

Michael took a deep breath. 'Miss Granby, I really do not think—'

She interrupted him. 'That it is any of my business?' she completed. 'You may not think so, sir. Perhaps you have not lived in a village before. I can assure you that everyone's business is everybody else's. You have been in the schoolroom mending the fabric of the place, when Miss Leicester could easily send for Ilam's carpenter. She irons your vestments; you go to Crossley farm to dine with her and you permit her to call you by your Christian name. If I have noted these things, then you can be sure that others have, too. In no time at all, your neighbours will have the banns called.'

He stared at her, appalled, but determined not to be browbeaten. 'You are mistaken, Miss Granby,' he said. 'I have lived in a village before and so has Miss Leicester.'

'In that case, it might be as well for you to ask yourself why she should be so ready to expose herself to such gossip.'

A grin began to spread across his features. 'Miss Granby, it strikes me that you might just be jealous.'

She drew her shoulders back. 'Jealous? I?' she asked with a scornful smile. 'And why do you suppose I should be jealous of the attentions that a lowly curate chooses to bestow upon a village schoolteacher? I simply seek to preserve you from gossip; that is all. Do not forget what I said to you before about informing the bishop about any improper behaviour on your part. We have been long enough without a clergyman here; it would be very unfortunate if you should be obliged to leave because of scandal.' She watched the flush of mortification flow into his cheeks and turned away, feeling strangely guilty.

He bowed with something less than his usual grace. 'I am obliged to you, Miss Granby for putting me in my place,' he said.

She nodded abruptly. 'Good day, Mr Buckleigh,' she said. For the second time, he put his hand out and caught hold of her arm. In response, she looked down at his hand and said again, with added emphasis, 'Good day, Mr Buckleigh.'

He released her then, and followed her to the door. She was about to mount Snowball with her groom's assistance, when the jingle of harness and the clatter of hoofs proclaimed the arrival of a newcomer. It was with a feeling of resignation that Michael observed Miss Belton handling the reins of a gig, pulled by one horse. She was accompanied by her maid sitting next to her and a groom riding behind.

'Here is another member of your court,' said Evangeline, smiling sweetly as her groom threw her into the saddle. 'Why don't you take her to meet Miss Leicester? There is safety in numbers, after all.' She turned to greet Amelia, who responded in kind.

'Good day, Miss Granby,' Michael said, before turning to his new guest.

'Oh, good day Mr Buckleigh,' said Amelia, her face wreathed in smiles as she allowed Michael to help her down from the gig. 'I have come to see how you are settling in.'

'That's very kind of you,' said Michael with a smile, as he handed the maid down. The presence of the maid was a relief to him. His conversation with Evangeline Granby had shaken him more than he liked to admit. It had simply not occurred to him that his friendship with Juliana Leicester might be subject to misinterpretation by the rest of the village.

They entered the cottage, whereupon Miss Belton turned to the maid, taking out her reticule. 'Go to the shop and procure for me some white thread,' she said, handing the girl a coin. When the maid had gone, she turned to Michael with a bright smile. 'Now,' she said, 'you can show me everything.'

There was a tiny pause. 'You have seen it, Miss Belton,' Michael replied frankly. 'There is just this one room downstairs, apart from the kitchen.'

Amelia looked about her. 'How delightfully cosy,' she declared. 'And upstairs, I suppose, are the bedrooms.'

Suppressing the urge to ask what else she might think would be up there, Michael simply said, baldly, 'Yes.'

'How much I would like to see the room where your sister will be sleeping,' she said, almost wistfully. 'Would you be so good as to take me upstairs to look at it?'

Evangeline began the journey by urging her mount into a bracing trot. Michael's words about being jealous had hit home. How dared he accuse her of such a thing? Just because they had kissed, he thought that he had some sort of claim upon her. The trouble was that if he could not forget that kiss, neither could she. She felt a twinge of guilt when she remembered how haughtily she had spoken to him. After all, he had saved her from highwaymen. Furthermore, he had refrained from telling her parents about her bad behaviour in Sheffield. She owed him something.

There were those in the village who would be all too pleased to pass on juicy gossip about the new clergyman. From personal experience, she was well aware how destructive gossip could be. She told herself that that was why she had been displeased to find Michael in such an intimate situation with the schoolteacher. Her warning to him had been completely genuine. If he was not more careful in his attitude towards the women of the village, he would find himself in trouble. Now Amelia was at the cottage, throwing herself at him no doubt, and if anyone was going to flirt with him, then it would be she and not that tiresome Amelia Belton!

Murmuring something to her groom about forgetting a handkerchief, she turned her mount, and within a matter of minutes, she was slipping out of the saddle once more, and entering the curate's house after knocking briefly on the door. She was just in time to see Miss Belton disappearing at the top of the stairs, whilst Michael looked on from the ground floor, an expression of utter consternation upon his face.

'Mr Buckleigh, pray come up and show me which is to be your sister's room,' Miss Belton called down brightly.

Evangeline looked up at him, raising her brows, before drawing a handkerchief from the pocket in her riding habit and allowing it to float to the floor. 'Why do not I go up also, since I am here?' she said. 'I, too, would very much like to see where your sister is to sleep.'

Michael gestured ruefully for Evangeline to ascend the stairs, then followed her up the flight. He was therefore able to see the expression on Miss Belton's face as they both emerged at the top. It was something akin to baffled rage. 'Why, Evangeline,' she said, summoning up a smile with an effort. 'I thought that you had returned home.'

'I had set off, but found that I had forgotten my handkerchief,' Evangeline replied.

'This way, ladies,' said Michael, showing them into the room that he had set aside for Theodora's use. It was a pleasant enough room, but did not really warrant the efforts that both ladies appeared to have made to see it.

'This is delightful,' said Miss Belton, overdoing things a little. 'When is she to come?'

'As soon as possible,' Michael replied devoutly.

Chapter Seven

It might have been supposed that a diligent curate could expect to have such a wish granted, especially since it was made not simply because he would take pleasure in his sister's company, but also for the very virtuous reason that he would then be more adequately chaperoned. Unfortunately, however, he received a letter telling him that as Theodora had caught a severe chill, travelling would be out of the question for some days. The following Sunday, therefore, instead of looking down upon the reassuring figure of his sister seated in the vicarage pew, he was greeted by the sight of a number of ladies, several of whom had, with varying degrees of delicacy, expressed an interest in him.

The lovely Miss Granby, who made his senses reel, whether by chance or by design he could not be sure, was seated with her parents. Miss Leicester, who had recently taken to wearing a rather more frivolous bonnet, was also there. Miss Barclay and Miss French were sitting together, in between a lady and gentleman who could only be Miss French's parents. Sir Lyle Belton was present, along with his wife and daughter, and a gentleman in military uniform whom Michael did not recognize.

Apart from them, there were two young ladies from a farming family, who gaped at him, then whispered behind their hands. All of womankind seemed to have gone mad. The landlady of the Olde Oak appeared to wink at him, but that might just have been a trick of the light through the stained-glass window. Miss Belton even waggled her fingers at him as he ascended the pulpit steps to deliver his sermon! Theodora could not possibly come too soon as far as he was concerned.

After the service was over, Sir Lyle made haste to introduce the young man in military uniform who was with his party. 'My nephew, Lieutenant Jeremy Fellowes. Jeremy, meet the new curate of this parish, Mr Buckleigh.' Barely had the two young men greeted one another than the baronet, remembering how he had been beaten off the mark on a previous occasion, invited Michael to dine.

'Are you staying with your uncle, sir?' Michael asked the lieutenant, when he had accepted the invitation.

'For a short time,' he answered. He was a handsome man, tall and slender, with golden hair that waved slightly. 'I will have to rejoin my regiment eventually, but for now I am a man of leisure.' At this point, Mr and Mrs Granby came out of church. 'What's more,' he added appreciatively, 'one needs leisure in order to explore the beauties of the area.' Fellowes could not be blamed, Michael conceded silently to himself. Evangeline was indeed a picture in a white gown trimmed with gold, and covered with tiny golden flowers. Suddenly he felt like punching the young officer for no justifiable reason.

Despite his feelings, however, there was nothing for it but to introduce the lieutenant to Evangeline and her parents. After a brief glance between Sir Lyle and his lady, the party invited for dinner was extended to include the Granbys as well.

'Is not my cousin handsome?' Amelia asked Michael, as they travelled in Sir Lyle's comfortable chaise a short time later. The lieutenant was on horseback and the Granbys were in their own chaise, so there was plenty of room for Michael to travel with the Beltons. 'I have to admit that I am exceedingly partial to fair-haired men,' she added provocatively.

'I am perhaps the wrong person to ask,' he replied, deliberately ignoring the second part of her speech. 'It seems to me that ladies and gentlemen can never agree upon what constitutes handsomeness in their own sex.'

Amelia shook her head. 'I cannot agree with you,' she replied. 'I can see that Evangeline is excessively pretty and I am quite prepared to say so.'

'Then perhaps it is merely gentlemen who are poor at recognizing good looks in other men,' Michael suggested.

'I think you may be right,' Sir Lyle agreed, and went on to relate an amusing anecdote that had come into his mind. Meanwhile, Amelia sat with a little smile on her face, thinking, I have made him jealous. It had not been part of her plan to have Evangeline present, but upon reflection it occurred to her that it might not be a bad idea. She would provide a useful diversion for Jeremy, leaving the field clear for her to pursue Michael.

Had the lieutenant been consulted, he would have confessed himself very ready to fall in with her plans. He had been struck by Evangeline from the very first and, having noticed the beauty of her face, had then gone on to take appreciative note of the luscious curves of her figure. He had not been unaware of the air of tension in Michael as he had made appreciative remarks about Miss Granby. A desperate flirtation was always to his taste. If it had the added benefit of making the curate jealous, then so much the better.

He had taken a dislike to the clergyman from the very first. He was rather inclined to dismiss men of the cloth as being unworthy of consideration. He was therefore annoyed with himself for sensing that there was something about Michael that meant that it would be very unwise to discount him in such a way.

They were a cheerful party at dinner. Michael was seated on Lady Belton's left opposite Mr Granby and with Amelia next to him on his other side. Evangeline was on Sir Lyle's left, and opposite her mother. On her other side was Lieutenant Fellowes, who seemed delighted to have the opportunity of getting up a flirtation with her.

Michael, for his part, resolved to take no notice of them and was soon deep in conversation with Amelia Belton, a fact that did not pass unnoticed by Evangeline, who immediately resolved to make herself even more agreeable to the soldier who was sitting beside her. 'I am wondering, Lieutenant, how it comes to be that you and I have never met,' she said. 'Amelia is your cousin after all, and I have lived in this vicinity for the whole of my life, as has she.'

'It does seem strange,' the young man agreed, 'but I can assure you that had we ever done so, then the encounter would have been graven upon my memory!' He laid his hand on his heart and sighed. Then, with a laugh, he abandoned his extravagant manner, noting with satisfaction that Michael had been glancing his way. 'In truth, it isn't so very strange. Remember that whereas Amelia is an only child, I have an older brother and two sisters who are now married. It was much more common when we were children for the Beltons to visit us at our home. Do you have any cousins, Miss Granby?'

Evangeline nodded. 'My father is an only child, but my mother's sister has two daughters. They are the bane of my life, I assure you.'

'No doubt they are constantly complaining at being compared to you,' he suggested.

'No no, quite the reverse,' Evangeline replied. 'It is I who suffer from odious comparisons.'

'I cannot imagine upon what grounds,' said the lieutenant gallantly. 'You are too kind.'

'Not at all. One does not complain about perfection.'

Evangeline found this compliment rather fulsome, but it made a welcome change to Mr Buckleigh's implied criticisms of her dress and conduct. 'My self-esteem is now very thoroughly soothed,' she remarked.

'Then my work is done,' smiled the lieutenant. 'Do you ride, Miss Granby?'

'Whenever I can get the opportunity,' she answered.

'Amelia does not. What a shame,' he murmured, his eyes sparkling.

For her part, Amelia had no hesitation in drawing Michael's attention to this flirtatious conversation. 'I can see that Evangeline is very taken with my cousin,' she remarked. 'I find that a little surprising in a way.'

'Indeed?' murmured Michael, trying not to sound particularly interested.

'She is generally more partial to dark men,' Amelia told him. 'Look at Lord Ashbourne. He has jet-black hair and Evangeline has been in love with him for years.'

After dinner was over and tea had been drunk, the party split up. Naturally enough, Mr and Mrs Granby offered to take Michael up in their chaise.

'What a shame that you cannot stay for longer,' said Amelia to Michael as Mr and Mrs Granby were making their farewells and Evangeline and the lieutenant were continuing their flirtation until the last possible moment. 'I have been making a collection of illuminated Bible texts, and was hoping that you might like to see them.'

'It will be something to look forward to,' Michael replied, inwardly thanking the Almighty for his lucky escape. Why people always supposed that clergymen must only like religious art he could not imagine.

To his surprise, on their arrival at Granby Park, Mr Granby said, 'I will hand the ladies down, then, with your permission, I will travel on with you to your home, Mr Buckleigh. I would like some further conversation with you.' Clearly Mrs and Miss Granby had not been informed of his intentions, for they both looked surprised. Michael readily gave his consent, and soon they were continuing their journey.

Mr Granby wasted no time in raising the matter that was on his mind. 'I needed to speak with you in private, Mr Buckleigh. I have a problem in which I would very much like your aid.'

'Of course, sir,' Michael replied, glad of the opportunity to return some of the kindness that had been extended to him. 'I shall do whatever lies in my power.'

'I am obliged to go to London unexpectedly,' Granby said. 'Had we not just arrived home from Sheffield, I would have taken my wife and daughter with me, but you have seen how a journey knocks my wife up. It takes her at least a week to recover. I therefore intend to leave them at home to look after each other. I shall not be gone much more than a week, I should think. In the meantime, I must ask if you will keep an eye on them and on Evangeline in particular.'

Michael hoped that he did not look as panic-stricken as he felt. Had Mr Granby asked him to give assistance in holding up the London stage, he could hardly have felt more horrified.

'I am very much concerned about her,' Granby continued anxiously. 'She is accustomed to having her own way. I freely admit that I am the one responsible for spoiling her, but my wife is not robust and should Evangeline subject her to a show of defiance, she would not be able to stand against her. In short, I would be exceedingly grateful if you would act as a kind of extra guardian for Evangeline.'

Michael could feel his heart sinking into his boots. The one young lady to whom he had acted as guardian from time to time was his sister, and she was obedient, unselfish, and sunny-natured. Miss Granby, though good-tempered when she chose, did not seem to possess either of the other qualities in abundance. Furthermore, the beauty of her face and the superb contours of her figure caused him to react to her in a manner that reminded him that he had been a man before he was ever a clergyman. He would be well advised to keep away from her as much as possible. To be obliged to advise her on her behaviour would be quite intolerable. Impossible to disclose all of this to her father! Nevertheless, for the sake of his sanity he attempted to make some protest. 'But sir,' he exclaimed, 'I cannot believe that she would be prepared to look upon me in such a way. I cannot be as much as ten years her senior. There must be someone else; Lord Ilam, for example.'

Granby shook his head. 'Ilam is still from home and I have no idea when he will return. What's more, he is much the same age as yourself. Evangeline has known him for years and he is married to one of her closest friends. I do not think that she would take him seriously.'

'Then what about Lord Ashbourne?'

'That would never do. In view of her past infatuation with him, I would rather not encourage her to go anywhere near him. Besides, he is from home as well and, even if he were not, his wife is nearing her confinement.'

'Sir Lyle Belton, then?' Michael suggested, growing desperate.

'Miss Amelia and my daughter are rivals and have never dealt well together, I fear,' Mr Granby answered smiling ruefully. 'Besides, there is now an additional danger. No doubt you noticed the attention that Lieutenant Fellowes was paying to Evangeline. I mistrust that young man. His family is quite large and he hasn't got a penny to bless himself with. I'm not wealthy, but Evangeline is our only child and she will receive a very respectable dowry and quite a pretty sum at my demise. She could easily become a target for a fortune hunter who wasn't over greedy. Now is not the time for me to go away leaving her unguarded.' Seeing that Michael continued to look doubtful, he went on, 'Mr Buckleigh, it would ease my mind so much if you would do this. You may not be much older than she, but you have an authority by virtue of the office that you hold. I will not leave Illingham happily unless I can be certain that someone will watch over her.'

Michael wanted to refuse, yet how could he? He had been very grateful for all the hospitality that he had received since his arrival in the village. He knew that he might never be able to return it. He could not refuse this opportunity of repaying the other man's kindness. What was more, the reference to the office that he held reminded him that he had a duty to care for every person in the parish. Yet he feared that Evangeline might well turn out to be more trouble than all the other parishioners put together.

'Very well, Mr Granby,' he said, trying not to sigh. 'I will act as an unofficial guardian to Miss Granby as you request.'

Mr Granby smiled with relief. 'My wife will be so thankful,' he said.

Later that evening, Mr Granby went to his wife's room to tell her about the arrangement that he had made with the curate. 'I must confess that I am very relieved,' he said.

'So am I,' Mrs Granby admitted. 'Don't stay away longer than you must, my dear. Most of the time she is a dear girl, but I do dread confrontations with her.'

'I will be back so soon that you will hardly notice I have gone,' he said reassuringly, planting a kiss upon her brow.

'Do you really think that Mr Buckleigh will be able to keep her in check?' she asked him anxiously, catching hold of his sleeve.

'I fancy he'll know how to make her do as she's told if necessary,' he replied. 'I detect a vein of steel in that young man.'

His interview with Evangeline the following morning was rather more stormy. He had toyed with the idea of simply not telling her of his decision, trusting to the fact that nothing of any significance would occur before his return. Then he reflected that such an action would hardly be fair to anyone in the case, especially Mr Buckleigh.

'Papa! How could you?' Evangeline exclaimed. 'I'm not a child!'

'I'm well aware of that,' he responded.

'Then why treat me like one?'

'It is not treating you like a child to make those arrangements that will most ensure your comfort,' he answered. 'If I were leaving Mama on her own, I would make the same request.'

'Really?' she said doubtfully.

'Well perhaps not exactly the same. Mama is not likely to become a target of fortune hunters.'

'Papa, how many London seasons have I had?' Before he could answer, she went on, 'Two! I have had two seasons, and I am to go to London later on this spring as well! Do you not think that I can detect a man who is after my money by now?'

'Evangeline, my angel—'

'Anyway, what makes you certain that Mr Buckleigh can be depended upon? He might not be as reliable as you suppose.'

'That is a very serious allegation,' said Mr Granby, drawing his brows together. 'I think that unless you have heard anything to his discredit you ought to withdraw it.'

It was the perfect moment for Evangeline to tell her father about how the curate had kissed her in Sheffield. She could alter the story so that it would not be so much to her discredit. Perhaps she could say that she had been lost and that he had led her astray. Even as the words were upon her lips, she found that she couldn't do it. She coloured. 'I beg your pardon, Papa. I didn't mean anything to his detriment. I was only thinking that he would soon be very busy with his sister's arrival. You might have given him too much to do.'

'Then it is up to you to make sure that his duties with regard to yourself are very light,' he responded, finding it easy to be firm with his angel when he was on the point of departure.

Determined not to shirk his duty, Michael set out for Granby Park the following morning. He could have thought of a thousand reasons for putting off the visit. In the end, he concluded that the sooner he went, the longer he could leave it before he had to go again. He devoutly hoped that Mr Granby had told Evangeline of his intentions, otherwise, he could not think of the smallest reason why she should take any notice of him. Not for the first time, he told himself that he bitterly regretted the encounter in Sheffield. It had made everything so much more complicated. The trouble was, every time he came to that conclusion, he ended up smiling as he recalled the taste of her lips.

Evangeline received him in the drawing room and, from the martial light in her eye, he could see that she was acquainted with Mr Granby's plans. Even though it was eleven o'clock, there was no sign of Mrs Granby. 'Well, here I am, as you see,' said Miss Granby. 'What instructions do you have for me? Shall I fetch my slate so that you can give me some letters to copy? Or would you prefer to hear me say my catechism?'

'Miss Granby,' he began.

'I have already practised the pianoforte this morning, but I will confess that I have rather neglected my mathematics,' she went on sweetly.

'Miss Granby,' he began again. He had come prepared to be conciliatory, but her aggressive attitude was damaging his intentions.

'What do you think about my posture?' she asked him, drawing back her shoulders. 'Would you like to see me sitting with the backboard on?'

Even while his temper was rising, he found himself noticing how her action had drawn his attention to her excellent figure. The powerful effect that this had upon him made him even more annoyed. 'Enough!' he said sharply. 'If you think that I wanted this charge any more than you, then you are very sadly mistaken.'

'Then why did you accept it?' she demanded.

'What else could I do? Your father has been everything that is kind to me since my arrival. How could I possibly refuse the one request that he has made? Believe me, Miss Granby, I cannot think of anything that I want to do less than keep an eye upon you and your affairs.'

'Then why do you not simply go away?'

'Because I cannot reconcile it with my conscience,' he answered.

She laughed. 'What a very compliant organ that conscience of yours is,' she said, laughing derisively.

'And what is that supposed to mean?'

'It conveniently enables you to forget about your own misdemeanours, but suddenly makes you holier than thou about mine.'

'I suppose that you are referring to that unfortunate incident in Sheffield,' he said, colouring.

'What else?' she asked. 'It was the one thing that would have prevented my father from asking you to keep an eye upon me, but, of course, you said nothing of it. Could it be because you know that what would be seen as simply a young girl's foolishness would be condemned as shockingly immoral behaviour in a clergyman? Oh fie, Mr Buckleigh!'

'You cannot possibly regret that incident more than I do,' he replied.

'No, I don't suppose I can,' she answered. 'I should not like anyone to know about it. It would make me look such a fool, after all – the girl who allowed herself to be kissed by a lowly curate. But I would over-come all that embarrassment, if I felt that it was for the greater good.'

'Miss Granby, are you threatening me?' he asked her.

She looked at him consideringly. 'Do you know, I think perhaps I am,' she answered. 'I haven't written to the bishop yet, but who knows, if you were to interfere in my concerns too much this week, I just might find it necessary. Did you want to speak to Mama, or have you discharged your errand for today?'

'I see no reason to disturb Mrs Granby,' he replied, picking up his hat from the table where he had laid it. 'It was, after all, to save her anxiety that your father placed upon my shoulders this most unwelcome responsibility. You might consider her feelings before you decide to go your length. Believe me, Miss Granby, you may threaten all you like but nothing will prevent me from doing what I see to be my duty. Good day to you.'

She stood at the window and watched him walk down the drive. For perhaps the hundredth time, she reflected upon how tiresome it had been of her father to put Michael in a position of authority over her. Just that morning she had dropped the copy of *A Vindication of the Rights of Woman* and it had fallen open at a page which had stated that:

Daughters should be always submissive.

Her father might have the right to demand obedience, but Michael certainly did not! She was now even more determined not to submit to the curate's authority. The fact that he was exceedingly handsome when angry did not change her view; rather, it made her even more annoyed for having noticed the fact. She was surprised to discover, too, that his principled response excited her admiration and this annoyed her as well. Strangely enough, the piece of his behaviour that rankled most with her was the way in which he had hung upon Miss Belton's lips at the dinner table the previous Sunday.

Her conscience might give a slight twinge at having spoken to him so insolently, but she firmly repressed it. After all, he deserved to be irritated after how he had behaved. It only remained to discover how best to do this.

Her opportunity came two days later when Lieutenant Fellowes arrived on horseback. 'I thought you might like to go for a canter – show me the countryside, and so on,' he said, his eyes sparkling. 'What do you say?'

'I say give me a quarter of an hour to change into my riding habit,' she answered. Perfect, she said to herself as she ascended the stairs. She would go for a lovely, refreshing gallop with the handsome soldier and she would not take a groom. What's more, she would make sure that Michael found out! She did feel a twinge of guilt as she walked past the door to her mother's chamber, but she did not allow it to disturb her. Mama would be abed for some time longer. They might even have returned from their ride by the time she had come downstairs.

As Evangeline descended the steps of Granby Hall, she saw that Snowball had already been brought round. Lieutenant Fellowes dismounted from his own horse and stood ready to throw her into the saddle. Really, he was quite handsome in an ordinary sort of way, she decided, looking at him surreptitiously as she took hold of the reins. Perhaps she might even allow him to kiss her. That would serve Michael right.

Chapter Eight

Michael had not intended to return to Granby Park so soon. It happened, however, that he heard in the village that Mrs Granby's housekeeper had suffered a bereavement, so he decided that he had better call upon her. This would also give him an excuse for seeing Mrs and Miss Granby at the same time, without looking as though he was spying upon their concerns.

Naturally, he called upon Mrs Granby first, and found her in the drawing room looking anxious. Her brow cleared at the sight of him. 'Oh, Mr Buckleigh, I am so pleased to see you,' she said. 'I am a little concerned about Evangeline.'

'Not already?' he exclaimed involuntarily. Then, conscious that he had leaped to an unwarrantable conclusion, he added hastily, 'I beg your pardon. Is she unwell?'

'No, she is well, at least as far as I know.' she said quickly. 'It is just that she has gone riding with Lieutenant Fellowes and she has not taken a groom.'

Michael could feel the anger rising up inside him. Her father had only been gone a matter of days and already she was worrying her mother by her wilful behaviour. Not only that, but she had ridden off with the very man from whom Mr Granby had wanted her protected. Involuntarily, he clenched his fists. Then, conscious of his hostess's anxious expression, he forced his expression to relax into a smile.

'Come, ma'am, she will not come to any harm, I'm sure. She is an excellent horsewoman, is she not?'

'Why yes, but—'

'And Lieutenant Fellowes is a cavalry officer; so no problems there.

What's more, she is of good family and well connected. He will not risk harming her, even if he has any such intention, which I very much doubt. It's just a case of high spirits, you may be sure. Remember that they are in the country, not in Hyde Park.' He smiled as reassuringly as he was able, and was rewarded when Mrs Granby smiled back at him.

'Of course you are right, Mr Buckleigh,' she said in relieved tones. 'I am making something out of nothing. You must blame my nerves, which have never been of the best. Would you care for a cup of coffee? And please stay for nuncheon.'

Michael had plenty to do, but he had no intention of leaving Mrs Granby until Evangeline had returned. He accepted her invitation, but pleaded the need to speak to the housekeeper about her recent loss.

'Oh yes, poor Mrs Gibbons. I know that her aunt's death was expected, but, even so, it was distressing to her.' Mrs Granby herself conducted Michael to the housekeeper's room, where she left him to offer what comfort he could.

When he returned to the drawing room nearly an hour later, he hoped he would find that Evangeline had returned. His hopes were to be disappointed and Mrs Granby was once more looking anxious. He sat down with her and proceeded to ask her about her family in Sheffield, gently drawing her out, so that she was soon talking freely, her worries forgotten.

The two riders had not yet returned when nuncheon was served and, for a few moments, Michael saw the anxious look return to Mrs Granby's face. In the nick of time, he had the happy notion of asking her about a portrait which hung over the fireplace. He seemed to detect a likeness between the lady in the portrait and Mrs Granby herself. Were they related, perhaps? This turned out to be a most fortunate choice of subject, for the portrait was of a distant relative of Mr Granby. There was a link between his family and that of his wife somewhere in the past, and they had been trying to discover where and when that link had occurred.

They had only just finished eating when noises in the hall alerted them to the fact that Evangeline had returned. Immediately, Mrs Granby's expression lightened. 'You said that everything would be all right,' she said to Michael. 'I wonder whether they would like anything to eat.' She turned to the footman. 'Christopher, will you be so good as to find out whether Miss Evangeline and Lieutenant Fellowes wish to join us?'

The footman bowed and withdrew.

'I am glad that your fears have proved to be groundless,' smiled Michael, wondering how he could contrive to speak to Evangeline on her own without distressing her mother. If he allowed this blatant piece of bad behaviour to go by unremarked, he might as well abandon any pretence at doing as Mr Granby had asked him.

The footman soon returned. 'Miss Evangeline has gone straight upstairs to change out of her habit, ma'am,' he said. 'The young gentleman who brought her home sends his regrets that he cannot stay.'

'Has he left?' Michael asked abruptly.

'He is doing so, sir.'

Michael turned to Mrs Granby. 'Excuse me,' he said. 'I must speak to the lieutenant.' He left the room as quickly as he decently could and was fortunate to find that Fellowes, having removed some burrs from his horse's mane, was only just climbing into the saddle. 'One moment, Lieutenant,' Michael called out from the top step.

'Yes?' answered the officer, raising his brows at Michael as if the curate were a stable boy who had exercised too much temerity in addressing him unbidden.

'You surely do not intend to ride off without speaking to your hostess,' said Michael, as he descended the steps.

'I am expected elsewhere,' Fellowes answered haughtily. 'I sent my regrets, as courtesy requires.'

'Unhappily, you were also expected *here* earlier and Mrs Granby has been anxious,' the curate told him. 'An apology from your own lips would be appreciated, I'm sure.'

The lieutenant knew this. Under any other circumstances he would have been out of the saddle, ready to soothe Mrs Granby with glib words, but Michael's criticisms had nettled him. Not for anything would he enter the house now, as if he were meekly obeying the clergyman's instructions.

'You may tender them for me,' he said insolently. 'I'm sure that you are better at grovelling than I am.'

Quick as a flash, Michael caught hold of the horse's bridle. He said nothing: his warning look was sufficient.

'Out of my way,' the lieutenant bit out, before setting his horse on its hind legs then galloping away.

Michael went back inside to where Mrs Granby was waiting. 'You will stay and see Evangeline before you go?' she said to him. Her tone seemed to him to be pleading.

'If you wish it,' he answered calmly. The last thing that he wanted

97

was another battle with Evangeline, but something needed to be said and he doubted whether Mrs Granby would say it.

A short time later, Evangeline came downstairs. She was dressed becomingly in a gown of her favourite shade of blue. 'Did you have a pleasant ride, dearest?' Mrs Granby asked her tentatively.

'Oh, delightful,' Evangeline answered. 'We rode towards Matlock and saw some very fine scenery.'

'Such a pity Lieutenant Fellowes could not stay for some refreshments,' said her mother.

'He had another engagement,' Evangeline replied. 'Anyway, we had already refreshed ourselves.' She looked at Michael with narrowed gaze. 'Good of Mr Buckleigh to bear you company,' she added.

'He has been so kind,' beamed Mrs Granby. 'He has been with me all morning.'

'How fortunate he is not to have had anything else more pressing to do,' Evangeline replied.

'Evangeline, dearest,' murmured Mrs Granby.

'I have also been visiting Mrs Gibbons, who has lost her aunt,' said Michael in an even tone. Evangeline had the grace to blush. An awkward silence fell.

Eventually Mrs Granby said, 'If you will excuse me, I think I will go and lie down.' She turned to Michael, holding out her hand. 'Thank you, Mr Buckleigh. You have been so kind.'

'Not at all, ma'am,' Michael replied warmly. 'I was glad to be of service.'

'I'm sure you were,' said Evangeline, after her mother had gone upstairs. 'I wonder whether my father ought to know about the way that you are lavishing your attention upon my mother.'

Michael bit back the angry words that he knew would start a confrontation immediately. 'She needed some attention this morning,' he replied. 'She was very anxious, and I fear that that must be laid at your door.'

Evangeline coloured. 'You are impertinent.'

'Impertinent – or rather uncomfortably truthful?' he asked her. 'Did it not occur to you how worried your mother would be when you rode off unchaperoned to God knows where with a man you hardly know? Or perhaps your chief concern in this matter was how best to annoy me.'

'Upon my soul, you take too much upon yourself,' replied Evangeline, uncomfortably aware that that had indeed been her chief motive. 'What makes you suppose that I should have the slightest interest in what you think? You, a threadbare curate!' She ran her eyes contemptuously up and down his figure.

'I do not suppose it,' he answered. 'The reason why you wanted to annoy me was because you cannot bear to be checked in any way. You have been spoiled all your life. Your father indulges you, your mother is afraid of you, and the consequence of that is that you think that you can do anything you like.'

Evangeline took a deep breath. 'Mr Buckleigh, you presume too much. Since when did my father give you permission to admonish me?'

'Let me see. He asked me to be your unofficial guardian, to keep an eye upon you, guard you, watch over you. He also reminded me of the authority of my position. I think he made his wishes perfectly clear.' Recalling one of Mr Granby's requests in particular, Michael went on, 'You mentioned that you had had some refreshment. May I ask where?'

'We stopped at an inn.'

'You took refreshment with him in a public inn?'

Evangeline shrugged carelessly. 'You know how it is.'

He crossed the room and caught hold of her by the shoulders. 'Tell me you have not permitted him to take any liberties,' he said fiercely.

She tossed her head. 'If I had, you should be the last person to criticize,' she said. In fact, they had taken their refreshment outside the inn, seated on a bench in the open. As for permitting liberties, that had been her intention, but when it had come to the point, she had not wanted to do so. Nevertheless, she would certainly not let the curate know that.

'I must insist that you tell me. Did you allow him to kiss you?'

She did not answer, but simply stared at him defiantly. For a moment the outcome hung in the balance. He wanted to kiss her more than he could remember wanting anything in his life before, but the temporary responsibility conferred upon him made such an action utterly inappropriate. He released her almost violently and turned away.

Evangeline had been holding her breath, half in anticipation. She was surprised at how disappointed she felt. To make up for that disappointment, she said the most hurtful thing that she could think of. 'You are forgetting the last conversation that we had in this room. Remember that I could destroy your reputation with one letter to the bishop.'

'I am aware of that, but I will not be blackmailed and I will not be brow-beaten. You may threaten all you like, Miss Granby, but you will not prevent me from criticizing your conduct when it is at fault.' He took a couple of steps closer to her, and lowered his voice. 'What is more, if I hear of any more childish behaviour from you, I shall do what your father should have done years ago.'

'And what is that?' she asked him suspiciously.

'Why, I shall simply put you across my knee and give you a good hiding. Good day to you. Make sure you apologize to your mother.'

Evangeline was so angry after he had gone that for a time she was quite unable to speak. The smashing of a small figurine which stood on the mantelpiece gave some relief to her feelings, but did not satisfy the urgent need that she felt to have her revenge upon Michael Buckleigh. How dared he criticize her conduct? She had only gone out riding for heaven's sake. It was enough to make her wish that she *had* allowed Fellowes to kiss her.

While her anger was still hot, she went upstairs to her room, sat down at her writing desk and, after mending her pen, she took a fresh sheet of paper and wrote a letter to the bishop, giving a colourful version of the curate's scandalous behaviour in Sheffield and describing his impertinence since then. This exercise soothed her feelings enormously and, after the letter was finished, she sat at her table in the window, her chin cradled on her hands as she thought about the excursion that she had just enjoyed with Lieutenant Fellowes.

The ride itself had been delightful. She was an experienced horsewoman, who enjoyed the challenge of tackling different kinds of terrain. Lieutenant Fellowes had been an ideal companion, keeping the kind of pace that she enjoyed and not noticeably making any allowances because she was a woman.

When they paused to admire the scenery, or got down to give the horses a rest, however, she found him less than congenial. If he was not paying her compliments that were a little too broad for her taste, he was boasting about his exploits as a serving soldier, or in the hunting field. Frankly, she had found his conversation rather dull.

Turning back to her letter, she folded it and wrote the bishop's name and address on the outside. The very writing of it had had the effect of cooling the heat of her temper, however, and she now found herself less convinced that she should take such a step which would almost certainly mean the end of Mr Buckleigh's career. He did seem to take his work very seriously, unlike a friend's brother, a vicar who appeared to look upon his parish as a means of gaining money to spend in London whilst his long-suffering curate did all the work. Evangeline could not imagine Michael behaving in such a way. She thought of how he had looked standing in the church porch, his vestments stirring about him in the breeze.

Out of the corner of her eye, she caught sight of her reflection in the mirror, her chin propped on her hands, a slightly dreamy expression on her face. Really, she must pull herself together at once! She was starting to feel sympathetic towards the tiresome clergyman and that would never do!

To turn her mind to other matters, she picked up Miss Wollstonecraft's book which lay open next to where she had been working. She had never done any more than flip through the pages, but now she picked it up, and chanced upon a most appropriate paragraph.

A man of rank or fortune, sure of rising by interest, has nothing to do but to pursue some extravagant freak; whilst the needy gentleman, who is to rise, as the phrase turns, by his merit, becomes a servile parasite or vile pander.

That was much better. 'A servile parasite,' she said, in tones of deep satisfaction. 'I must remember that next time he chooses to throw his weight about.' Feeling calmer, she left her room and walked along the passage to her mother's bedchamber. She found her mother lying down on the bed but not asleep.

When Mrs Granby saw her daughter, she sat up. 'You have not quarrelled with Mr Buckleigh, have you, dearest?' she asked anxiously.

'What if I had?' Evangeline asked defensively.

'Oh, nothing,' was the quick reply.

Made sensitive by Michael's words, Evangeline suddenly felt almost as if she was observing her mother for the first time. She saw the older lady's eyes slide away from hers and was horrified to find herself wondering whether her mother really was a little afraid of her. She sat down on the bed. 'Don't worry, we were just talking,' she said, taking the other woman's hand.

'I should hate you to quarrel with him,' said Mrs Granby earnestly. 'He was so kind to me today; and to Mrs Gibbons as well. I cannot imagine Mr Lusty giving up so much of his time just to allay someone's fears.'

'You shouldn't have been afraid, Mama,' said Evangeline. 'I'm a very good rider, you know.'

'Yes, I know,' Mrs Granby replied simply. 'But you are all I have, dearest.'

'I'm sorry, Mama,' Evangeline replied remorsefully. 'I won't make you worry like that again.'

After Evangeline had soothed her mother's anxieties, she returned to her own room. Miss Wollstonecraft's book was still open at the passage that she had been looking at earlier. She recalled the phrase 'servile parasite'. Why had Michael Buckleigh agreed to 'keep an eye' on her? He could have said no. Probably he was hoping to reap the reward of her father's gratitude by battening on to her family for evermore! Her annoyance with the clergyman came back afresh. It had at least been partly his fault that her mother had been upset. He had probably been encouraging her fears, not comforting her as he had said. Wretched man! He need not think that he could walk away without her taking revenge. She would just have to think of a way of annoying Michael that did not involve upsetting her mother.

As Michael walked down the drive, he berated himself for handling the whole matter so badly. How could he have threatened to put Evangeline over his knee? What had he been thinking of? No one else seemed to be able to make him lose his temper as did she. He knew why, of course: it was all due to that powerful attraction that she had for him.

That was not the only part of the affair that he had handled clumsily. He should not have confronted Lieutenant Fellowes in the way that he had. After all, he could hardly have taken Evangeline on the outing had she not accepted his invitation. Nevertheless, in Mr Granby's absence it was his, Michael's, duty to point out that to expose a young lady to possible public censure was not the action of an officer and a gentleman. Even so, he wondered whether he had made too much of it, not because of his responsibility to Mr Granby, but because he was jealous. What would he not have given to be able to gallop across the countryside with Evangeline! He sighed. With any luck, war might be declared and the lieutenant's regiment might be summoned overseas.

Anxious for an encounter that did not involve confrontation, he wandered down to the school where Miss Leicester, who did not have any pupils at that time, welcomed him with a cup of tea and home-made scones. This kindness was very welcome and he sat with her for a comfortable hour, drank two cups of tea and consumed at least three scones. When at last he left, he was unaware of how much this visit had caused her hopes to lift.

The next time he saw Lieutenant Fellowes was at church two days later, and the circumstances were particularly annoying. When Michael had entered the church from the vestry, he had supposed initially that Miss Granby was not at worship, for her family pew was empty. Then, as the congregation rose to sing the opening hymn, she came in, not with her mother, but with Sir Lyle and Lady Belton, Miss Belton and Lieutenant Fellowes. The whole party proceeded to enter the Granby family pew, with Evangeline sitting next to Lieutenant Fellowes. Throughout the service, it seemed to Michael that the two of them did nothing but make eyes at one another. So distracted was he by this spectacle that he even lost his place in his sermon and was obliged to leave rather a long pause while he found it again. This incident seemed to provide the two young people with cause for further amusement. By the time Michael pronounced the final blessing, he was convinced that this must be the worst service that he had ever conducted. He was very thankful that Mr Lusty had not appeared by chance to discover how he was getting on.

Miss Granby and the lieutenant came out of church a little later than the rest of the party, and Michael had a chance to speak to them. 'Is Mrs Granby unwell today?' he asked.

'She has a slight headache,' Evangeline answered. 'She is prone to them when there is an east wind. I dare say she'll be glad to see you if you are looking for an excuse.' The lieutenant hid a smile.

'I do not need an excuse to visit the sick,' Michael answered, his tone more pompous than he liked. 'I see that you are still staying with your relatives, Lieutenant Fellowes,' he went on, stating the obvious. Splendid, Buckleigh, he added in his own mind, you're not just a pompous windbag, you're a slow top as well.

'Indeed,' the young officer answered. 'I have an excellent incentive for remaining, as you see.' He bowed in Evangeline's direction.

'I was very thankful for his presence in the area,' she said, darting a flirtatious glance at the lieutenant. 'A simple message that I had no escort brought him to my side in the most gallant way possible.'

'How convenient,' Michael drawled.

Evangeline darted a startled look in his direction. The intonation of his voice had been remarkably like that of Lord Ashbourne. Before she could give that idea any further consideration, her attention was claimed by Miss Barclay and Miss French. Michael took advantage of this by saying to the other man, 'Have you had the opportunity to express your regrets to Mrs Granby?'

Fellowes drew himself up straight. 'I beg your pardon?'

'I am sure that she will be pleased to receive your apologies,' Michael replied.

The lieutenant glared at the man facing him. For a few moments, he forgot where he was and nearly thrust his fist into the face in front of him. Then a lady behind him spoke and he realized what a shocking thing it would be to punch the curate in the church porch. He allowed a false smile to cross his features. 'It was only a country ride,' he said in a patronizing tone. 'I suppose that Mrs Granby is a rather delicate lady and easily made nervous.' He stared at Michael as if to imply that he was made of the same kind of stuff.

'Knowing that, it would have been wise to avoid upsetting her,' Michael responded, determined not to lose his temper. 'I would ask you to give that matter a little more thought in the future.'

Fellowes glared at him, before turning on his heel and strolling up to Evangeline who was still standing with Miss Barclay and Miss French. Sir Lyle approached Michael and asked whether he would like to dine with them. 'Miss Granby is to join us,' the baronet explained. 'We had made arrangements to collect both her and her mother this morning, but Mrs Granby is not well. It would be a dull dinner for her at home I fear, with her mother abed and her father away.'

Michael glanced across at Evangeline. So she had lied to him. Obviously flirting with Fellowes meant more to her than being honest with him. Knowing this, he was glad that he had already accepted another invitation to Crossley Farm. Despite his promises to her father, the last thing that he wanted to do was to watch Evangeline with Fellowes.

Evangeline had not been unaware of the conversation going on between the curate and the soldier, and she glanced at the two of them standing in the doorway, Fellowes in his dashing cavalryman's uniform which flattered his figure so enticingly, and Michael in his vestments. What would Michael look like in uniform, she wondered. She tried to picture him thus attired, but while the picture that she managed to conjure up was seductive enough, she found to her surprise that she actually preferred him in his vestments. Perhaps it was because he looked so at ease in them. Then, as the soldier appeared to take umbrage at something that the clergyman had said, she remembered how annoyed she still was with Michael. For a brief moment or two, her eyes met his. She thought that he looked disapproving and she lifted her chin defiantly. It would be satisfying to flirt with Lieutenant Fellowes under his nose at dinner, she decided. It was only when Sir Lyle's party began to walk to the carriage that she realized Michael was not coming. Glancing round, she saw him exchanging a laughing remark with Miss Leicester, then nodding at

Mr Crossley. Miss Leicester, seeing the direction of her gaze, lifted her chin and smiled in a rather proprietary way. When Lieutenant Fellowes next addressed a playful remark to Evangeline, she had to ask him to repeat himself.

Chapter Nine

Mr and Mrs Crossley were as hospitable as always, and the meal that was served was excellent, but half of Michael's mind was at the Cedars. What was he to do about Evangeline? At times, he was convinced that her sole purpose for flirting with Lieutenant Fellowes was to annoy him. On other occasions, he castigated himself for being so conceited as to imagine any such thing. Why should Miss Granby not be drawn to Lieutenant Fellowes? He was just the kind of dashing young man whom she must have been meeting constantly in London. He had a good seat on a horse, and was able to accompany her when riding, a pursuit which she obviously enjoyed. He, Michael, was also an excellent rider, but unfortunately he had nothing to ride. The property he lived in was his on loan and by an act of charity. He did not even have his own parish. Why would a lovely, well-dowered young woman ever look at such as he?

Such thoughts as these were running through his head during the meal at Crossley farm, so much so that on one occasion, Mrs Crossley had to address the same remark to him three times. He really must pull himself together, he decided. He must face facts. He was infatuated with Miss Granby. He had conquered such feelings before and he could do so again. Indulgent Mr Granby might be, but he would never agree to his only daughter marrying a penniless curate. Had he not spoken just before he left about his fears that Evangeline would fall prey to a fortune hunter? He would never have done such a thing had he even considered that same curate as a son-in-law. In the meantime, he would be better employed seeing more of Miss Leicester, or of Miss Belton, whose parents clearly favoured him.

Unfortunately, however, he could not dismiss from his thoughts the fact that Evangeline was his responsibility, entrusted to his care by her father in his absence. How could he best discharge this responsibility? After Mr Crossley's gig had taken them back to Illingham, Michael got down at the same time as Miss Leicester and told her that he needed her advice.

Miss Leicester was too wise to show how delighted she was at this eventuality. His seeking her out in this way was evidence that he felt the need of the counsel of a mature woman. She invited him into the schoolmistress's house and asked him to be seated whilst he told her in what way she might be of service. So sympathetic was her expression, and so ready was she to listen, that he soon found himself telling her the whole story of his unwilling temporary guardianship of Miss Granby, concluding with an account of the unchaperoned riding expedition.

'No doubt you will tell me that I am being over-scrupulous,' he said, a little self-consciously at the conclusion of his tale. 'Having shared the matter with you, I am more than half wondering whether I am making a mountain out of a molehill.'

'I cannot agree with you,' she replied. 'A young woman cannot be too careful of her reputation. Such a prank could easily make her appear fast.'

Oddly enough, Miss Leicester's support of his original view had the effect of making Michael want to defend Evangeline. 'Surely not in the country,' he replied. 'In London now, it would be a very different matter.'

'This problem would not have occurred in London,' Miss Leicester pointed out. 'She would hardly have been left alone in the house with no company but an ailing mother. Besides, I suspect that even Miss Granby would obey the rules when in Town. Here, near her home in this comparatively isolated place, she thinks that she can go her length.'

'It is unfortunate that her mother's health is so uncertain,' said Michael. He was beginning to feel uneasy and was more than half wishing that he had never begun this conversation. It was starting to feel uncomfortably like gossip.

Miss Leicester sighed. 'That is to be laid at Miss Granby's door, at least in part,' she said. 'She is an only child and shockingly spoiled. She is undoubtedly a great beauty, but her very looks are marred by all the airs that she puts on. She knows that she only has to lift a little finger and Mama and Papa will leap to fulfil her desires.'

Michael looked at her, startled at the vigour of her sentiments. 'Is that not a little harsh?' he asked her, wrinkling his brow.

Miss Leicester blushed, conscious that she had gone too far. 'Perhaps,' she agreed. 'You must blame the fact that my own background was very different. I always knew that I would have to make my way in the world – as did you, of course.'

He nodded. 'That is so,' he agreed. 'Anyway, I have spoken to Lieutenant Fellowes and I do not intend to take the matter any further. I am sure that I have allowed the weight of responsibility to bear too heavily upon me. You must blame the fact that I am expecting my sister to arrive any day now. The thought of having to look to the needs of two young ladies is rather daunting.' He stood up to leave. 'Thank you for allowing me to share this with you,' he went on, as he picked up his hat. 'I feel much easier in my mind now.'

'Yes of course,' Miss Leicester answered, smiling. 'Please let me know if there is anything that I can do to help; and do bring Miss Buckleigh to visit me when she arrives.'

'Thank you. I shall be pleased to do so.'

As he took hold of the door handle, she surprised and slightly alarmed him by laying her hand on his. 'I cannot wait to meet her,' she said.

Michael thought no more about his conversation with Miss Leicester for, just two days later, he met his sister off the stage in Ashbourne. That he was doing so in style was thanks indirectly to Lord Ilam. Michael had made enquiries at the Olde Oak about hiring a conveyance and this information had found its way back to Illingham Hall. That same day, the head groom had come to the cottage with the news that his lordship's gig would be available for his use, either for him to drive himself, or for one of his lordship's grooms to do so if he did not feel competent. Should the weather be poor, then a closed carriage would be made available.

Michael was staggered by Lord Ilam's generosity. He had come across noblemen who were sympathetic to his calling and ready to throw the occasional piece of largesse in his direction. This would usually come in the form of dinner, or a joint of meat, or perhaps a basket of fruit. Never before had he encountered this kind of consistent open-handedness. He could hardly wait for an opportunity to thank the viscount. He decided that he would obtain the direction of Lady Ilam's parents so that he could write immediately. He did not want to be backward in attention towards one who had showered him with such disinterested benevolence.

As the time approached for the stage to arrive, he found himself becoming very excited and, when his sister got down, it was all that he could do not to elbow all the other passengers aside so that he might pick her up and swing her around.

Theodora was small and dainty, with ash-blonde hair of exactly the same shade as Michael's, a colour that they had inherited from their mother. Theodora's brows, though well marked, did not have either the startling colour or the pronounced arch of Michael's, and her eyes, rather than grey, were something between hazel and green. Just now, the delight on her face reflected that on her brother's.

'Thea, my dear, you look blooming,' Michael declared. 'I cannot tell you how much I have looked forward to your coming.'

'No more than I have looked forward to being here,' she replied, pointing out her luggage to the groom, who had been sent with the gig. As she put her hand on Michael's arm and walked to the carriage, it could be seen that she limped quite badly, a disability that she had carried from birth. 'You have a servant to accompany us,' she remarked. 'That's very grand.'

'It is all thanks to Lord Ilam, whom I have yet to meet,' Michael replied. 'Did you have a comfortable journey?'

Theodora smiled bravely. She very seldom complained, but because she was not tall, the seats of most travelling conveyances were a little too high for her and tended to aggravate her condition. 'I am glad that it is nearly over,' she said. 'Is it far to Illingham?'

'Only a few miles,' Michael said reassuringly.

Theodora found the gig more comfortable than the chaise, for she was not squashed up amongst strangers. All through the journey, she was looking around eagerly, asking whether such a building was known to her brother, and if he knew who lived there.

It did indeed take only a very short time to travel to Michael's cottage. When Theodora saw it, she exclaimed with delight and could barely wait for Michael to help her down before hurrying inside. The groom carried Theodora's luggage upstairs to her room, but when Michael took out some coins in thanks for his services, the man shook his head. 'It's his lordship as pays me, sir. He won't see me short.'

'Remarkable,' murmured Michael, as the groom left.

'Lord Ilam is indeed generous,' said Theodora, from the top of the stairs.

'I'm beginning to wonder whether he's even human,' said Michael. 'His Christian name is Gabriel. Perhaps he is an angel, as well as being named after one.'

'Like you,' put in Theodora.

'Yes; like me,' Michael agreed, struck by the notion as he had not been before, even when the verger had pointed it out to him. 'Do you like your room?' he went on, climbing the stairs two at a time.

After carrying Miss Buckleigh's luggage upstairs, Lord Ilam's groom returned to Illingham Hall and, when he had stabled the horses, he went to the kitchen for some refreshment. He was immediately quizzed by the staff who wanted to know what the curate's sister was like. No, she wasn't much like her brother, except in the colour of her hair. She was a dainty little thing; not much to her, really. A pity that she walked with a bit of a limp.

One of the kitchen maids was sent to the Olde Oak later with a message, and she conveyed the news that Miss Buckleigh was very slight, with pale hair and a limp. Some of the customers heard the news, among them Old Jed, who told his sister that Miss Buckleigh was thin and pale with very light hair and a nasty limp. By the time Miss Leicester had heard the news of the arrival, which was on the following day, Miss Buckleigh had not an ounce of flesh on her bones. Her face was chalk white, as was her hair – what bit there was of it – and her limp was so severe that she could barely walk.

Miss Leicester had to admit to being a little disturbed. She had already decided that despite Mr Buckleigh's obvious physical attractions, she had a reasonable chance of snaring him. After all, thanks to her occupation, she was able to converse with him on an easy, almost professional basis, something that was denied other ladies. Even his lack of wealth was to her advantage. The young ladies of the village might giggle over his charms, but their parents would never consider a serious match. If she could attach him, she was almost certain that she would be able to persuade Lady Ilam to take the unusual step of allowing her to continue as village schoolmistress after her marriage.

The presence of Miss Buckleigh made all of these calculations much more difficult. Despite Michael's protests, in her heart she had been convinced that with a little encouragement, Theodora could be persuaded to go out to work. The news that she had received would appear to make that impossible, which therefore raised other difficulties. The little schoolhouse would be just about big enough for a married couple with two or three children, but there would be no space there for the curate's invalid sister. There would be nothing lost by showing a caring attitude towards the newcomer, however, so, with this in mind, she picked some spring flowers from her tiny garden and was about to put on her bonnet in order to walk to the curate's house when there was a knock on the door. She opened it to find Michael himself on the threshold, a small but perfectly healthy-looking young woman standing beside him. Her hair, Miss Leicester noticed, was quite plentiful and exactly the same shade as his.

'Miss Leicester, good day,' said Michael. 'I hope you will forgive the intrusion, but I very much wanted to present my sister Theodora to you. Thea, this is Miss Leicester, the village schoolmistress.'

The two women curtsied and Miss Leicester begged the visitors to come in, gratified that she was the recipient of one of their first calls. 'This is most fortuitous,' she said, 'for I was on the point of visiting you with some flowers from the garden. Do, pray, be seated, and I will make us some tea.' The limp was only very slight, the teacher decided, as she put the cups and saucers out on the tray in the kitchen. There was no reason why Miss Buckleigh should not find employment eventually, so long as the duties were light. Certainly she did not need to live upon her brother's charity.

'For how long are you intending to reside with your brother?' Miss Leicester asked her visitor, when they were all settled with their tea.

'As long as possible, I hope,' said Michael with a smile. 'Thea's father has gone abroad and, when he returns, he will want to settle in Oxford.'

'It has been his dream,' Miss Buckleigh agreed. 'My father is very much an academic, Miss Leicester. He does not really need or even want other people around him, unless they are scholars. Such people are quite difficult to live with.'

'I am sure that they must be. However, I am certain that he made sure you had a good education.'

'Oh yes,' Theodora agreed. 'I know Latin and some Greek, and have also studied Mathematics.'

'Do you know French and Italian?' Miss Leicester asked.

'The former yes, the latter, no.'

'And do you paint or draw?'

Michael laughed. 'Miss Leicester, you sound very earnest: are you interviewing her for some post?'

The teacher laughed, flushing a little. 'By no means,' she answered a little self-consciously. 'It is just that I expect Miss Buckleigh will be wanting to make her own way in the world before too long. I would be more than happy to advise her about the kind of post that she could be looking for.'

Michael raised his brows and lifted his chin in a completely unconsciously arrogant gesture, for this was not the first time that Miss Leicester had made this inference. 'My sister will not be going out to work while I can prevent it,' he said firmly.

'I can assure you that I am no clinging vine, Miss Leicester,' put in Theodora, sitting up straight. 'I have every intention of housekeeping for my brother.'

'Yes, of course,' Miss Leicester replied, wanting to retrieve her position. 'Naturally I would never try to interfere in your concerns.'

'I would never have supposed it, Miss Leicester,' Michael said politely.

Miss Leicester offered them more tea then added, 'By the way, I thought that I had assured you that you could call me Juliana?'

'You did indeed. I had not forgotten. However, it has occurred to me that people in our situations ought to be very guarded about their reputations. Perhaps we agreed to use Christian names too soon.'

'Perhaps,' Miss Leicester replied, not looking entirely pleased.

The visitors finished their tea, but did not linger for more than the correct half-hour. 'She seems very pleasant, but a little managing,' said Theodora, after they had left. Michael smiled. A number of childhood illnesses, together with receiving her education at the hands of a comparatively old, scholarly father, had given Theodora a maturity of outlook that some eighteen-year-olds lacked.

'She is, isn't she?' Michael responded ruefully. 'I hadn't noticed that before. As if I would let you go out to work.'

'You might not have had a choice if I did not have something to come to me from Father.'

'She has been very friendly towards me, though. She has even ironed my vestments.'

'Very wifely,' remarked Theodora.

'I beg your pardon?' said Michael, as much alarmed as taken aback.

'I'm sorry,' said his sister colouring. 'I was only thinking that Miss Leicester would not need to do so now that I am in residence. What's more, I shall be able to warn off all the young ladies who are beating a path to your door,' she added playfully.

'Why do you think I wanted you to come so soon?' he asked, trying not to sound anxious. Theodora had confirmed his own latent fears and reminded him of the warning that Miss Granby had given him earlier.

The walk back to the cottage was uphill; by the time they were close to home, Theodora's limp had got worse.

'Don't fuss, Michael,' she said. 'I'm not in pain – or at least, not very much. Just give me your arm and I shall manage splendidly.'

They were negotiating the last incline when the jingling of harness was heard. Miss Belton approached, driving a one-horse gig, accompanied by her groom. She smiled brightly. 'Good day,' she cried. 'I had heard that you had arrived, Miss Buckleigh, and I have come to welcome you to the dis—' Her voice faded as Theodora took a few steps forward, smiling in response. Miss Belton's eyes were fixed upon what she could see of the newcomer's feet. '—trict,' she finished, a little faintly.

'That is very good of you,' said Michael, his lips tightening a little. 'We have just been visiting Miss Leicester. Pray come inside and sit with us.'

'Thank you, but I cannot stay for long,' Amelia replied, her smile a little fixed. She did come in and join them, but after that first anguished stare, she took great care not to look anywhere near Theodora's feet.

'Why do people have to be so ridiculous?' Michael demanded, after she had gone. 'Anyone would think that you had two heads.'

'They are supposed to be better than one,' Theodora reminded him with a rather unconvincing laugh. Suddenly Michael felt guilty. In the village where they had always lived, people were so accustomed to Theodora's limp that they had ceased to remark upon it. Only the occasional visitor might stare. He had forgotten how coming to a new place might expose her to unwelcome scrutiny, and he felt at once angry and protective. How many other people would make her feel awkward because of their own stupidity? He hoped desperately that Evangeline Granby would not be one of them.

In the event, his next encounter with Miss Granby had nothing whatsoever to do with Theodora; for when Miss Granby rode into the village the following day on an errand for her mother, she chanced to see Miss Leicester outside the school and dismounted in order to speak to her. On this occasion, Evangeline was very properly accompanied by her groom and, as she was about to leave after a brief conversation, Miss Leicester commented on the fact, remarking that Mr Buckleigh would be glad to see it.

'He was very concerned when you decided to go riding with Lieutenant Fellowes without a chaperon,' she said.

'Indeed,' Evangeline answered coldly.

'You must not be surprised that he should choose to share his anxiety with me,' Miss Leicester assured her kindly, laying a hand on Miss Granby's blue velvet sleeve. 'Remember that we are of similar standing in the neighbourhood. In addition, Michael – that is, Mr Buckleigh – and I have become quite close.' She lowered her eyes coyly. 'It is only natural that he should want to ask my advice.'

'And what advice did you give, Miss Leicester?' Evangeline asked, her tone civil and pleasant, but her eyes cold.

'I reminded him that a young woman needs to be careful of her reputation,' answered the teacher, 'but I am sure you know that.'

Evangeline could barely speak for rage as she rode back up the main street of the village. That Michael should be placed in authority was bad enough; that he should discuss her with the village schoolmistress was intolerable. The ride did nothing to cool her temper, so consequently when she got down from her horse at the curate's cottage, she was fairly boiling. It was something of an anticlimax when her groom rapped on the door to have it opened by a fair-haired young woman whom she had never met before.

For a moment or two, Evangeline was completely nonplussed. Then eventually she said, 'I beg your pardon. I was wondering whether I might speak to Mr Buckleigh?' She was aware that as she uttered the curate's name she was almost grinding her teeth.

'I'm afraid not,' the young woman replied. 'My brother has gone over to the church. Would you like to step inside, Miss...?'

'Miss Granby,' Evangeline replied. 'Welcome to Illingham, Miss Buckleigh. Thank you very much, but I cannot stay. I have a very urgent need to speak to your brother.'

She must have sounded rather aggressive, for Miss Buckleigh stepped backwards a little awkwardly, her hand to her throat. 'To speak to him?' she echoed.

'To murder him, actually,' replied Evangeline, before turning to stride hastily in the direction of the church, leaving her groom with a terse command to take care of the horses until her return.

Michael had formed the habit of going to the vestry in the church in order to write his sermons and prepare other work. He had been very tempted to change his routine when Theodora arrived, but reluctantly he decided against it. Doubtless when winter came, he would study at home, but for now, it was important that his parishioners should see that he was just as diligent when his sister was living with him, as when he had been a bachelor living alone. As he had walked to the church that very morning, he had looked again at the handsome vicarage standing empty and sighed. It seemed such a waste. If he were the vicar, now, and not simply the curate, he would at least have something to offer a future bride.

He noted ruefully that his thoughts travelled directly from this notion to the person of Evangeline Granby. He remembered how severe he had been with her when he had visited Granby Park. Now that his first anger had worn off, he was obliged to acknowledge that most of it had been due to jealousy. His only hope was that she would not guess his feelings. How she would laugh at him! Whatever happened, he must master this. With an enormous effort of will-power, he dragged his mind away from this tantalizing subject as he entered the church.

Once in his vestry he sat for a long time with his Bible open, some blank sheets of paper in front of him and a quill in his hand, whilst he gazed into space. Then, determinedly, he found the passage allotted for the following Sunday and bent his mind to his task. He was wrestling with a particularly difficult interpretation when he heard the sound of footsteps in the church and stood up in order to investigate. He had only taken a few steps away from the desk, when the door was pushed open with some vigour and Miss Granby came striding in, her eyes aflame.

'How dare you!' she demanded.

'I beg your pardon?'

'You might well,' she retorted. 'Bad enough that you should take it upon yourself to censure my conduct; to discuss it with someone else is the outside of enough!'

Michael had been thinking exactly the same thing, but perversely her accusations made him want to defend his actions. 'I suppose you mean Miss Leicester,' he replied.

'Why? Have you been gossiping about my concerns with any other people?' she demanded.

'I have not been gossiping,' he responded, his cheekbones touched with spots of colour. 'There is nothing unreasonable in wanting to share anxieties with a mature lady.'

'Believe me, you might share any other matter with Miss Leicester with my good will,' answered Evangeline. 'I have absolutely no interest in which mature ladies attract your attention.'

'Miss Leicester does not attract my attention, as you put it,' said Michael angrily.

'That is not what *she* thinks.' Evangeline replied. 'She told me that you had become quite close.'

'Close friends, was her meaning, I have no doubt.'

'Really? You did not see her eyelashes fluttering downwards!'

'Don't be so ridiculous,' Michael said scornfully. 'There is nothing romantic going on between us and, if there were, you may be assured that I should be discreet.'

'Implying, I suppose, that *my* romantic dealings lack discretion,' declared Evangeline in an accusatory tone.

'That is not for me to say,' he replied, drawing his lips together.

'Oh, but it is,' she protested in sarcastic tones. 'You are my guardian, remember. Pray, give me some instruction. No doubt you have plenty to say with regard to my conduct concerning Jeremy Fellowes.' Her employment of the lieutenant's first name was done with the intention of provoking Michael. She was not to be disappointed.

The curate looked furious. 'Your use of a man's Christian name when you are only slightly acquainted with him is quite improper for a start,' he said.

'Oh pooh,' she replied provocatively. 'He is the nephew of a neighbour – almost a brother, really.'

'You have not been behaving towards him as though he was a brother.'

'You have no idea how I have been behaving towards him. When we dined with the Beltons, at least my conversation was perfectly audible to the whole table, unlike the intimate exchange which was going on between you and Amelia.'

'It was not an intimate exchange.'

'It certainly looked like one. You were practically sitting on her knee.'

'Nonsense!' he exclaimed. 'Anyway, my conduct is not in question.'

'Well perhaps it ought to be. I would have thought that a clergyman would have felt obliged to set a better example of propriety. But then you are leading at least two young ladies up the garden path, and probably more beside. I wonder what the bishop would say to such behaviour?'

He crossed the room swiftly, catching hold of her arms. 'Miss Granby, if you speak to the bishop,' he began.

'You will do what?'

He looked down at her face, turned up towards his, a faint smile rendering it lovelier than ever. At once, his anger dissolved as he became consumed with passion of quite another kind. Her smile died away and he could see that she was similarly affected. The bishop, Miss Granby's reputation and his own were completely forgotten as he crushed her to him and covered her mouth with his in a long, passionate kiss. She did not struggle. Had she done so, he would have released her immediately. Instead, as he embraced her, she wrapped her arms around his neck and held him closer, making little sounds of appreciation as he deepened the kiss, exploring the inside of her mouth with his tongue. Time melted away and they were both transported back to Sheffield when, as Miss Evans and Mr Leigh, they had been unshackled by questions of restraint and position.

Eventually, something made them draw apart, both breathless. They became aware almost at the same time of a rustling sound from inside the church. 'Did you hear that?' Michael asked.

'Yes. What was it?'

'I'm not sure.' Michael released her and walked to the door into the church in order to investigate. Hurriedly, Evangeline turned away, put her bonnet back on – for it had been pushed off her head during their embrace – and tucked a few stray curls inside. 'No one there,' he said in a relieved tone.

'I think that I had better leave,' Evangeline murmured, colouring now at the memory of what they had just been doing. She pushed past him and hurried to the front of the aisle below the chancel steps.

'Miss Granby – Evangeline,' Michael began, following her. They both heard heavy footsteps as someone entered the church and then Old Samuel appeared. Pulling himself together with difficulty, Michael cleared his throat and said, 'I am very sorry, Miss Granby, but I do not think that your prayer book has been found. Ah, Samuel, you come in a good hour,' he said. 'Miss Granby has mislaid her prayer book. Have you found it anywhere?'

The old man shook his head. 'Doubtless it's lost for good, now,' he said, his tone no more cheerful than usual.

'Were you looking for me?' Michael asked him. He was acutely conscious of Miss Granby a few steps away.

'Aye, I was,' Samuel replied. 'Lady Agatha's back. You'll find her in the Halfpenny House.'

'Thank you,' Michael answered a little stiffly. 'I will call upon her. Where is the Halfpenny House?'

'I can show you, if you like,' Evangeline suggested.

Michael stared at her. God alone knew what would happen if he was alone with her again. On one level there was nothing that he wanted more than to pull her into his arms and hold her close, yet that was the last thing that he ought to be doing. What he needed was a walk in solitude to think about what had occurred. 'There is no need, Miss Granby. Samuel will tell me the way.'

The old verger stomped out into the porch.

'Was it he whom we heard before? Do you suppose he saw?' Evangeline asked anxiously, her voice a whisper.

'I've no idea,' Michael answered in the same low tone. 'I pray not. If he says anything, I'll let you know. Are you coming?'

'I will remain here for a little while, if you do not mind,' she said. He looked at her steadily, not wanting to turn away. Her cheeks were faintly tinged with colour. Never had she looked lovelier.

'Of course.' He paused, wanting to say something else, but with no idea in his mind of what it should be. Eventually he simply added, 'We will speak of this again.' She nodded and they stared at each other for a long moment. She was the first to turn away, then after a moment or two, she heard the sound of his footsteps as he walked down the nave of the church.

She stood with her hands pressed to her hot cheeks. She had exchanged a kiss or two before with the occasional young man who had attracted her, but never had she experienced such a passionate embrace. If she closed her eyes, she could remember how it felt to be in his arms, to experience the touch of his lips.

She had come to the church furious with him and feeling that his interference was unjustifiable. Passion had washed away all those other feelings, so that none of them seemed to matter. She might try to tell herself that she was only flirting with Michael for fun, as she had flirted with others before. She might even pretend that she was only a little smitten with the handsome new clergyman. The truth was that she had fallen head over ears in love with him and the whole process had begun in Sheffield when they had first met. While she had no idea what her father would say about it, she really did not care. Lieutenant Fellowes might behave as beguilingly as he could and strut about in his scarlet coat for all he was worth, but Michael was the only man that she wanted.

What did Michael want, though? They had shared more than one passionate kiss, but that did not necessarily mean anything. True, he was a clergyman; but Evangeline had met other clergymen, including her friend's brother, the vicar, who had been terrible flirts. She now recalled that Michael had been obliged to leave two previous curacies. Could this have been because of some kind of misdemeanour with the opposite sex? Could his heartfelt wish that Samuel should not have seen them be more to safeguard his reputation than hers?

Suppose though, just suppose that he really was sincere. What had she herself done? She had defied him, mocked his poverty, and threatened his calling. It was hardly the kind of behaviour designed to endear herself to him. Meanwhile, Miss Leicester was serving him tea and scones and proffering wise advice, whilst Amelia Belton looked at him as though he was the Archbishop of Canterbury. No wonder if he preferred both of them to her!

Deciding that this kind of reflection could do her no good at all, she left the vestry and walked back to the curate's cottage.

Chapter Ten

'Is he dead?' Theodora Buckleigh's question so startled Evangeline that all she could do was simply stand and stare.

After a moment, she said, 'I beg your pardon?' in rather a blank tone.

'My brother; is he dead?' said Miss Buckleigh, enlarging upon her point. 'The last time I saw you, Miss Granby, you were on your way to murder him.'

Evangeline laughed self-consciously. 'Oh, that,' she answered. 'No, I decided to let him live for the time being. To kill him now would be to leave nothing for later.'

'Will you not come in?' Theodora asked. 'I was just thinking how refreshing it would be to have a cup of tea.'

'Thank you, I would be glad to,' Evangeline answered, crossing the threshold.

'You will have to excuse me while I get it myself,' said Theodora, as she limped towards the kitchen. 'Someone comes in to clean and do some of the cooking, but in between we make shift for ourselves.'

'Of course,' Evangeline answered.

'Before you say anything, Miss Granby, you will have noticed that I walk with a limp.' Theodora's tone was something between matter of fact and defiant.

'Yes, I had noticed,' Evangeline replied gently, watching as Theodora carefully put tea into the pot and took the kettle from where it was hanging over the kitchen fire. 'Was it the result of an accident, or were you born with it?'

'I was born with it,' Theodora answered. 'My mother died when I was born, after a difficult delivery. People in the village where I have lived all my life are used to it, but those who do not know me tend to stare.'

'I went to the wedding of a cousin in Sheffield recently,' said Evangeline. 'She has a slight limp, but she has had some shoes specially made and you hardly notice it.'

'I had not thought of having special shoes,' murmured Theodora thoughtfully. 'I wonder if they are very expensive.'

'I'll write to my cousin if you like,' Evangeline suggested.

Once they were enjoying a cup of tea, Theodora said, 'Miss Granby, I must tell you that I am very pleased to meet you, for ever since my brother wrote to me about your first meeting, I have been consumed with curiosity.'

Evangeline turned bright red. For one horrible moment, she wondered whether Michael had actually told his sister about the meeting between Miss Evans and Mr Leigh. 'Our first meeting?' she echoed cautiously.

'You are the young lady who was in the coach with my brother when it was attacked by highwaymen and defended herself so heroically,' Theodora declared.

'We were attacked,' Evangeline replied, much relieved, 'But I cannot agree that I was heroic. Whoever described me so has exaggerated, I fear. I was just exceedingly annoyed.'

'It was my brother who described the events,' said Theodora with a twinkle, 'but he is a clergyman, so he cannot possibly have exaggerated. I am so pleased to meet you, Miss Granby, for I have been longing for you to tell me the one thing that my brother has withheld concerning the hold-up.'

'And what is that, Miss Buckleigh?' Evangeline asked.

'Whether any of the highwaymen was handsome, of course,' was the reply. 'He cannot seem to be able to tell me.'

'I hate to disappoint you, Miss Buckleigh, but they were all exceedingly plain,' Evangeline replied.

'Well I *am* disappointed,' Theodora admitted. 'One of them ought to have been handsome and gallant like Claude Du Vall, or Dick Turpin.'

'They were neither handsome nor gallant,' Evangeline disclosed. 'In fact, one of them was exceedingly rude. In any case, I don't suppose that your brother would have been able to tell you even if one of them *had* been handsome. Gentlemen are remarkably uninterested in the looks of other gentlemen, I find.'

'I don't know many gentlemen,' Theodora responded. 'Not well, anyway; only Michael and my father.'

'I take it that your own journey here was not as eventful as mine.'

'No, it was not, but it was not very comfortable either,' Theodora replied. 'The seats on the stage are a little too high for me and I cannot get comfortable. I do wish that I was a little taller.'

'I have always wished that I was shorter,' Evangeline said. 'Perhaps none of us is ever satisfied with our appearance.'

At this moment, there was a knock on the door and, when Theodora opened it, it was to find Lieutenant Fellowes standing on the threshold. 'Forgive me for intruding upon you,' he said with a gallant bow, sweeping his hat off his head. 'I think you must be Miss Buckleigh.'

'Yes, yes I am,' answered Theodora, sounding a little breathless. Evangeline could understand why. The sight of the young lieutenant in his red coat and white breeches, his black boots shining and his golden hair waving in the sun was enough to gladden the heart of any maiden – any maiden who was not already smitten with the curate, of course.

'I had ridden into the village and on seeing Miss Granby's groom outside, I thought I might discharge two delightful errands at once – making your acquaintance, and offering to escort her home when her visit is concluded.'

'This is Lieutenant Fellowes, Miss Buckleigh,' said Evangeline, stepping forward. 'He is related to Sir Lyle and Lady Belton, and is thus perfectly respectable, although he will not be pleased with me for saying so.'

'Please come in and sit down, Lieutenant,' said Theodora courteously, with a touch of shyness in her voice. Evangeline recalled her saying that she did not know many gentlemen. She had probably not had the chance to talk with a handsome young man before. 'May I offer you some tea?'

'I will decline, thank you,' the young soldier replied, taking the seat that Theodora had offered him. 'Tea is a drink that I do not enjoy. But I would be very glad to have a little conversation with you; unless, of course, you are talking secrets that a gentleman may not hear?'

'If we were, we certainly would not own it,' Evangeline told him.

'That's given me my own,' he said. He turned to Theodora. 'You have only just arrived I believe. How are you liking Illingham so far?'

Evangeline took careful note of Theodora's behaviour and found that she was self-conscious without being silly, and her remarks showed that she had an intelligent mind. It would not do her any harm to receive a little attention from a handsome young man who would soon be rejoining his regiment. Nevertheless she, Evangeline, might take the opportunity of warning him not to flirt too desperately with the curate's sister. For herself, she did not feel in any kind of danger from him. He smiled too much, his laughter was a little forced, and without a scarlet coat he would be nothing special.

After about a quarter of an hour, Evangeline and the lieutenant stood up to go. 'You must come and spend the day with me soon,' Evangeline told Theodora before she left. 'Mr Buckleigh must often be out and about his duties and you may then feel a little dull.' Remembering how she had interrupted Michael in his duties that morning and what had happened as a result, she coloured, a fact which Fellowes noted.

'I should be delighted to do so,' Theodora replied.

'Perhaps I might fetch you, Miss Buckleigh,' suggested Lieutenant Fellowes. 'I could borrow my uncle's gig.'

'Do not expect to be invited to stay,' Evangeline warned him. 'Remember we might be talking secrets again.'

'I have no doubt,' the lieutenant replied with a smile. As they were riding back up the village street with Evangeline's groom very properly in tow, he said, 'A charming little thing. Quite pretty, too.'

'As well as being far too young for you,' Evangeline pointed out.

'I know that,' he agreed. 'I thought that I had made it plain that my interest lay in quite another direction.'

'You are such a flirt that I cannot imagine your interest remaining in any direction for very long,' she replied.

'You wrong me,' he complained mournfully. 'I thought I had made it clear to you that I am your slave.'

'I'm afraid that wouldn't suit me at all,' she told him. 'My family support the abolition. Shall we canter?' The conversation had begun to make her rather uncomfortable. She could hardly believe that only a few days before she had encouraged him in a desperate flirtation whilst they were out for the morning, and had almost allowed him to kiss her.

An experienced philanderer, the lieutenant was sensitive to the changing moods of women. 'Are you trying to get rid of me?' he asked her, when they slowed their pace to accommodate some cows coming the other way.

'Certainly not,' she answered rather defensively.

'You see, last time we talked together, you were mad as fire over the curate's interference and were ready to annoy him in any way possible. Now, today, I find you in his cottage, protecting his little sister and blushing at his name.'

'Nonsense,' Evangeline answered, hoping that she was not blushing again. 'The other day I spoke in the heat of the moment. I can see that for Papa to ask the local clergyman to care for me and Mama in his absence is perfectly reasonable, if rather annoying. I called upon his sister to be civil. If I am trying to protect her from you, it's only because I know what a rogue you can be.'

He left the matter at that, but, after he had escorted her home and declined an invitation to go in for refreshments, he rode thoughtfully back to the Cedars. News from the capital had revealed that his debts were becoming rather pressing. He had not had any intention of marrying for a long time, but a marriage for money might be the wisest course after all. Evangeline was not only very beautiful but she was also the only child of a man in comfortable circumstances. He had no intention, therefore, of allowing her to slip through his fingers. Furthermore, it did not suit his vanity to find himself dropped in favour of a curate, particularly one who had behaved towards him in such a high-handed fashion.

Evangeline's attitude had bruised his vanity, so he found it quite soothing to be the object of admiring looks from two young ladies who had come to visit his cousin. He had met Miss French and Miss Barclay at church, and he was by no means averse to dallying with two ladies who were obviously impressed by one of England's gallant heroes. So absorbed was he with flattering and flirting that he did not notice that Amelia was much more subdued than usual. It was only when she slipped quietly out of the room that he realized something was amiss.

'Oh dear! I fear we were the bearers of rather unwelcome news,' said Miss French, not sounding particularly regretful.

'Quite shocking, in fact,' contributed Miss Barclay, covering her mouth with her hand.

'You intrigue me, ladies,' remarked Lieutenant Fellowes.

'I do not think that we ought to enlighten you,' Miss French replied.

'Oh, but you must,' answered Fellowes, knowing his duty. 'You cannot possibly tell me half a story, then refuse to disclose the rest.'

'But it is, it must be, a very wrong thing to spread gossip about a clergyman,' Miss French replied, before giving a little gasp.

Fellowes pricked up his ears at this point, but was far too cunning to reveal his interest. 'I am sure you are right,' he answered. 'In any case, I have heard my hostess say that Mr Wilson, the vicar of this parish, is beyond reproach.'

'But a curate is a very different matter,' murmured Miss Barclay. 'And to think that we had been so impressed with Mr Buckleigh.'

'Oh hush, Maria,' said Miss French. 'We ought not to mention names!'

'But scandal is no fun without names,' said the lieutenant coaxingly. 'Come, ladies, this is so exciting! Such stories make me feel as if I was back in London again.' This remark did its work, making both young ladies feel very sophisticated and cosmopolitan.

'Promise you will say nothing,' Miss French demanded, looking round.

'I swear,' he replied, raising his hand as if taking an oath.

'We were in Illingham this morning, just to take the air, you know, and Maria thought that she might like to consult Mr Buckleigh on … on a point of … of theology.'

'Really,' said Fellowes.

'Yes … yes indeed,' Maria corroborated. 'So I went into the church, and when I got to the vestry, I saw them.'

'Them?' He echoed.

She dropped her voice. 'Mr Buckleigh and Miss Granby; they were kissing!'

'Indeed?' So this was the reason for Miss Granby's sudden coldness!

'Oh yes! Mind you, I cannot say that I am surprised,' said Miss French. 'She has always boasted that she can get any man she wants. We challenged her with seeking to enslave Mr Buckleigh and she did not deny it. It seems that she has gained her objective.' She eyed Fellowes with a shrewdness that he had not expected. 'I do hope that she has not broken *your* heart as well,' she added.

'By no means,' he answered with a flirtatious laugh and an arch look. 'I am still heart whole – for the present.' With this, he turned the subject and eventually sent them away very well satisfied.

In a thoughtful mood, he was about to go up to his room when Lady Belton diverted him as he was heading for the stairs. 'Can't it wait until later?' he asked, anxious to think over what he had just heard.

'No it can't,' she replied rather sharply. 'Something disturbing has occurred and I wondered whether you might be able to throw any light upon it. Come into the drawing room.'

He was not a man of deep affections. Even though he had known his aunt's family for as long as he could remember, his only purpose for coming to stay had been in order to escape his creditors for a while. Nevertheless, he was well aware that he might want to use this retreat on another occasion. Schooling his features into an expression of polite acquiescence therefore, he followed her into the drawing room. After his conversation with Miss Barclay and Miss French, he had a suspicion that he knew what the disturbing incident might be.

'It is so unfair,' her ladyship protested, as soon as the door was closed. 'Amelia is upstairs crying her eyes out.'

'Why, what's happened?'

'Those two gossips have come with such a tale about Mr Buckleigh and Miss Granby. Apparently they were kissing in the vestry at Illingham church.'

'Really?' he replied, reflecting that his suspicion had been confirmed. 'Is every blessed woman in the area in love with the curate?'

'I thought you might be better placed to answer that question than I,' she retorted. 'After all, you have been spending quite a bit of time with Miss Granby recently.'

'Very true,' he acknowledged. 'It hadn't occurred to me that she had any real interest in the curate. Now, though, when I come to think of it, I wonder whether her chief reason in seeking my company was to annoy him.'

Lady Belton gave a snort of annoyance. 'Amelia was smitten with him from the beginning and would not rest until we had had him to dinner and heard him preach. Needless to say, he accepted our hospitality without a qualm. Doubtless you were too busy flirting with Evangeline, but if you had noticed him sitting with his head close to Amelia's last time he dined here, you would have said that things were as good as settled. Now, it seems as if it is Evangeline Granby who will snap him up. As usual, she has acted as though she were queen of all she surveys, but Amelia had set her heart on Mr Buckleigh. I must say, I am very disappointed in him.'

'It's very regrettable, but I don't see what can be done,' replied Fellowes. 'Pity. Amelia's a nice little thing.'

'She is a heartbroken little thing at the moment. He shouldn't be arousing expectations and then not fulfilling them. It makes me wonder how many other ladies he has deceived by his behaviour.'

'I'm surprised that you were willing to agree to the match,' he remarked. 'It's not as though he is a great catch, after all.'

'No, but Amelia is our only child and I have no desire to see her go far away from here. With what her father will leave her, she will be very comfortably off one day. She has no need to marry for money. Buckleigh must have guessed that we would be willing to allow a match between him and Amelia.'

'He has obviously decided that Miss Granby will be a better bet.'

Lady Belton sniffed. 'The Granbys will never allow a marriage between their daughter and the curate. Why do you think they keep taking her to London? They hope to make a great match for her, mark my words. I hope that I am not so mercenary! Buckleigh ought to be punished for what he has done.'

Fellowes smiled to himself, suddenly seeing a way of settling a score. 'Poor little Amelia. You could always lodge a complaint against him, I suppose.'

'A complaint?'

'With the bishop. I doubt he would be very pleased to hear about such behaviour.'

'An excellent idea,' Lady Belton exclaimed. 'At one and the same time, he will be punished for what he has done, and, with any luck, removed from Illingham where Amelia is bound to keep seeing him. Then perhaps we may see more of Lusty, and he is not yet spoken for. I shall write at once and you may deliver it for me.'

'I should be delighted,' Fellowes replied, remembering how the curate had questioned his conduct whilst secretly pursuing Evangeline Granby at the same time. When he took the letter to the bishop he would be sure to add a few words of his own.

Chapter Eleven

—⚬◌⚬—

As Michael walked to Halfpenny House, which was situated at the
other end of the village from his own home, it would have been
hard to exaggerate how deeply troubled he was about what had
occurred in the vestry.

Evangeline was not the first woman to whom he had felt drawn, but
he could not remember a woman ever tempting him as much as did she.
What was more, he now found that he was thinking about her to the
exclusion of other women. As a young man at university, his lustful feelings had been characterized by what he could only describe as a kind of
roaring in the blood. When he looked at, or even thought about
Evangeline, that same roaring came back. It had been a wonder that Old
Sam had not discovered his curate half devouring the prettiest member
of his congregation on the top of the vestry table!

Not for the first time, Michael wondered about his ancestry and
about what kind of man had fathered him. His mother had never
spoken about him, but would not hear anything said against him either.
Michael's belief was that his father had been a libertine, for whom his
mother had simply been one in a long string of conquests. She had been
barely sixteen when he was born, for goodness' sake! What kind of a
monster seduced a child of that age? The actions of his father repelled
him; but when he looked at a woman and felt that powerful surge of
primeval desire, he feared that this was his inheritance from the man he
had never known. The very idea disgusted him.

His musings came to an end for a time as he arrived at Halfpenny
House. It was something between the vicarage and his own cottage in
size, and looked to be Jacobean, like Illingham Hall. A stately butler

admitted him, assured him that Lady Agatha was within, and conducted him to a drawing room, where a lady dressed all in black was sitting at a table, writing.

'Mr Buckleigh,' she exclaimed, rising after the butler had announced him. 'Welcome to Halfpenny House. Grimes, bring us some wine. You're not a teetotalling Methodist, are you?'

'No, my lady,' Michael replied, making his bow. As he rose from his reverence he saw standing before him a diminutive lady of about fifty years of age. Her figure was neat, and her hair very dark, with a smattering of grey. Her eyes, too, were grey, under strongly marked brows, and her chin seemed to indicate strength of character. At once, he gained the distinct impression that this lady would make a powerful ally, but a formidable foe.

'Hmm.' She looked him up and down. 'At least you *look* like a man; not like that insect, Lusty. Are you married?'

'No, my lady,' Michael answered, recalling his earlier reflections.

'A pity. I would advise you to marry as soon as possible. You're far too handsome to be single. The village wenches will be sniffing round you like dogs after a bone, if indeed they aren't already doing so.' The butler came in with wine, and set it down on a table. 'Mr Buckleigh will pour,' she said.

Michael walked to the table, unaware that Lady Agatha was observing him with a narrowed gaze as she took in the unconscious grace of his movements. He poured two glasses of wine and took one to his hostess. 'What do you think?' she asked him casually. 'It's a new wine I'm trying. I don't know much about it myself.'

He held the glass up and observed the play of light on the deep red liquid. Then he held the glass under his nose and took a sniff. Finally he sipped it. 'I would say order some more,' he said eventually. 'This is quite exceptional.'

'You relieve me,' she answered. In fact, the wine had been given to her by Lord Ilam from his own cellar. She had simply asked Michael's opinion in order to test the quality of his palate. 'Please be seated; no, not there.' She indicated two seats near the window and placed him where the light would fall upon his face. 'Now, Mr Buckleigh, you must tell me how you come to be in Illingham, acting as Lusty's curate.'

'My previous curacy came to an end,' he told her. 'Mr Lusty, I believe, has found it difficult to perform his duties here as well as continue as chaplain to the bishop, so I was appointed to assist him.'

'Your curacy came to an end,' Lady Agatha repeated. 'Left under a cloud, did you? Got yourself entangled with a woman, no doubt.'

'No indeed,' Michael replied indignantly. 'That was the previous—' He halted, conscious that he had been indiscreet. 'I beg your pardon,' he concluded, embarrassed.

'Not at all. I like to see that you've some passion in you. Are you pleased with the cottage that Ilam prepared for you?'

'I'm delighted with it,' he replied frankly. 'Last time, I was in lodgings above a butcher's shop.'

Lady Agatha wrinkled her nose in distaste. 'I cannot see why you do not have the use of the vicarage, but I suppose you would be hard pressed to maintain it on a curate's stipend.'

'The cottage is big enough for myself and my sister.'

'Oh, your sister lives with you.'

'She merely stays with me at present while her father travels abroad. I am hoping that she will make her home with me permanently.'

'Of what age is she?'

'She is eighteen.'

'Indeed?' Lady Agatha raised her brows. He looked at her, puzzled. There was something familiar about her features. He could not decide of whom she reminded him. 'She must be considerably younger than yourself.'

'I am twenty-eight, my lady.'

'Indeed,' said her ladyship again. Her expression had slowly relaxed during the last exchange until at this point, she was smiling in rather a knowing way. 'You are much of an age with Ilam, then. Have you met him yet?'

'No, you are the first member of your family whom it has been my privilege to meet.'

There was a short silence, then Lady Agatha said, 'I notice that when you spoke of your sister, you said "her father" and not "our father". Was there a reason for that, or was it a slip of the tongue?'

Michael narrowed his gaze. 'Are you always so acute?' he asked her. 'I have never met my natural father. My stepfather married my mother shortly after I was born. My sister was the only child born of their union.'

'I see.' Possibly judging that she had been quite intrusive enough, Lady Agatha now proceeded to talk about parish business, encouraging Michael to ask questions and giving him a good deal of useful information.

'Why is this called the Halfpenny House?' was one question he asked her curiously.

She smiled. 'It was built by one of my ancestors to house his mother-in-law,' she replied. 'Apparently, it was either that or have the interfering old crone under his feet all the time. She only consented to live here on condition that she should pay rent for it. She wanted to shame him, you see. Instead, *she* was shamed, for he set the rent at just one halfpenny a year. After she died, my ancestor was so entertained by the notion that he set the rent at one halfpenny in perpetuity. There has been no one who has needed it recently, so Ilam has had to have quite a lot of work done in order to make it habitable. I'm sure he thinks that it is a small price to pay when set against the unpleasant prospect of having me living with him.'

Michael inclined his head gracefully. 'I'm very far from contradicting you, ma'am,' he said.

'No doubt you'd agree that I'm an interfering old crone as well,' she added.

'Certainly not,' he answered. 'Why, there is scarcely a grey hair on your head.'

'You're damned impertinent for a parson,' she said bluntly, making him wonder for a moment whether he had gone too far. Then she added with a twinkle, 'I can see we shall get on splendidly.'

At the end of the visit, he rose to go. 'I must thank you very much for your hospitality and for your interesting observations on parish life,' he said, bowing with a grace which did not escape his hostess's eye.

'I was pleased to be of assistance,' she said. 'You must come again, but next time bring your sister. I do not think you told me her name?'

'She is Theodora,' he replied. Then, anticipating her next question, he added, 'And mine is Michael.'

Her smile broadened. 'Of course it is,' she replied elliptically. After he had gone she said aloud to the empty room, 'Oh Raff, my dear brother, you have no idea! How very entertaining this is going to be.'

The news that Michael received from Theodora on his return to the cottage caused him to be a prey to mixed feelings. On the one hand, he was delighted that his shy little sister should have taken so strongly to another young woman. That the young woman in question should have been Evangeline Granby was doubly pleasing to him. The very fact that she had come to his cottage had proved that he had not offended her beyond forgiveness. What had touched him the most, though, was the matter-of-fact way in which Evangeline had spoken about Theodora's limp. It was a welcome contrast to Amelia's barely concealed revulsion.

What had made him less happy had been Theodora's description of the arrival of Lieutenant Fellowes. A fair-minded man, Michael could well understand why his little sister had been impressed by a red-coated officer with blond waving hair. Knowing that to express disapproval would be to invest the soldier with a certain glamour, he merely smiled and said that he was pleased that she had had some company.

Once upstairs in the privacy of his room, however, his expression took on a grimmer look. Lieutenant Fellowes might look all that was glamorous. Unfortunately, he had seen the soldier at work and he feared the influence that he might have upon a young girl who had very little experience of men of the world. What was more, he suspected that Fellowes would not be averse to using Theodora as a means for taking some revenge upon him for the way in which he, Michael, had questioned his conduct. It had never occurred to Michael when he had invited her to come and stay that he would have to watch out for predatory young men.

Then, in a sudden moment of self knowledge, he realized that he was fooling himself. When he had discovered that Fellowes had been in the cottage in his absence, the thing that had angered him the most was not the thought that the man had been talking to his sister, but that he had ridden off with Miss Granby. Casual questions directed to Theodora had revealed that it had been a merry party, with everyone joining in with the conversation.

He thought back to the kiss that he and Evangeline had shared. Had she actually returned his kiss, as he had supposed at the time, or had she simply suffered an embrace that he had forced upon her? Or, worst of all, was she actually the kind of flirt who enjoyed teasing more than one man at the same time? His heart protested against this idea; but his mind recalled that their very acquaintance had begun when she had sent him a come hither look. Her own father had disclosed that she had been infatuated with Lord Ashbourne. Miss Belton had told him that Evangeline was still in love with the notorious earl. What was more, only a few days ago she had ridden off with Fellowes in defiance of his wishes; she had never told him what had transpired during that ride. Had she permitted Fellowes to kiss her? He felt sick at the very thought.

Chapter Twelve

───❦───

Lady Ashbourne was awoken from her afternoon sleep by a light touch on her lips. She opened her eyes to see her husband smiling down at her. 'Are you rested, my love?' he asked her. 'I asked Polly to bring some tea.'

They were very comfortably situated in the best room that The Old Hall Hotel in Buxton could provide. Her ladyship had drunk the waters that morning at her husband's insistence, after which they had returned to their room so that they could have a light nuncheon and she could rest.

She smiled, and allowed him to help her to sit up. 'I am feeling much better,' she replied, 'but I will be glad when he – or she – decides to be born.' She ran a hand over her stomach.

Possessively, he took hold of her hand, raised it to his lips, then placed his own where hers had been. He looked into her eyes. 'You cannot possibly imagine how much I love you,' he said tenderly.

'Even though I am fat, and plain, and my ankles are swollen?' she said, half joking, half in earnest.

'You are carrying my child; to me you are as desirable as you have ever been,' he answered, bending to kiss her.

The maid came in at this point and Ashbourne got up to allow her to set the tray. Jessie looked across the room at her husband. Tall, with broad shoulders, his dark hair was caught behind his head in a bow, the silver flashes at his temples giving him an air of distinction. As always, his clothes fitted him immaculately, from his dark-blue coat, to his snowy shirt, his dull gold brocade waistcoat and his buff breeches. 'I feel slovenly next to you,' she grumbled, after the maid had gone out again.

ANN BARKER

He eyed her carefully. 'You do look rather entrancingly blowsy,' he said eventually, with a hint of a drawl.

'In this condition?'

''Tis only your condition that prevents me from ravishing you,' he responded, with an exaggerated leer.

She laughed, placing a hand on her stomach once more. 'Raff! You will shock him or her!'

'You mean that, unlike my daughter-in-law, you have no idea of the sex of the baby?' Lady Ilam had told everyone from very early in her pregnancy that her baby was a girl and, sure enough in due course of time, she had presented her delighted husband with a beautiful daughter.

'I haven't a clue,' she freely admitted.

He poured them both tea, then after he had given her her cup, he was silent for a long time, his gaze far away. 'Are you thinking about Gabriel?' she asked him eventually.

'No,' he answered after a pause. 'Strangely enough, I was thinking about Michael.'

'Do you want to seek him out?' she asked. He had told her the story of his love for Dora Whitton, and of the child born of their love, a child he had never seen, although he had heard scraps of information about him over the years.

'Part of me wants to; part of me is saying, leave well alone. After all, he's managed for twenty-eight years without the dubious pleasure of my acquaintance. Don't tell me he'd ever have become a priest if I had had any influence over him.'

'All I wanted to say, Raff,' said Jessie putting down her cup, 'is that if you wanted to find him, even to bring him home, I wouldn't mind.'

'You are a queen among wives, my dear Jez,' answered Raff, putting down his own cup, and leaning across to kiss her once more.

'Raff,' she said coaxingly, allowing her fingers to play with his cuff. 'Do you think that *we* might go home now? I have had quite enough of Buxton spa water, and I don't want to risk not getting back for the birth.'

'My darling, of course,' he answered. 'I'll give instructions immediately.'

A few days after his first visit to Lady Agatha, Michael received a note summoning him to Halfpenny House, where her ladyship was waiting to receive him. 'Ashbourne's home,' she said. 'He brought Jessie back from Buxton yesterday.'

'Jessie?'

'His countess. She's expecting a baby shortly and they both want it to be born at the abbey. I'm visiting them tomorrow and thought you might like to come with me.'

'I should be glad to,' Michael replied. 'It's very thoughtful of you to suggest it.'

'Not at all, dear boy,' Lady Agatha replied with a mischievous little smile. 'I very much want to be present when you meet.'

Not really understanding her sentiments but appreciating her suggestion, Michael returned home to find Theodora reading a note, which she folded and put away. 'Miss Leicester has asked me to help her in the school tomorrow,' she said. 'Do you think I should go?'

'I have been invited by Lady Agatha Rayner to go and meet Lord Ashbourne,' he told her. 'Would you not prefer to go with me?'

Theodora looked very nervous. 'Must I?' she asked. 'I would much prefer you to go on your own the first time. I will come with you on another occasion, perhaps after I have met him at church.'

'Very well,' Michael answered with an understanding smile.

No sooner had they finished their conversation than there was a knock at the door. Michael opened it to find himself face to face with a man of about his own height, more heavily built, and with dark-brown hair tied back in a queue. 'Good day, Mr Buckleigh,' he said. 'I'm Ilam. May I come in?'

'By all means,' Michael answered, surprised but delighted. 'Please allow me to make my sister known to you. Thea, Lord Ilam.'

'My pleasure, Miss Buckleigh,' Ilam said with a bow that was vigorous and business-like rather than elegant. 'I regret that my wife has not been able to accompany me,' he went on, as he took the chair that Michael indicated. 'She is staying with my father and his wife, but hopes to visit you on another occasion. Are you well settled in here? Do you have everything you need?'

Michael smiled. 'When I try to express my gratitude for your generosity, words fail me, my lord,' he replied.

Ilam interrupted him before he could say more. 'Just as well. You've already thanked me in a handsome letter. There's no need to add to it. To know that you have all that you need to live here comfortably and carry out your duties is enough for me.'

'I am more than comfortable,' Michael responded. 'May I offer you a glass of wine, my lord?'

'Not at present,' Ilam replied. 'I really must not stay. One point I would make, though: you are not my servant, so I would infinitely prefer it if you would call me Ilam, rather than "my lord". If you find that you need anything, apply to me. When my wife returns, you must both come and dine.'

'Thank you, my ... Ilam,' Michael corrected himself.

Ilam was on the point of leaving when he turned in the doorway. 'One more thing: how do you get around?'

'I walk,' Michael replied. 'I have no horse at present.'

'Come to the Hall any time you need to go a distance, or even if you want the exercise. I've plenty of mounts that need riding and I'll be glad if you'll oblige me in that way. You too, of course, Miss Buckleigh.'

'I ... I don't ride, my lord,' Thea stammered. 'I'm ... I'm lame.'

'Are you?' said Ilam, in a matter-of-fact tone. 'I'm sorry. I hope I didn't embarrass you. Stacia – my wife – will tell you that I'm so tall, I don't notice what's going on a foot below me anyway. You'll have to get her to take you out in the barouche.'

'Thank you,' Michael replied, bowing in his usual graceful manner, as Theodora curtsied.

Ilam drew his brows together. 'I've met you before, haven't I?' he asked the clergyman.

Michael rose from his elegant bow, and raised his brows. 'I do not think so,' he responded.

Ilam directed a sharp look at him. 'What is your given name?' he asked.

'Michael.'

Well, I'll be damned, Ilam said to himself as he walked home.

Nearly two years before, he had discovered that his aunt was manipulating everyone from the bishop to himself in order to prevent a new vicar from being appointed, so that she could stay in the vicarage. The consequence had been that the villagers had been denied the solace of a priest for some months. Despite this, he had not been pleased when Henry Lusty was installed as vicar, since he felt that this would be an embarrassment to his stepmother. When he had learned that a curate had been appointed to reside in the village, therefore, he had been delighted. He had decided, for truly disinterested reasons, to make the curate as comfortable as possible.

He had known for a long time that his father had another son, born before he had married his, Gabriel's, mother. He also knew that this other son was a clergyman named Michael. When he had first seen the new curate, however, he had not been struck by any similarity to his father. Although of a similar height to the Earl of Ashbourne, his features were finer, with higher cheekbones, and the effect of the blond hair with the dark brows was sufficiently startling in itself to divert one's mind from any other similarity. Not until he had been on the point of leaving had he truly begun to think that they might be closely related.

It had been the elegance of the clergyman's bow that had first caught his attention, for it had exhibited all the natural grace that characterized his father's every movement. Then when Ilam had asked if they had met, Michael had denied it, with a slight lifting of those brows. Suddenly, for no reason that Ilam could put his finger upon, he felt sure that he was face to face with his half-brother. The man was certainly of the right age. The discovery of his Christian name had confirmed his suspicions.

All of these thoughts ran through his mind as he walked home, but as he crossed the threshold of Illingham Hall, his dilemma was this: how the devil was he going to tell his father?

Chapter Thirteen

———◦◦◦◦———

The following day, Lady Agatha Rayner called at Granby Park. Evangeline could never decide whether she liked the formidable lady or not. She did have a habit of saying the most outrageous things, often designed to irritate. On the other hand, she was a good deal more amusing than many people in the village. From the moment that she was shown into the drawing room, her ladyship proved herself to be on form.

'Just as pretty as ever, so I see,' she said, looking Evangeline up and down. 'No doubt you're just as spoiled.'

Evangeline was on the point of declaring boldly that if she was, it was not her fault, when she cast a glance at her mother's anxious face. 'That is not for me to say,' she answered demurely.

Mrs Granby, who had opened her mouth to say *Evangeline, dearest* in protest, realized that there was no need and surprised both herself and her daughter by saying, 'Indeed, Lady Agatha, she is a great comfort to me while her father is away.'

'Really?' said Lady Agatha, her brows raised. 'Well that's as it should be, I suppose. How is Granby? What takes him away from home at this time?'

As Mrs Granby explained to a rather dubious-looking Lady Agatha that her husband was in London on business, Evangeline thought about the extraordinary notion that had come into her mind. There was an unmistakable family likeness between Lady Agatha and Lord Ashbourne. From the very first Evangeline, had caught glimpses of Lord Ashbourne in Michael. Now, as she watched Lady Agatha listening to her mother speaking, she could see that same likeness between the earl's sister and Michael. She knew that Michael's father had deserted him before his birth. Could his father possibly be Lord Ashbourne?

She was just telling herself that this must surely be absurd when her thoughts were interrupted by something that Lady Agatha was saying. 'And how is the new curate settling in? From what I have heard, he seems to be well liked.'

'He has made a very good impression, has he not, Evangeline?' Mrs Granby responded.

'Interesting that Lusty chose to send him,' Lady Agatha observed, as Evangeline nodded. 'I wonder, what was his motive?'

'Surely the better to provide spiritual care for his flock,' Mrs Granby suggested diffidently. She had always found Lady Agatha Rayner more than a little intimidating.

Lady Agatha snorted. 'That insect! He's after revenge, more likely,' she answered.

'Revenge?' echoed Mrs Granby, puzzled.

'I shouldn't let it worry you,' her ladyship answered airily. 'I am sure it will all prove to be very entertaining. Did you know that Dr Littlejohn is back home, by the way? I called on him only yesterday.'

Lady Agatha stayed for a glass of wine, then left in order to pay another call.

'I do not know how it may be, but I always find Lady Agatha's visits quite exhausting,' said Mrs Granby after that redoubtable dame had gone.

'I'm not surprised,' Evangeline replied. 'What do you think she meant when she was talking about Mr Lusty wanting revenge?'

'I have no idea,' her mother answered frankly. 'I suppose it must be something to do with the fact that he was engaged to Lady Ashbourne.'

After a short silence, Evangeline said, 'Mama, am I really a comfort to you, or were you just saying that to put her in the wrong?' The previous evening, Evangeline and her mother had played cards together. Perhaps her love for Michael had made her more sensitive to her mother's needs. Certainly, Mrs Granby had opened out more, whatever the reason might have been, and had turned out to have a talent for mimicry that Evangeline had never suspected. She had even done a passable imitation of Lady Belton, which had made her daughter laugh heartily. They had spent the most companionable evening together that either of them could remember.

Mrs Granby coloured a little. 'Well, dearest, I cannot deny that there are times when you have made life a little difficult. But over the last few days, you have been nothing but a comfort. Would you like to come with me to call upon Dr Littlejohn? I know that you always enjoy speaking to him.'

'Yes, I would,' Evangeline replied, feeling strangely moved by what her mother had just said.

Doctor Littlejohn was delighted to see Mrs and Miss Granby and was eager to tell them something about his visit to the lakes, where he had spent many happy hours walking in the hills. Evangeline gave his account less than half her attention. She was thinking about Lady Agatha's extraordinary statement concerning Mr Lusty's possible desire for revenge.

She was brought back to the present by Dr Littlejohn's voice saying Lady Agatha's name. 'Yes I have called to see her,' he said, looking troubled. 'I am a little concerned, I confess.'

'She seemed in very good health to me,' Mrs Granby assured him.

'Oh yes yes,' Dr Littlejohn agreed, his thin scholarly face anxious. 'I am just afraid that she may be plotting something.'

'Oh, I see,' responded Mrs Granby, her expression concerned. They had both known Lady Agatha for long enough to be well aware of her mischievous streak. 'She has hardly been back for long enough to be doing so, surely.'

'I suppose not,' the academic agreed. 'She is taking the new curate to visit Ashbourne Abbey today. Perhaps her glee is because she has met him before her brother has.'

'Good God!' exclaimed Evangeline, leaping to her feet.

'Evangeline?' said Mrs Granby, as Dr Littlejohn got politely to his feet.

'Oh ... oh, it's nothing,' Evangeline responded in a flustered tone as she took her seat once more. 'I thought that I saw a ... a wasp.'

The conversation resumed, but Evangeline played no further part in it. When her mother suggested that it was time to leave, she sprang to her feet with alacrity, bidding Dr Littlejohn farewell in a manner that was only just civil. What she was to do, she could not imagine. She knew that she must do something, for suddenly she had guessed what mischief Lady Agatha was probably planning.

When they arrived at home, she accompanied her mother indoors, but, as they prepared to go upstairs to take off their outdoor things, Evangeline said, 'Mama, do you mind if I hurry ahead of you? I must change into my habit in order to go out again. I have just thought of an ... an urgent matter that I must attend to.'

'Oh! Oh, yes, yes, of course my dear,' answered Mrs Granby in puzzled tones.

'I'll tell you about it later,' Evangeline called back over her shoulder as she ran up the stairs. She rang the bell and, when Elsie arrived, she was already scrambling into her riding habit.

'Now do have a care, Miss Evangeline,' said the girl. 'You'll tear it.' Catching her mistress's urgency, however, her fingers flew across the fastenings and in no time at all, Evangeline was running round to the stables.

She had become convinced that Lady Agatha was taking Michael to Ashbourne Abbey so that in her own wicked way she could enjoy the shock and consternation that would surely be felt by father and son as they faced one another for the first time. Her first instinct had been to go and see Michael, but a moment's thought had convinced her that that would be the wrong strategy. Nothing that Michael had said or done had given the slightest indication that he suspected that Lord Ashbourne was his father. If she was right in her suspicions, then Lord Ashbourne must be the one to be warned. He could then decide how best to confront his own son.

She dispensed with a groom, despite the vociferous protests of the head stableman who had put her upon her first pony. Riding cross country so as to make the best time, she headed for Ashbourne Abbey, praying that she would arrive there before Lady Agatha and Michael. At least she knew that they had not set off before she and her mother had visited Dr Littlejohn.

She had visited Ashbourne Abbey on previous occasions and knew it well enough to be sure of where the family would probably be sitting. Avoiding the drive, therefore, and galloping round to the back of the house, she rode up to the terrace, and summoning a rather bewildered gardener to hold her horse, she ran up the steps and pounded on the French door.

To her great relief, Lord Ashbourne himself was inside and he opened the door for her, ushering her in with a bow. As always, he looked immaculate, clad in a coat of dark green with buff breeches, his black hair with its distinctive white wings swept back into a queue. His brows were raised in surprise at her entrance. 'Miss Granby, this is unorthodox, but none the less welcome,' he said politely.

A few years ago, Evangeline had convinced herself that she was in love with the rakish earl. Even today, there was something about his undoubted good looks that made her heart beat faster; now she realized that this was due to the similarity to Michael that she perceived in him.

The other occupants of the room looked as surprised as Ashbourne. Ilam was standing by the fireplace, somehow much more the country squire than his father. Lady Ashbourne was lying on a *chaise-longue*, very heavily pregnant and looking rather tired. Sitting close to her was Lady Ilam, who sprang up intending to embrace her friend.

'No! No time,' Evangeline gasped, for she was a little out of breath from her exertions.

'My dear Miss Granby, do come and sit down,' said Ashbourne urbanely, as he attempted to guide her to a chair.

'Listen, please,' said Evangeline, tugging at his sleeve. 'Lady Agatha is coming to see you with the new curate.' Ilam straightened at once. He had come that day with the very intention of telling his father of his suspicions, and had not yet thought of how to bring the subject up.

'Indeed,' replied Ashbourne. 'I am delighted of course, but—'

Again Evangeline interrupted him, catching hold of his arm this time and looking up at him desperately. 'Please be quiet and listen! He has your eyebrows and his name is Michael.'

Ashbourne whitened. He bent towards her now, searching her face keenly. 'Say that again,' he breathed.

At that moment, the door was flung open, and the butler announced 'Lady Agatha Rayner and Mr Buckleigh, my lady.'

Michael made his bow, took a step forward, then stood staring at Lord Ashbourne for what seemed to Evangeline to be an eternity. She was still holding on to the earl and was therefore able to witness the unfolding scene from his point of view. What she could not have known was how the scene looked to Michael as he entered. Lady Agatha stood to one side, a faint, slightly malicious smile playing across her lips.

Lady Agatha's carriage had collected Michael from his cottage not very long after Theodora's departure for the school. After he had waved his sister off, he had gone back inside in order to make sure that his appearance was immaculate for his meeting with Lord Ashbourne. With this end in view, he had hurried up the stairs and into his bedroom, so that he could check the arrangement of his neck cloth and his hair. He was so used to his own face that he seldom thought deeply about the remarkable contrast between his hair and his brows. Then, for some reason, he had stared at his features and raised his brows. It was as if he was seeing himself in a different way; a way that was confusing and strange. With a flash of awareness, he had remembered looking at Lady

Agatha and thinking that she reminded him of someone. Suddenly he had understood of whom she reminded him: it was of himself.

On her arrival at the cottage, Lady Agatha had smiled at him, more than a hint of mischief in her eye. 'I trust you'll find this outing entertaining. I know that I shall.'

'Really, ma'am?'

'Oh yes. An encounter between a virtuous young clergyman and my rakehell of a brother; what could be better? How much have you heard about him?'

'Only a few rumours,' Michael had confessed, with a feeling of foreboding that he would have been at a loss to explain.

'There was a time when there were plenty of those,' Lady Agatha had told him. 'No female was safe from the Fallen Angel.'

'The Fallen Angel?'

'His nickname amongst the *ton*. Now, of course he's married to my Jessie and supposedly reformed, but with Raff anything is possible.'

'With whom?' Michael had asked sharply.

'Raff – my brother; another nickname, only used by his nearest and dearest.'

Lady Agatha had continued to talk, but Michael had heard no more of what she was saying. He had found himself remembering a number of disconnected ideas that he had previously failed to put together, but which, added together, made a very disturbing picture. His name, Michael, that of one of the angels, after whom all men in the family of the earls of Ashbourne were named; his features, notably his brows, so like those of Lady Agatha; the view expressed by some whom he had met locally, who were convinced that they had met him before; lastly, the nickname of Lord Ashbourne, 'Raff' – a name which had just been disclosed to him. Her ladyship could not possibly have known that this was the name which had been upon his mother's lips just before she died. Michael had been with her at the time. She had looked up at him, her face suffused with a happiness that he had never seen before. Then she had reached up to touch his cheek and breathed the word 'Raff' before quietly slipping away. He had not understood the significance of that until now.

There was only one solution: Ashbourne, the Fallen Angel, the rakehell from whom no female, including Michael's own mother, was safe, was his father.

All of these thoughts and ideas came together in Michael's mind as they travelled to Ashbourne Abbey. They were still buzzing about in his head when he stood upon the threshold and saw the man who must surely be his father bending over Evangeline whilst she clutched at his arm. Suddenly, for Michael, the whole scene was overlaid with a red mist. There were other people in the room, but Michael was barely aware of them. He saw before him a man in his forties, immaculately dressed, with jet-black hair save for the white wings at his temples. His face was faintly lined, perhaps with dissipation. There was elegance in his every movement. In Michael's mind, it seemed as if everything was slowed down, as he watched Ashbourne gently lift Evangeline's hand from his sleeve, touching her skin as he did so. The earl straightened and took a step forward to meet him. In his eyes, Michael saw the truth of his suspicions. He crossed the room, almost at a run, drew back his fist, and struck Ashbourne down with a blow to the jaw. Then, entirely ignoring the mayhem that resulted from his precipitate action, he turned on his heel and half stumbled, half ran from the room.

Chapter Fourteen

'R aff!' Jessie exclaimed anxiously, swinging her feet to the floor. From where she was sitting she could see the prostrate form of her husband.

'I'll attend him,' said Gabriel, as he crossed the room to kneel at his father's side. The older man was already stirring. 'He's all right; just slightly shaken.'

Eustacia, Lady Ilam took hold of Jessie's arm and urged her to remain seated. 'Let Gabriel attend to him,' she said soothingly. Then, to her husband, she said in a puzzled tone, 'What is the meaning of this? That cannot be the curate of whom you have spoken so highly, my love.'

'It is,' Ilam replied shortly.

'But why would he do such an outrageous thing?' Eustacia demanded, puzzled.

'I think I know,' said Jessie softly. 'He's Raff's son, isn't he?' Ilam nodded.

It was left to Evangeline to speak the words that everyone else in the room had in mind. She crossed the room until she was face to face with Lady Agatha. 'You evil old witch,' she said.

'Oh tush, they had to find out some time,' Lady Agatha said carelessly. 'The rest of you were tip-toeing around the matter in the most inept way possible.'

By this time, Ashbourne was sitting up, but was still looking a little shaken. 'Sensitive as always, my dear sister,' he said, chuckling faintly. 'Your penalty can be to ring the bell and order me some brandy. Are you all right, Jez, my dear?' He allowed Ilam to help him to his feet, and thence to the *chaise-longue* where his wife was sitting.

'Perfectly all right, if you are well,' Jessie responded, taking his hand.

'I shall do,' said Ashbourne, rubbing his jaw ruefully with the other. By good fortune, he had not struck his head as he fell. He turned to his son. 'Ilam; would you...?'

Ilam nodded. 'I'll go after him.'

After the viscount had left the room, Jessie said, 'Stacia, take Evangeline up to my dressing room so that she can compose herself.'

'Good idea,' remarked Lady Agatha, utterly unconcerned about the furore that she had set in motion. 'She looks as if she's been dragged through a hedge by her feet.'

Evangeline stared at her disdainfully, but when she looked in the mirror in Lady Ashbourne's room she gave a squeak of dismay. Never had she appeared in public looking so untidy. Eustacia gave a chuckle, but bid her sit down and was soon brushing out her hair.

'Remember how you did my hair for me when I came to stay with you before I was married?' she said. Evangeline nodded. A few minutes later, Eustacia whispered in her ear, 'He is very pretty, isn't he?'

Evangeline turned her head abruptly, to the imminent danger of the arrangement that Eustacia had almost finished. 'Oh Stacia, I don't know what to do.'

'About Mr Buckleigh?'

Evangeline nodded. Then she told her friend everything that had happened between herself and the dashing curate, beginning with their first encounter in Sheffield. 'I have to admit that I ... have a fondness for him,' she said eventually. 'But what will Mama and Papa say? A penniless, illegitimate clergyman is not at all what they had in mind for me.'

'My dear Evangeline, when did that ever worry you?' Eustacia asked. 'I seem to recall a time when you declared that all you had to do was to drum your heels upon the floor and they would accede to your demands.'

'I hope I have grown out of that by now,' Evangeline replied with dignity.

'You have said that you've a fondness for him. Now I have a fondness for a good many people but I'm only in love with one man.'

'You're very lucky,' Evangeline answered. 'The man you fell in love with met with your parents' approval.'

'Not straight away, he didn't,' Eustacia answered with a chuckle. 'It was almost more than Mama could stomach to see Lord Ashbourne, a former dishonourable suitor of hers, become my father-in-law.' After a brief silence, Eustacia went on, 'If it is the thought of living in poverty with him that you cannot bear, then be honest enough to say so straight away. It is not fair to keep the young man dangling.'

'I am not keeping him dangling,' Evangeline answered wretchedly. 'He has not declared himself. Not that I blame him. I … I haven't been very nice to him, Stacia. I do not even know whether he loves me as—'

'As you love him?' Eustacia concluded softly. 'Well, now might be a good time to go and find him. After what has transpired this afternoon, he must have all kinds of ideas going round in his head and he is probably hurting quite badly.'

'But I may not be the person that he wants to see. I know that Amelia likes him; I suspect that Miss Leicester does too.'

'But neither one of them knows what has transpired this afternoon.'

'You think I should go?'

'You will have to decide that for yourself – but would you feel at ease if you did not?'

Michael had almost reached the end of the lengthy drive of Ashbourne Abbey when the jingling of harness told him that someone was coming in pursuit.

'Climb up,' said Gabriel as he drew the gig to a halt next to his half-brother.

Michael looked up at him, his face stormy and troubled. 'You're very good, but I'd rather walk,' he said.

'If it's any comfort to you, I've frequently wanted to take a swing at him myself,' said Ilam. He paused. 'It was Ashbourne who sent me after you, by the way.'

'My lord, I don't want to be rude, but I need some time to myself – to clear my head.'

Ilam sighed. 'Very well,' he answered. 'You know where to find me. My name's Gabriel, by the way.' Michael looked at him, startled. 'We are brothers,' the other reminded him, before turning the gig and driving back towards the house.

Michael had no idea for how long he walked in the end. In his first anger, all he wanted was never to see Ashbourne again. He had always known that to bear resentment against another was incompatible with his calling as a clergyman, and he had been convinced that he regarded his father with indifference. He had just discovered that to discount a theoretical father was very different from seeing the real man face to face, especially when that man was leering over the girl with whom he was in love.

By the time he reached his cottage, his thoughts were calmer but no clearer. What was certain was that he had struck down a peer of the realm, a nobleman on whose estate much of his work was based, and upon whose good favour his position must partly depend. Such an action could not possibly be overlooked. He would be exceedingly lucky to keep his situation after this.

He then realized that the post had arrived whilst he was out. Lord Ilam employed a man to collect letters from the inn. His lordship had been kind enough to arrange that Michael's letters should be brought to his door as well. On this occasion, he had only received one letter. A brief glance at it told him that it was from the bishop.

Dear Mr Buckleigh
It is with a feeling of deep disappointment that I write to inform
you that I have received a most serious complaint about your
conduct.

He read the opening greeting and the first sentence. For some minutes he stood staring into space, his mind unable to take in any more. He looked down at the letter again, but it contained very little more information. The bishop was very much shocked. He feared that he would have no alternative but to remove Mr Buckleigh from office. The curate was to attend him at his palace in Sheffield.

A complaint! From whom? With a sinking heart, he remembered that Evangeline had threatened to complain to the bishop on more than one occasion. Now it seemed that she had done it; with that action she had destroyed both his fledgling hopes of gaining her love and also his career. He had now failed as a curate for the third time. No doubt Ashbourne would also complain to the bishop after the day's events. As a consequence, he would be unfrocked, and all his plans for Thea's safety and future comfort would come to nothing. The poor girl would probably be better off going as a governess, as Miss Leicester had suggested. It couldn't possibly be less secure than attempting to depend on the provision of her idiot brother!

He poured himself a large glass of brandy. It had been a gift from Lord Ilam, he recalled; Ilam, called Gabriel – his half-brother. For the first time, he remembered that Gabriel had acknowledged the relationship. However ignorant he, Michael, had been, his half-brother clearly had known something about him before. What was more, the violence that he had exhibited towards Ashbourne had not noticeably shocked him. At least the viscount had been favourably disposed towards him, until today. Perhaps talking to him might be a good idea. It was a tiny spark of hope in a very dark landscape. He could not speak to Gabriel now, however, for he was still at Ashbourne Abbey. Michael tossed back the rest of his brandy and, early though it was, he prepared to drink his way through the bottle.

When Evangeline tapped on Michael's cottage door, there was no answer to her first knock or even her second. Tentatively, she turned the handle and walked in. Michael sat sprawled in his chair, a brandy glass in one hand, one leg carelessly thrown over the arm of his chair. He did not stand as she entered, but looked at her, his brows raised. He had pulled off his stock and his hair was loose and in disarray. Never until this moment had she seen him looking as much like the rogue whom she had met in Sheffield.

His drunken appearance confirmed all her worst fears, but strangely, she did not think any the worse of him. Perhaps Miss Belton and Miss Leicester would be shocked to see the curate drunk, but Evangeline had always thought of him as a man who simply happened to be a clergyman.

'Mr Buckleigh, you really do look the most complete rake,' she said, without thinking.

'All the more attractive to you then, no doubt,' he replied.

'What do you mean?' she asked, honestly puzzled.

'You obviously have a liking for rakes. Take Fellowes, for instance; you were disporting yourself all over the county with him. Then there was Ashbourne who was pawing you today, leering over you like some debauched roué, without your making any obvious objection. And don't let us forget Mr Leigh, shall we? You were very happy to go off with him, weren't you? Didn't like him so well when you found out that he was a parson, though.'

Evangeline stared at him. A good deal had happened to upset him that day. Furthermore, she could see by the bottle that he was far gone in drink, and he probably did not mean half of what he was saying; but his words hurt nevertheless. 'You are quite mistaken,' she began; though to what she was referring she would have had difficulty in saying.

He did not wait for her to explain. 'Well, don't worry. I won't be a parson for too much longer. You can't blot your copy-book much more than I've done, can you? How many curates lay their most distinguished local landowner to the floor on first meeting him? I'll be unfrocked, then I'll become a rake, just like Ashbourne and perhaps you'll find me as desirable as you find him.' He stood up, swaying slightly. 'Well? Shall I put my arm around you, rest my cheek against yours, run my hands up and down your arms like he did?' He suited his actions to his words. 'How do you like that, eh? Not so much as when he did it, I'll bet.'

She made no reply, and neither did she struggle. She was not sure that he would listen to anything she said anyway. Eventually her patience was rewarded when he released her. 'It can't be as bad as you say, surely,' she said eventually.

'Can't it?' He walked unsteadily to the table, and picked up a sheet of paper that lay upon it. 'Just cast your beautiful eyes over that, then look me in the face and tell me that you are not to blame.' He thrust it into her hand.

'Infamous!' she exclaimed, after she had read it. 'Who could do such a thing?' Then, as the meaning of the letter sank in, she suddenly remembered that she herself had written a letter of complaint to the bishop: a letter which she had signed, and addressed: a letter that she could not remember having seen in her room recently.

She turned hot and cold. As she looked up at him, shock and consternation were written all over her face. 'No, it can't have … Michael, I never meant—'

'You didn't mean me to find out. No, I don't suppose you did. I just wish I could have done so before you ensnared me like all the others. Don't worry. I won't be pestering you with my *threadbare curate's* attentions. I know; I'll join the army and put on a scarlet coat. Then you might want to go cantering around the countryside with me.'

'Michael,' she ventured.

Before she could say any more, he threw himself back down in his chair again. 'God, I'm tired.' He closed his eyes.

Evangeline stared at him in consternation. Was he really going to fall asleep in front of her, in the middle of a conversation? She looked around for something with which to cover him, and in the end ran upstairs, pulled the coverlet off the bed in one of the rooms and brought it back down with her. How young and vulnerable he looked, she thought as she tucked it around him.

She had only just straightened when she noticed that Michael had opened his eyes. 'Evangeline,' he murmured in puzzled tones. 'What are you doing here?' Then before she could say anything, he covered his eyes with his hand. 'God, I remember. What a bloody fool I've made of myself.'

'No, I—' she began.

'You know damned well I have,' he interrupted. 'Would you please go now? I don't want to talk to anyone just now, least of all you.'

His words had an ominous ring, but she could see that her presence here was not doing any good. He would never listen to her while he was drunk. 'Very well,' she answered. She walked to the door, then thought of one thing that had been upon her mind when she had set off for Illingham. 'Where is your sister? She should not see you like this.'

He wrinkled his brow, as if he were trying to remember. 'She's at the school,' he said eventually.

'I'll fetch her and take her home with me,' she said. She had suspected that Michael might welcome the removal of his sister to another location and had come prepared to take Theodora back with her to Granby Park in the gig.

'Thank you,' he answered, closing his eyes again. She went out, softly closing the door behind her.

Michael woke up, he did not know how long after Evangeline's visit. Indeed, he could have convinced himself that her appearance had been a dream, but for the coverlet around him which carried the faintest hint of her perfume. He wandered into the kitchen for something to eat and, on finding a hunk of bread and cheese, consumed that and some ale. Then he went up to his room to lick his wounds. Janet arrived in order to cook his dinner, but he called down, telling her not to bother. He was not well and his sister was from home.

She was much concerned and could not be dissuaded from preparing a hot drink for him, but after she had brought it upstairs, she left, promising to return in the morning. He did not feel in any condition to argue with her. After she had left, he went downstairs for the rest of the brandy, and finished the work that he had started earlier.

The following morning he felt as though a whole battalion of elves armed with little hammers had taken up residence inside his head. As well as feeling in poor shape physically, he felt thoroughly ashamed of himself. He was the resident clergyman and ought to be setting a good example to the community. Instead, he had behaved like the village drunkard. What if there had been some emergency the previous evening? He could never have gone.

He went downstairs for hot water so that he could shave and wash and, having taken the jug back to his room and attended to his ablutions, he felt a little better. Then his eyes lit upon his prayer book and once more he felt covered with shame. How could he read the Morning

Office when he had behaved so disgracefully? To make matters worse, there was the letter from the bishop that still lay on the table downstairs. In his present mood, he could only feel that the complainant had had the right idea. He was utterly unfit for his office.

He went downstairs at a pace that was quite at variance with his usual athletic stride. Janet had seen him the previous day when he was the worse for wear. He could hear her moving about in the kitchen. He did not know how he was to look her in the face.

He had just reached the bottom of the stairs when Janet came into the room. 'Good morning, Reverend,' she said softly. 'How are you feeling today?' She was holding a tankard in her hand. 'His lordship sent this for you,' she said. 'Lord Ilam, I should say. He said he thought it would make you feel better.'

Michael looked at her with narrowed eyes. 'Did you tell Lord Ilam that I was … ill?' he asked her.

'Oh no, sir,' Janet replied. 'His lordship just seemed to know that you might be in need of something. He said if you drank it down quickly, it would be best.'

Michael flushed with mortification. Did the entire village know that he had got drunk the previous day? Nevertheless, he took the tankard and, after a sniff of distaste, tossed the mixture back. For a moment, he thought that his head and his stomach might both explode. Then, imperceptibly, the cloud in his brain began to disperse, the tight band around his head loosened and he began to feel better. When Janet rather tentatively suggested breakfast, he realized that he was ready for something. It was only after he had begun to eat that he remembered that Theodora was not in the house. Of course! Evangeline Granby had taken her home. His heart gave the customary lift at her name, before he recalled that it was she who had complained against him. All at once, his appetite left him. He eyed the remaining food on his plate with disgust and could not finish it.

He went upstairs and again caught sight of his prayer book. This time, after a brief hesitation, he picked it up and, going downstairs, he left the cottage and walked to the church. There, in the quietness, he read the Morning Office, after which he felt calmer. Then he went into the vestry to try to decide upon his next course of action. He took out a clean sheet of paper, mended a pen and dipped it in the ink, in order to make a list. All he could do after that, however, was sit and stare into space.

In his mind's eye he had recalled over and over again the moment when he had walked into the drawing room of Ashbourne Abbey and seen Evangeline holding on to the earl's arm whilst he bent over her. Now, as he thought about the matter, he remembered that Evangeline had been in riding dress, and looking decidedly the worse for wear, as if she had ridden there hell for leather. Had she hurried to tell Lord Ashbourne that she thought that he, Michael, was his son? Somehow, that notion hurt as much as the memory of the earl leering over her. Why had she not come to him instead? It was simply another instance of her betrayal.

The church clock sounded the hour and he realized to his surprise that he had been sitting there for nearly half the morning with a blank sheet of paper in front of him. He was no closer to deciding what to do than before.

He walked out of the church, blinking in the bright sunshine. One of the parishioners was passing on the other side of the road, and she bobbed a curtsy. He forced himself to smile and wave a greeting. For how much longer would he be able to do this, he asked himself with a sinking heart?

Chapter Fifteen

Once back inside his cottage, Michael looked round, and was overwhelmed by another wave of unhappiness. How pleased and proud he had been when he had welcomed Thea just a short time before! He walked over to the fireplace and looked down at the kindling and the logs laid ready in the grate. He felt as if all his hopes were destined to turn to ash, just as surely as the next fire that was lit.

From what seemed to be very far away, he heard a sound that he could not identify at first. Then, shaking off the mist that had enveloped his brain, he realized that someone was knocking at the door. The last thing that he wanted was a visitor. For a brief moment, he had a wild idea that it might be the bishop, until he realized that his lordship would not deign to call upon a curate in this kind of way – particularly a disgraced curate! Reluctantly he opened the door to find an extremely pregnant lady standing on the threshold.

Apart from Lord Ashbourne and Evangeline, he had taken very little notice of those who had been present in the room at Ashbourne Abbey the day before, although he vaguely remembered this lady's shocked face as he had left. He now realized that she was very near her time, and rightly concluded that she must be Lady Ashbourne. He blushed inwardly at the thought of the distress that he must have caused her by knocking her husband down.

'My lady,' he exclaimed. 'Please come in.'

'Thank you,' she said with a smile. 'I regret I do not move with my usual facility at present.'

'Doubtless time will mend it,' Michael replied. 'Please sit down.' He conducted her to a chair.

'Thank you,' she said again.

'May I get you something to drink? A cup of tea?'

'Perhaps in a little while,' she answered. 'Pray come and sit down with me, Mr Buckleigh, for I have come to talk to you.'

He eyed her warily. She did not look angry. 'I must apologize for the shock that I gave you yesterday,' he said. 'It must have been distressing for you.'

'It is the first time that a visitor has made his entrance in such a way,' she agreed. 'My husband has suffered no permanent damage, but then I don't suppose that will concern you particularly.'

Michael got up. 'Forgive me, my lady,' he said. 'I do not know; I ...' His voice tailed off. He covered his eyes with his hand.

'I do not suppose you ever expected to meet your father,' Jessie suggested gently.

He looked at her. 'He has told you, then. No, I did not expect to, nor did I ever want to,' he answered frankly. 'I had no wish to meet the man who had despoiled my mother, then left her without a word.' He flushed, remembering to whom he was speaking. 'I'm sorry, but it is the truth.'

'The truth as you see it, sir.' Jessie looked down at her hands, then looked up at him. 'Mr Buckleigh, how old do you suppose my husband is?'

It was not the question that he had expected to hear. 'Why, forty-eight or forty-nine, I suppose,' he hazarded.

'He is forty-four,' Jessie answered. 'How old are you, Mr Buckleigh?'

'Twenty-eight,' Michael answered, his eyes widening. 'But—'

'He was only sixteen when you were born,' Jessie interrupted. 'How much control over his own destiny do you suppose he had?'

'Enough to get a young woman with child,' Michael answered, his tone hardening. Nevertheless he could not help remembering that his own mother would have been just forty-four had she lived.

'You must see him again; give him a chance to explain.'

'There is nothing to say,' said Michael. 'And now, if you will excuse me—'

Jessie sighed, and pulled herself to her feet. 'Mr Buckleigh, if you only knew—' She broke off with a gasp, bent over, and clutched her stomach. Her eyes opened wide. 'Oh, my goodness!' She gasped again.

'Allow me to assist you into the carriage,' said Michael concernedly.

There was a short pause while they both waited for the contraction to cease. She shook her head. 'It's too late for that, and also for the cup of tea that you promised. I very much regret that I will be giving birth in your cottage, Mr Buckleigh. Will you have my husband fetched, if you please?'

Michael went outside hastily and sent the carriage away with a succinct message. Then he went back into the cottage, where Lady Ashbourne was doubled-up with another contraction. 'The maid changed my bed linen only today,' he said. 'Will you allow me to help you upstairs?'

She shook her head. 'I would rather wait until my husband comes,' she said. 'Talk to me. Tell me how you like Illingham. Have you made many friends?'

He talked gently to her, holding her hand, and placing his arm about her to steady her each time she was seized by another contraction. He was just nursing her through the most powerful one yet when galloping hoofs came to a halt outside. The door of the cottage opened and Lord Ashbourne stood on the threshold. Michael noted with a sense of satisfaction of which he was immediately ashamed that a faint bruise across the chin marred the earl's masculine beauty. As the two men's eyes met, Michael realized that Lord Ashbourne must be seeing a very similar sight to the one that had met his own eyes when he had entered the drawing room and seen the earl bending over Evangeline. With a sudden moment of insight, he understood that the earl's stance could have been protective rather than lecherous.

'Raff,' Jessie breathed thankfully.

'I'm here, sweetheart.' Lord Ashbourne crossed the room in two strides and bent to smooth his wife's hair away from her brow and drop a gentle kiss upon it, whilst Michael rose and stepped back.

'Mr Buckleigh wanted to help me upstairs, but I waited for you.'

'We must get you home,' the earl insisted. 'The chaise is coming.'

Lady Ashbourne shook her head. 'It's too late. My waters have broken.'

'My room is to the left at the top of the stairs, my lord,' said Michael.

Ashbourne nodded. 'My thanks. Now, up with you, my dear.'

When Michael had first seen his father, the earl had looked the very picture of an elegant gentleman, not a hair out of place. Today he was dressed for riding, but despite the fact that he must have ridden from Ashbourne Abbey hell-for-leather, he still looked as though he had only just left the ministrations of his valet. If asked, Michael would have hazarded that the earl was just a little effete. Now, to his surprise, Ashbourne bent down and, without noticeable effort, picked his wife up in his arms.

'Raff, I can walk if you will assist me,' she protested gently.

'Yes, but I like to carry you,' the earl replied, smiling tenderly at her.

Jessie sighed and leaned against his shoulder in the manner of a woman who has found a longed for place of safety in which to rest. Michael hurried up the stairs and into his room, to make sure that all of his belongings were out of the way. Then he drew back the covers so that the bed would be ready for the unexpected occupant.

'Thank you, Mr Buckleigh. This is most kind,' said Jessie as Ashbourne brought her in.

'I will fetch one of my sister's nightgowns,' said Michael, going into Theodora's room and coming back with the garment in question. Luckily, since Lady Ashbourne was bigger than Theodora, particularly now, the garment was a voluminous one.

'Ilam has gone for the doctor,' said the earl. 'Would you be so good as to go downstairs and look out for them?'

Michael had only just descended the stairs when Ilam arrived at the door with the doctor and a sensible-looking woman, who turned out to be the midwife. 'Lady Ashbourne is upstairs,' said the curate. 'Her husband is attending her.'

It was not very long before Lord Ashbourne came back down. In his eyes was an expression of deep anxiety. 'Dismissed already?' Ilam asked him.

The earl inclined his head. 'As you say. I have nothing to do but wait, apparently.'

'My home is naturally at your disposal,' said Michael a little stiffly. With all the excitement, and the need to see Lady Ashbourne safely disposed, he had briefly forgotten about the circumstances in which he and the earl had last met. Now, he hardly knew how to face the man. 'I will withdraw to the Olde Oak, so that you may have more room.'

'There's not the least necessity for that,' Ilam replied. 'You are more than welcome at Illingham Hall.'

'You are very good,' Michael answered.

Gabriel turned to his father. 'By your leave, sir, I think I should go back to Ashbourne Abbey and acquaint Stacia with what is happening.'

The earl grinned reluctantly. 'No doubt she'll want to come back with you. Women, I find, all want to be closely involved with these kinds of events.'

'Michael?' The curate looked up, startled to hear his Christian name upon the lips of his half-brother. Ilam had said that he might call him

Gabriel. It had not occurred to him that the viscount would assume that the privilege should be mutual.

He read the message in Gabriel's eyes without difficulty. He was asking him to remain at the cottage so that Lord Ashbourne would not have to wait alone. Briefly, Michael hesitated, his gaze turning away. There was nothing that he wanted to do less. In that instant, he caught sight of his own reflection in the mirror. Unlike yesterday evening, he was once more neatly dressed, his high plain stock proclaiming his calling and reminding him of his responsibilities. One of the two men with him now was a parishioner. The other was deeply anxious about his wife, who was even now giving birth upstairs. He could not refuse to help.

'Of course I will remain,' he said.

Ilam nodded. He picked up his hat, crossed to where his father was standing, reached out and gripped his shoulder. 'Jessie is in good health, and the doctor is reliable. I'm sure that all will be well.'

Ashbourne smiled bleakly. 'I'm grateful to you for your reassurance, but my experience in this aspect of life has not been very happy so far.'

Ilam nodded. 'I must be on my way,' he said.

Seized by a sudden thought, Michael said, 'My lord, I wonder … I scarcely like to ask, but—'

'Ask anything you like, but for God's sake stop calling me "my lord",' Ilam interrupted.

Michael smiled reluctantly. 'Very well – Gabriel. Miss Granby took my sister home with her yesterday when I was … was …'

'Indisposed?' Gabriel suggested. 'You'd like me to look in upon them?'

'Only if you have time. Perhaps they could be informed about what is happening here. I think that it would be for the best if Miss Granby could keep Theodora with her, but only if it's of no inconvenience. Obviously I understand that any errands to do with Lady Ashbourne must come first.'

'Consider it done,' Gabriel answered. 'I'll get a message to her somehow.' He turned again to his father. 'Bear up. Jessie would expect it of you, you know.'

As Michael watched him go out of the door and close it behind him, he thought of how Gabriel was going to see Evangeline. He had not had leisure to think about her since Lady Ashbourne had arrived. Now, he thought of her again, and remembered the letter. For the first time, it occurred to him that her offer to take care of his sister did not fit with his picture of a spoiled woman who cared nothing for him. He frowned in puzzlement.

He had not realized that at the mention of his sister, Lord Ashbourne had turned his attention from what was happening upstairs, and had become curiously still. Now he spoke. 'No one told me that you had a sister,' he said, his expression puzzled.

'A half sister,' Michael replied. 'Our mother died when Theodora was born.'

'Not when *you* were born.'

'Not when I was born,' Michael agreed. 'It's what I was told.'

At that moment, there came a cry from upstairs. 'Jez,' Ashbourne breathed, and without hesitation, he sprang from his chair, and ran up the stairs. Michael heard the murmur of voices and moments later, the earl came back down.

'It is not uncommon for women to cry out in this situation,' the curate told him, feeling that he ought to say something reassuring.

'You're an expert, are you?' the earl asked, his eyes hard with anxiety.

'Not an expert, but at least I was there when Theodora was born,' Michael answered coldly.

'Meaning that *I* was not there when *you* were born, I suppose,' Ashbourne suggested.

'You may draw what inference you please, my lord,' said Michael, turning his back. 'I am quite uninterested in your opinions.'

'If you would but allow me to explain,' Ashbourne began.

Michael whirled round. 'Explain what? How you despoiled a young woman who was little more than a child? How you deserted her and left her to explain the situation to her cold-hearted family? How your desertion meant that she was all but sold into servitude, from which she was rescued, not by you, but by my stepfather? How you never, ever made any attempt to find me, or take an interest in me?' To his horror, he could hear his voice trembling as he spoke that sentence. He forgot all about his promise to Gabriel. All he knew was that he could not remain in this man's presence for a moment longer. 'No, I'm afraid I have no interest in your spineless excuses. You're a libertine and a coward, and I despise you with all my heart.' He walked to the door and stood, his hand on the handle.

'Where are you going?' Ashbourne asked, white-faced.

'Does it matter? I'm simply doing what you did: I'm walking away.'

Michael left the cottage not knowing where he was going and caring less. The words that he had just spoken to Ashbourne were whirling round and round in his brain. Where had all that bitterness come from? He had thought that he was largely indifferent to the man that had fathered him. Now, Ashbourne's desertion was ripping and tearing at him, as if it had only just happened. After he had been walking for some time, he realized that he was breathing heavily, as if he had just taken part in some strenuous exercise. He stopped to catch his breath, unsure of how far he had walked or in what direction. Without surprise, he noted that he was within sight of Granby Park.

Before coming to Illingham, his sole aim had been to serve as well as he might, and progress nearer to gaining his own parish. He had known what he wanted, who he was, and where he was going. Now, his life had become complicated and none of these issues was clear. His reverie was interrupted by the advent of a man on horseback. Michael recognized him almost immediately as being Lieutenant Fellowes.

It had been with a sense of satisfaction that Fellowes had delivered Lady Belton's letter to the bishop. He had ridden into the village with the intention of calling upon Michael to try to discover how he had taken the news. The curate's appearance was everything that he could have hoped for. The man looked absolutely stunned. 'A delightful day,' remarked the soldier, enjoying looking down upon one whom he perceived as being a rival.

Michael looked about him blankly. He was so oblivious to the state of the weather that he would hardly have been surprised to discover a light covering of snow. 'As you say,' he replied in distracted tones.

'I fear I interrupt your thoughts,' said the lieutenant, with more than a touch of malice. 'Doubtless you are preparing next week's sermon – your text drawn from one of the *letters*, perhaps.' He gave his penultimate word a little extra emphasis.

'Yes, my mind is elsewhere,' Michael admitted, not catching his inference. 'Forgive me. I am not good company today.'

'Think nothing of it,' answered Fellowes, torn between pleasure that Michael was so clearly disturbed and annoyance that he was not rising to the bait. 'I will leave you to your walk. I am about to call on the divine Miss Granby and I must not keep her waiting.' So saying, he turned his mount and rode off towards Granby Park. He had made no arrangement to call upon Evangeline, but it suited him to give Michael that impression.

Such a revelation could hardly make Michael more miserable than he already was. He turned and walked in the opposite direction. So

Evangeline, having raised a complaint against him, was now encouraging Fellowes. His duty to Mr Granby perhaps dictated that he should discourage this state of affairs, but he could not do it; he simply could not.

Still bent upon avoiding the village, he took one of the many paths that criss-crossed the countryside thereabouts. He did not want to meet anyone. Just now he needed to lick his own wounds.

After walking for some little time, his thoughts becoming no clearer as he went, he eventually came upon a house that he thought he recognized. On circumnavigating it, he found that he had approached Halfpenny House from the back. Lady Agatha Rayner was in the garden cutting some flowers. She stood looking at him as he approached. 'You look awful,' she said frankly, as soon as he was close enough to speak to. 'Come inside for a glass of wine.'

'Thank you, but I'm averse to company at present,' he answered.

She picked up the basket at her feet and handed it to him, giving him no choice but to take it. 'Do as you're told, Nephew,' she said, before walking into the house, leaving him to follow behind.

They entered by a glass door at the back which gave on to a book room. From there, Lady Agatha led him through a door which led into the drawing room where they had sat when he had first visited her. She rang the bell, then when Grimes came, she gave him the basket and instructed him to bring wine.

'How did you know?' Michael asked curiously.

She did not ask him to explain what he meant. 'You have our eyebrows to start with,' she replied. 'Mind you, with that hair the effect is so freakish that one doesn't notice them straight away. Where did you get it from? Your mother?'

'Yes,' Michael answered. 'You'll find that my sister has the same hair colour, but fortunately without the eyebrows.'

'But then Ashbourne ain't her father. What else? Oh, your bearing.'

'My bearing?'

'That smooth elegance of movement, added to the way you lift your chin – it's all Ashbourne. What's more, I knew that Raff's bastard was a clergyman named Michael. Add all those things together and it makes an obvious picture to one who knows him – or you – well.'

Grimes returned with the wine and, as on the previous occasion, Lady Agatha asked her visitor to pour. 'I have to say that I immensely enjoyed the visit to the abbey the other day,' her ladyship remarked, when they both had a glass in their hand. 'I haven't been entertained so well in ages.'

Michael grinned wryly. It seemed to be a long time since he had had cause to smile about anything. 'You'll forgive me if I take a different view of the matter,' he said.

'I expect you do,' she conceded. 'Perhaps you think I ought to apologize to you. After all, it was Raff's skin I wanted to get under and not yours. But I'm afraid that I never apologize for anything.'

'I expect *I* got under his skin far more thoroughly,' he answered, looking down into his wine.

'I doubt that. Men never seem to resent being hit by one another as much as one would suppose. Was he what you expected?'

Michael thought of the moment when he had first seen his father, then recalled his encounter with him in the cottage earlier that day. 'Yes and no,' he answered.

'I always thought that I hated him,' remarked Lady Agatha conversationally. 'It was only when he nearly died following a duel which he fought over Jessie that I realized my feelings for him were far more complicated. There's eight years between us, you see, and we've never been close. Our father saw to that.'

'You'll have to talk to my sister, ma'am,' said Michael. 'She'd like to exchange views with you on what it is like to bear with an older brother.'

Lady Agatha smiled mischievously. 'That's just the kind of flummery that Raff would come up with, but Ilam would never say in a million years.'

'If you're going to say I'm like him—'

'You'll do what? Knock *me* down? You can't deny your inheritance. Be thankful. There's plenty of worse people you could have been like. At least Raff doesn't take after our father in nature. He was an evil old bastard.'

'Presumably you take your own advice and don't seek to deny *your* inheritance, ma'am,' said Michael.

She laughed. '*Touché*. Your Evangeline called me an evil old witch the other day.'

'She's not my Evangeline.'

'Oh, I think that perhaps she is.'

From Halfpenny House, he walked into the village and stood for a long time looking into the duck pond. Somewhere in the distance he heard a baby crying. For the first time, he recalled that even though he had been asked by Gabriel to stay at the cottage, he had walked out after less than five minutes. No doubt he had by now lost the good opinion of the one member of the family who until now had been predisposed in his favour. He wondered idly how deep the duck pond might be and whether it would be possible for him to drown himself.

Chapter Sixteen

As soon as Theodora was settled in at Granby Park and Evangeline could decently leave her, she ran to her room to look for the letter. She would have liked to have rushed home to look for the wretched thing straight after she had left Michael's cottage. Unfortunately, she had committed herself to collecting Theodora from the school. To make matters worse, since Michael's sister had no inkling of the tumultuous nature of recent events, Evangeline was forced to put on a bright façade, even though she was feeling quite the opposite.

Once alone, she was freed from the need to dissemble. Frantically, she searched through her drawers, then checked underneath all the furniture, between her chest of drawers and the wall. Finally she was obliged to acknowledge that it was nowhere to be seen. Surely no one could have picked up the letter and sent it? She was not so careless with her letters normally. Eventually, she sent for Elsie who put an end to all hope by saying, 'Oh yes, miss, I found it and made sure it was sent.'

After she had spent some time berating herself to no purpose, she decided that the best thing to do would be to contact the bishop directly. He would surely listen to her! If necessary, in order to convince him that she had a high opinion of the curate, she would inform him that she and Michael intended to marry. She could even say that she had only written the letter because they had had a lovers' quarrel. It would be a shocking piece of mendacity, not to say presumption, on her part, particularly now that Michael no doubt considered her to be the lowest person who ever breathed. She now admitted to herself, however, that there was nothing that she desired more. She loved him and she wanted to marry him. It was as simple as that. It did not matter two straws to her that he was Lord Ashbourne's bastard. Nor did it matter that he had scarcely a penny to his name. If he loved her – and she was by no means convinced that he did after everything that she had done – then she would somehow persuade her father to accept him as a son-in-law.

She had enjoyed her London seasons hugely. Now, she did not want to attend any more, unless it was as Mrs Buckleigh. But first, she must sweep away the nightmare of this complaint, so that Michael could continue to do the work that he loved. Even if he could not forgive her, she owed him that much.

Theodora was delighted to have the chance to spend some time with Miss Granby at her home, providing that Michael could be informed. They did not collect Theodora's things from the cottage. Evangeline made her invitation sound as if it was just for the rest of the day. She had no doubt that she would be able to persuade her guest to stay the night. Then someone could be sent to get her things, or she might be able to borrow some clothes that Evangeline had outgrown and had not yet thrown away.

Evangeline's mother took to the curate's sister immediately, and was soon showing the younger woman her embroidery, a craft which Evangeline did not enjoy, but which Theodora found very absorbing and in which she had some skill. Mrs Granby was also in good spirits because she had had a letter just that morning telling her that her husband would be home any day now.

Evangeline was obliged to conceal how much she dreaded such an eventuality. As a supporter of Michael's, he would be horrified at what she had done. He could not be any more horrified than she was herself. She felt like a traitor, entertaining Michael's sister when she might quite possibly be the means of his ruin.

After a late breakfast the following morning, Evangeline took Theodora for a walk around the rose garden, not yet looking its best, but showing promise for the future. Theodora made a comment about the garden of the vicarage in which she had lived with her father. Evangeline answered her, well aware that she was only giving a small part of her mind to what her guest was saying.

The more she thought about it, the more it seemed to her that the best thing for her to do would be to go to Sheffield in person. The whole situation would be far too complicated to explain in a letter. What was more, she could not be certain that it would arrive before Michael had to appear before the bishop. In any case, she felt certain that a personal approach would be the best. She was well aware of the effect that her remarkable beauty had upon most men. If she could charm the bishop into listening to her, then so much the better.

The only question was how to get there. Her father was not available to take her. She dared not ask Lord Ashbourne or Lord Ilam for favours on Michael's behalf, for she had no idea how either of them felt about this new relative. Lady Agatha might come out of sheer mischief, but in order to persuade her to do so, Evangeline would have to reveal more than she wanted about her personal feelings.

If she could once get to Sheffield everything would be easy. She would be able to stay overnight with her relations if necessary. Doubtless they would think it very odd of her to turn up unexpectedly, but they could not possibly have a worse opinion of her than they already had.

Evangeline and Theodora were just going inside when Lord Ilam came out into the garden, moving with his usual energetic stride. He bowed to them both, bade them good day, then turned to Theodora. 'I come to you with the latest news,' he said. 'My stepmother is at your house, Miss Buckleigh, as is my father.' Evangeline bit back an exclamation. Ilam looked pointedly in her direction. They were both remembering what had happened in the drawing room of Ashbourne Abbey. 'She went to call upon Michael and went into labour. She is presently giving birth upstairs.'

'And Lord Ashbourne?' Evangeline ventured.

'He remains there. Michael is keeping him company.'

'Is that wise?' Evangeline asked, forgetting for a moment that Theodora did not know what had happened the previous day.

'Why should it not be wise?' Theodora asked anxiously. 'What is happening? Is Michael all right?'

'Your brother is perfectly all right,' Ilam answered reassuringly. 'He has things to talk about with my father, that is all.' Before Theodora could ask what those things might be he went on, 'I have been to Ashbourne Abbey to collect my wife. She has stepped down from the carriage to have a brief word with Mrs Granby, but I must not delay.'

'Please tell Mr Buckleigh that he need have no concern for his sister,' Evangeline said. 'She may stay here for as long as is necessary.' As he left them, Evangeline reflected that here was another reason why she could not possibly ask Lord Ilam or his father for help to get to Sheffield.

She was still pondering anxiously over the matter that afternoon when Lieutenant Fellowes was announced as she and Theodora were looking over some new fashion plates that had arrived from London. Mrs Granby was resting on her bed.

The last time Evangeline had spoken with Fellowes, he had accused her of having an interest in Michael and she had denied it. It was obvious that he could not abide the curate. Suddenly it seemed to her that Fellowes might be someone that she could make use of. With this in mind, she suggested that the three of them should stroll about the garden a little. Then, as she and Theodora stepped on to the terrace, she whispered, 'Miss Buckleigh, in a little while, would you make an excuse for coming back inside? I need to speak to Lieutenant Fellowes alone.'

Theodora looked at Evangeline rather reproachfully. She had been hoping that this new glamorous friend might make a match of it with her brother. Nevertheless, she nodded and, after only a short time, she exclaimed over a broken shoestring and hurried into the house.

'Miss Granby,' said the lieutenant, 'may I take advantage of your companion's absence by asking you if you have decided to relent towards me?'

'Relent?' Evangeline echoed, turning away so that he had just a tantalizing glimpse of her perfect profile.

'Last time we spoke, it seemed to me that you had decided to favour the church over the army,' he explained.

She gave a trill of laughter. 'Good heavens, no,' she answered. 'You appeared to me to be presuming rather a lot, so I thought to teach you a lesson. Have you learned it, sir?' She glanced up at him through her lashes.

'I was never a good scholar, but if you were my teacher, then I vow I would try harder,' he replied, his eyes full of laughter that was not entirely free from malice. In view of what he had learned about her activities in the church vestry, this was bidding fair to become a most entertaining conversation. He would allow her to take the lead and see where it took them.

'So I can expect to see some improvement.'

'Never doubt it, Miss Granby. And now that little Miss Buckleigh has gone inside, you will be able to favour me with some … ah … individual tuition.'

This was just the opening that Evangeline had been hoping for. 'I am glad she has left us, I confess,' she sighed. 'I felt obliged to invite her to stay, but now I am regretting it.'

'And why is that?'

'Well, you know that Mr Buckleigh is supposed to be acting as my guardian while Papa is away. I am convinced that his little sister will spy upon me, telling him everything that I do. It is most vexatious. No doubt she will tell him that I have been walking alone with you in the garden, for instance.'

'In that case, I wonder why you sent her in,' he observed.

She smiled at him. 'I thought it worth the risk,' she replied, with a saucy toss of her head. 'What I would not give to make sure that he had a taste of his own medicine!'

'What do you mean?'

'Well, he has been trying to rule my life. I would very much like him to discover what it is like to be lorded over by someone else – the bishop, for instance.'

'Really?' He leaned closer to her. 'Well perhaps your wish might be fulfilled.'

'In what way?' she asked.

'Someone has written to the bishop to complain about him. He'll be summoned to Sheffield to have his wrists slapped very soon, no doubt.'

'How do you know?' Evangeline asked sharply, forgetting her role for a moment.

He stared at her curiously. 'How does anyone know about these things? News gets about.'

'Is it known who sent the letter?' she asked cautiously.

'That would be telling.' His reply convinced her that by some means he had found out about the complaint, but did not know its source.

'Anyway, this is excellent,' Evangeline declared. 'Oh, how I wish I had known sooner.'

'Why?' he asked.

'Well, I … I could have sent a letter at the same time,' she answered, improvising rapidly. 'Now, I expect it will be too late, and perhaps just one letter will not be sufficient to get him removed.'

'Removed? You surprise me.'

'Do I?' she asked ingenuously.

'Last time we spoke upon the subject, I gained the impression that you were thinking more favourably of him.'

'Certainly not,' Evangeline replied indignantly. 'He is presumptuous and takes far too much upon himself. He needs to be taught a lesson. I wonder …' She allowed her voice to tail away.

'You wonder?' he prompted.

'I was just thinking that if I could only get to Sheffield, I could speak to the bishop in person.'

'So you could,' he replied in a conversational tone.

She looked at him, as if taken by a sudden thought. 'Would *you* consider escorting me there tomorrow?'

'I? Tomorrow?' Even Fellowes was startled.

'It may seem rather sudden, but you see, my mother has heard that my father will be back any day. It will be much harder to get away when he is around. He approves so heartily of Mr Buckleigh that he will not hear a word against him. I will never be able to lodge a complaint once Papa is home.'

'Suppose I did take you tomorrow, how would you get away with it?'

'Oh, quite easily,' Evangeline replied. 'Mama never rises much before noon. You could come to fetch me first thing and we could be in Sheffield by midday. If the bishop can see me straight away – and I do not see why he should not – we will be back by dinner time.'

'Will your mother not be anxious? Remember what a ridiculous taking she got herself into when we simply went out riding.'

'Miss Buckleigh is staying,' Evangeline replied, biting back a sharp retort at his implied criticism of her mother. 'She can tell Mama that I have gone to see Lady Ilam.'

'But won't it seem odd that Miss Buckleigh has not gone as well?'

'Not really,' Evangeline replied. 'Miss Buckleigh is a little lame, as you may have noticed. She can pretend that her foot is paining her and that she would rather stay at home.'

'How do you propose we should go?' The lieutenant asked.

She looked nonplussed. 'I had not thought of that,' she said truthfully.

Lieutenant Fellowes thought for a moment. 'I have an idea,' he said. 'Why don't I persuade Amelia to come with us? I need not say anything to her about the nature of your errand. You could pretend that you were visiting your cousin or something, and I could take her shopping. That way, you would be chaperoned without having to bother about bringing a maid.'

Evangeline nodded thoughtfully. She did not relish the prospect of sitting with Amelia in a confined space for the best part of three hours. On the other hand, it would be a relief not to have to take Elsie who had nearly let the cat out of the bag on more than one occasion concerning their adventure in Sheffield. 'If you are sure that Amelia will be willing to go.'

'I will convince her of it,' he replied. 'By the way, what reason do you intend to give Miss Buckleigh for your protracted absence?'

Evangeline smiled brilliantly. 'Oh, that's simple,' she replied. 'I'll tell her that I'm going to Sheffield to plead her brother's case with the bishop.'

He laughed. 'Miss Granby, you are positively Machiavellian,' he declared. And so am I, he added silently, an unpleasant smile on his lips. Moments later, he excused himself in order to make arrangements for the next day's outing.

'But whoever would do such a thing?' Theodora exclaimed indignantly. In order to explain her absence on the morrow, Evangeline had felt obliged to tell Michael's sister about the complaint that had been made about him and about his summons to attend upon the bishop. They had gone up to Evangeline's bedchamber so they would not be overheard.

Evangeline glanced at her swiftly, before looking away. After a very long pause, she said in a small voice, 'I am very much afraid that it was … was probably I.'

'*Probably* you?' Theodora questioned, torn between puzzlement and shock.

'Yes, probably,' Evangeline responded hastily, before Theodora could take this information in. 'I don't know for sure, I wrote a letter, but—'

'How could you?' Theodora cried, her eyes full of confusion and distress. 'What has Michael ever done to hurt you? When has he ever done anything but his duty with regard to you and your family?'

'I know, I know,' Evangeline answered, wringing her hands.

'You know what will happen now, don't you?' Theodora went on, her distress turning to anger. 'He will be removed from Illingham and very likely unfrocked as well.'

'Surely not,' Evangeline answered, horrified.

'You do not understand. He was removed from his first curacy because a young lady fell in love with him without the least encouragement, and her fiancé picked a fight with him. Then in his second curacy, his vicar made himself objectionable to a woman and Michael thrashed him. This was his last chance. Now you have spoiled it for him.' She turned towards the door.

'Where are you going?' Evangeline asked.

'I am going to see Lord Ashbourne,' Theodora replied, her voice trembling. 'I have never met him, and it terrifies me to death to think of it, but I cannot believe that he would be so unjust as to let a good man suffer through your spite. He must be persuaded to use his influence with the bishop.'

'No, wait,' said Evangeline urgently, catching hold of her arm.

'Let go of me,' Theodora flashed angrily. 'Michael is my brother and I love him. I must do what I can.'

'Wait,' Evangeline said again. She took a deep breath. 'I love him too, and I have a plan that will save him.'

'What do you mean, you love him?' Theodora asked scornfully. 'How could you love him and do such a thing?'

Evangeline explained how Michael had made her so angry that she had written the letter. 'It relieved my feelings, but I never intended to send it,' she assured Theodora. 'Have you never written something – in your diary perhaps – about someone just because they made you angry, but later regretted it?'

Theodora stared at her for a few moments then turned away. 'I *did* write something horrible in my diary once,' she confessed. 'My father made me stay in to construe some Latin instead of going on a picnic with friends. I wrote that I wished he was dead. I was so frightened that it might come true that I scribbled and scribbled over it, then tore the page out and burned it. Even so I was terrified for several days that I might have wished it upon him.' They were both silent for a short time. 'If you did not intend to send it, how did it get there?'

'I don't know,' Evangeline replied wretchedly. 'I left it in here. Nobody usually takes letters from my room, but I asked Elsie if she had taken my letter and she said yes.' She pulled Theodora over to the window seat, urged her to sit down, then knelt at her feet with a rustle of skirts. 'Please believe me. I never planned to hurt Michael. I do love him, I promise you. And I have a plan to undo the dreadful damage that I have done.' Seeing that Theodora no longer looked as if she might be on the point of leaving the room, Evangeline sat down next to her and explained what she had been saying to Lieutenant Fellowes. 'I am hoping that speaking to the bishop in person will make a difference,' she concluded. 'Anyway, I have got to try.'

'You are doing all of that – for Michael?' said Theodora, glancing at Evangeline sideways.

'I must – even though he probably won't want to speak to me ever again.' Her voice broke on her final words.

She had only shed a few tears before Theodora's small hand pressed a handkerchief into hers. 'I believe you,' the younger girl said, 'and I want to help. What can I do?'

'Sheffield? But why upon earth would I want to go to Sheffield with Evangeline Granby? I would prefer not to go to the end of the street with her.'

Lieutenant Fellowes prepared himself to deal patiently with his cousin. He had plans which he did not want spoiled at this stage by a young woman's tantrums. 'Calm yourself, my dear coz,' he said, as he guided her to a chair in the little withdrawing room at the back of the house which she liked to think of as her own. 'Such violence of feeling is ruinous to the complexion, I'm told. Besides, I thought that you got on quite well with her.'

'I've never liked her,' Amelia answered bitterly, 'and since she was seen kissing the curate in the vestry I have positively detested her.'

'Well, if you come with us to Sheffield tomorrow, I can guarantee that she will soon be out of your way – for good.'

Amelia paled. 'For good?' she echoed, her hand going to her throat. 'You are not intending to … to …'

'Good God, Amelia, get your imagination under control,' said Fellowes scornfully. 'She won't come to harm. You do want her out of the way, don't you?'

'Well of course; as long as you aren't going to hurt her. Then perhaps …' She twisted her handkerchief in her hands.

'You have hopes of getting him back?' he suggested.

'Evangeline bewitches all the men,' Amelia burst out. 'I've seen her do it so many times before. With her out of the way, I might have a chance with him.'

'Then come with me tomorrow.'

'You're going to help me? Then of course I'll come. What are you planning? What do I have to do?'

'You don't have to do anything. Just be civil to Miss Granby and let me do the rest.'

Chapter Seventeen

⁘

'Damnation, he *knew* that I wanted him to stay,' said Ilam exasperatedly when he arrived back at the cottage and found his father waiting alone downstairs. 'If I do not give him a piece of my mind ...'

'No, Gabriel,' said Ashbourne, laying down a book which he had taken from Michael's bookcase and which he had been perusing off and on without taking in any of the contents. 'It was really far too much to expect that he would be able to stay in the same room as myself, you know.'

'But given the circumstances—'

'Whatever the circumstances.'

'But, Father—'

A slow smile spread across Ashbourne's face. He made no reference to the fact that this was the first time that Gabriel had ever addressed him in such a way. 'Give him time,' he said. 'But don't let him be alone for too long.'

Gabriel was very torn. On the one hand, he felt for Michael, for he knew from experience how difficult it was to come to terms with old wrongs. On the other, his father ought not to have been left alone. Looking at the man whom he had once thought he detested, he realized to his surprise that he had become fond of him. With a flash of insight he understood that this might be partly to do with Ashbourne's impending fatherhood, an experience that he himself remembered and with which he could empathize. As he paused in indecision, the door opened softly and his wife stood on the threshold. 'I couldn't bear to keep away,' she said. 'How are things going?'

There was a cry from Jessie upstairs. Ashbourne looked at his daughter-in-law. 'You tell me,' he said, with the air of one completely at a loss.

'It sounds quite normal to me,' she responded.

'That's more or less what Michael said,' the earl told her.

'He was right,' she said. 'Where is he, by the way?'

'If you are able to stay, my love, then I shall go and look for him,' Gabriel replied.

Thinking that this might be done more easily on horseback than on foot, Gabriel set out to walk to Illingham Hall to get himself a mount. He went the long way round, rather than taking a short cut to the stables, as he reckoned that he might then be more likely to see someone who had bumped into Michael. As he got to the entrance gates, however, his eye was caught by the figure of a man standing by the duck pond which marked the far end of the main street of the village. Something told him that this would be Michael. As he drew closer he could see his half-brother looking down into the pond, his whole body giving a picture of deep dejection. At that moment, the last vestiges of anger melted away. He approached the clergyman, laying a hand on his shoulder.

Michael looked straight at him. 'I was thinking of throwing myself in,' he said.

'Not seriously, I hope,' Gabriel responded. 'David Crossley and I had a fight when we were boys and we finished up in there. It's only three feet down at its deepest, and you'd look rather foolish, I fear.' Michael gave a little half smile. Taking this as a hopeful sign, Gabriel added, 'Come on; let's go home. I've a decent Madeira I'd like you to try.'

The entrance of Illingham Hall was cool and dark and, in some strange way, it felt comforting to Michael as he walked in. He looked about him as he had not done when he had visited the housekeeper on a previous occasion. Gabriel, observing him, said, 'Has it occurred to you, Brother, that had our father married your mother, that you would be Lord Ilam and I would not exist?'

'No, it had not occurred to me,' Michael responded. He thought for a moment, remembering the well-tended acres, the cottages in good repair, and the contentment of the people. 'That would have been a pity, I think.'

Gabriel laughed, led him into the library and indicated a comfortable chair, whilst he poured them a glass each from a decanter on a side table. He felt that there was more that Michael needed to know, but was very unsure as to how to proceed. He was glad when Michael spoke first.

'The Crossleys seem an excellent family.'

'They are indeed,' Gabriel agreed. This was the kind of opening that he had been hoping for. 'They were my salvation.' He settled himself easily in another chair.

'Your salvation? That's a curious turn of phrase.'

'In order to explain it, I'll have to go over quite a bit of old history,' Gabriel continued. 'My mother died when I was born and, apparently, my grandfather blamed Raff.' Michael stood up and turned away abruptly. 'If you don't want to listen, we can talk of something else,' Gabriel said gently.

Michael shook his head as if to dispel some of the confusion in his mind. 'No; I mean, yes, of course I want to listen. I'm sorry. Do go on.'

'I should have said "*our* grandfather". Of all the relatives that you've gained, I think he's probably the most unpleasant.'

'Lady Agatha said that he was an evil old bastard.'

'Yes, well, she should know. He exacted revenge for my mother's death by sending me to be brought up by the Crossleys. My father was not allowed to approach me without permission.'

'But how could he have done such a thing to his own son?' Michael exclaimed. 'Did your father make no attempt to rebel?'

Gabriel noticed Michael's use of the word "your" when "our" would have been more correct, but did not remark upon it. 'I think great pressure was put upon him. He's never told me the details. Remember, too, that he was only seventeen. How much control did you have over your own life when you were that age? In any case, by then he had more than one son to worry about.'

Michael wrinkled his brow in puzzlement. 'You mean me? But he never took the slightest notice of me. How can I possibly come into all this?'

'In your early years, your financial support came from my grandfather. Raff had to do as he was told as far as contact with me was concerned. If he didn't, the threat was that your support would be withdrawn.'

'Dear God!' Michael whispered, so shocked that the blasphemy escaped from his lips without his even being aware of it. 'I had no idea. I suppose that if he seemed likely to seek *me* out, then ...'

'Then he would threaten *my* comfort in some way. I shouldn't be surprised. Small wonder that my father – our father – concluded that the best way to guard us from his malice was to keep away from both of us. Most of what I've told you I've had from my father. You might be tempted to dismiss it as fabrication on his part. All I can say is that it rings true when measured up against what I've heard from the Crossleys, Aunt Agatha and others, and also when I bring to mind my own vague memories of my grandfather.' They were both silent for a while. Eventually Gabriel said, 'I know now that although he sent me away for the worst of intentions, he actually did me a favour. At least I had the chance to grow up as part of a happy family, which is more than my father had.' He paused. 'What of you? Were you happy?'

'Yes, I had a happy childhood,' Michael answered, smiling reminiscently. 'My mother was gentle, kind and loving. I still miss her. When she died …' He paused. 'When she died, I knew that I had to pass on that kindness to my sister. Although a good man, my stepfather is rather formal and serious. He has always done his duty by us – more than his duty, as far as I am concerned – and for that I am thankful; but in some ways, I have been more like a father or an uncle than a brother to Theodora.'

After this, Gabriel deliberately changed the subject, and they were soon talking about some of the more eccentric characters in the village. One concern continued to hover at the back of Michael's mind. How was he to tell Theodora about his parentage?

Eventually Gabriel said, 'I'll show you where you are to sleep.' Michael's things had already been brought to Illingham Hall from the cottage. The room that was to be his was larger than all the top floor of the cottage put together and was handsomely appointed in shades of blue and gold. 'I'm not sure what Eustacia wants to do about dinner,' the viscount told him. 'In any case, I feel that I ought to go back to the cottage and see how my father is faring.'

Michael squared his shoulders. 'I'll come with you.'

'Only if you're sure. To be blunt, he's got enough to think about without you causing him further disturbance.'

'I don't want to distress him. I just want to understand.'

On their arrival at the cottage, they found Lord Ashbourne and Lady Ilam sitting and talking quietly together. Ashbourne rose to his feet. 'There's no sign of the baby just yet,' said her ladyship. 'Jessie is doing very well.'

'I wish I could say the same,' replied Ashbourne wryly.

'Stacia, my love, you have been here for quite a time,' said Gabriel, after a short silence. 'Allow me to take you for a short walk down the lane.'

'Are you offering to lead me up the garden path, my lord?' asked Lady Ilam, as she rose gracefully and put her hand on her husband's arm.

'Undoubtedly,' Gabriel answered, lifting her hand and kissing it before laying it back on his arm. 'We shall be back anon.'

After the couple had left, there was a short silence. Eventually Lord Ashbourne said, 'I'd offer you a seat, but for the fact that it's your house.'

Michael hesitated then sat down. There was another silence. Eventually he said rather tentatively, 'Before I ... I left earlier, you said that you were told my mother had died at my birth. Who told you that?'

'My father, your grandfather. He told me gleefully that your mother had died in giving birth to you.'

'But why, when it was not true?' Michael asked, puzzled.

'He took pleasure in inflicting pain. More importantly, though, he knew that if she was still alive, I would manage to seek her out, somehow. He wanted me to concentrate upon establishing a legitimate family, you see. Once I was assured that Dora was dead, nothing mattered to me anyway.'

'But you got married,' said Michael. 'You married someone else when you knew that ... that ...'

'I knew that your mother was with child. Yes.' He turned away. 'You'll say that I was a coward. No doubt you'd be right.'

'I always thought you were a heartless libertine,' Michael said frankly. 'Lady Ashbourne told me that you were only sixteen when I was born. That makes such a notion rather improbable. But your reputation ...' His voice tailed away.

'My reputation was gained after Gabriel was born.'

'And what of my mother?'

Ashbourne sighed. 'Your mother's family kept a farm near to the school I attended. I met her one day when I was out riding on a horse supplied by my father. I never lacked for material comforts, you'll notice. She was no happier at home than I, and I was her first love as she was mine. When she discovered that she was with child, I went to my father and told him that I intended to marry her. It was not a very pleasant interview.' He was silent for a long time, remembering the past. Eventually he spoke again. 'My father made it clear to me that there was no chance of my marrying Dora, and that he would exact his revenge upon her if I ever approached her again. He had always held the purse strings. He promised that if I married the girl that he had chosen for me, he would support you and Dora financially. I had no choice but to agree.'

'The girl you married was Gabriel's mother.'

Ashbourne nodded. 'Laura Vyse. She was two years older than I. With hindsight, I have to wonder whether she and my father were actually in love, although, to give the devil his due, I am convinced that he never behaved improperly. I was married in the April of 1768, you were born in August when, as I thought, your mother died. Gabriel was born the following May. *His* mother *did* die at his birth. But yours lived on. Did she … was she…?'

'Was my mother happy?' Michael thought back. 'She was content, I think. My stepfather was always kind to her.'

'I'm glad of that. You are like your mother in many ways,' Ashbourne went on, looking at him thoughtfully. 'Your colouring and your bone structure, for instance. I would have known you for her son anywhere. Your manner has something of her gentleness as well.'

'My sister is like her,' Michael told him.

'I should like to meet your sister,' said Ashbourne, his expression softening.

All at once, Michael's suspicions hardened again. 'If you dare—' he breathed, getting to his feet.

Ashbourne also rose. 'I make every allowance for your prejudices, but that is going too far,' he said firmly. 'I am in love with my wife and, even if I were not, I don't believe I'm depraved enough to seduce the innocent child of my first love who must be almost young enough to be my granddaughter.' He paused, looking at Michael's fists clenched by his sides. 'I warn you, you'll not catch me unawares again. If you hit me, I'll give as good as I get. My father would have said that you had coalheaver's shoulders. You get them from me, you know – as does Ilam.'

Michael laughed reluctantly, unclenching his fists. 'I beg pardon, sir; also for hitting you—'

Ashbourne waved his hand dismissively before Michael could finish his apology. 'There's no need,' he said. 'Your reaction was quite understandable. I rather admired your spirit. Did you box at university?'

Michael nodded. 'I didn't have a lot of money to spare, but I found the work quite easy. I used to trade essays and translations and the like for boxing and fencing lessons.'

'In any case, it would be foolish to brawl in here,' Ashbourne observed. 'There isn't enough space – and it would be a tragedy if that were damaged.' He walked over to the table in the window and picked up Michael's bowl with what the clergyman could see at once was an expert touch. 'Roman, I believe. It's a fine specimen. Where did you get it?'

'An elderly neighbour, James Warrener by name, left it to me in his will.'

Ashbourne's face lit up with recognition. 'Warrener! The old rogue. I knew him well, although I hadn't seen him for a good many years. Wait though. I remember getting a letter from him telling me about a lad from the village who had a feel for pottery. That would have been you, I suppose.'

'Indeed, I think it must have been.'

'I'll have to look it out and show it to you.'

'He also gave me this book,' said Michael, as he went to the book-shelf to get his copy of *Tom Jones*. As he was doing so, Ashbourne remembered something that Warrener had written in another letter.

None of my family is interested in antiquities, so I've planned to leave my entire collection to that young lad I told you about. He's got his own way to make in the world, and it would help him a good deal. He has a way of handling pottery that reminds me so much of you....

It might be worth sending his man of business to discover whether his old friend had really left Michael only one bowl.

A few minutes later, Janet came in from the kitchen. 'Good evening, Reverend,' she said, dropping a curtsy. 'Mrs Davies sent me—' She broke off as she caught sight of Lord Ashbourne. 'Excuse me, my lord,' she said, curtsying again. 'I didn't see you at first. Mrs Davies wondered whether you gentlemen'd like something to eat, and if'n you want to eat here or at the Hall. I know you didn't feel up to having anything much this morning, Reverend.'

Ashbourne raised his brows. 'Like that, was it?' he said, strolling over to his son's side. Michael returned his gaze. There must have been some similarity in their expressions, for Janet looked from one to the other and said quite involuntarily, 'Oh, my goodness!' Then she coloured. 'I beg your pardon,' she added, in a mortified tone.

'Not at all,' Ashbourne replied. 'You are one of the first to see me and my son side by side. It must be rather an alarming sight. As for food, I'm not sure that I could eat anything at present.' He cast his eyes up in the direction of the bedroom.

'Begging your pardon, my lord, but it will do Lady Ashbourne no good for you to be fading away,' said Janet diffidently, still eyeing the two of them in fascination.

'Lord and Lady Ilam will be back in a few minutes,' said the earl. 'We'll decide then.' They both sat down again.

After she had gone into the kitchen, closing the door behind her, the earl looked at Michael who was still staring at him in astonishment. 'What is it?' Ashbourne asked.

'I never expected to meet you,' Michael replied simply. 'I certainly never thought that you would acknowledge me.'

'I'm not ashamed of you,' said the earl.

For Michael, his words were like a blow to the stomach. He had tried never to think about his natural father. When he had done so, he had dismissed him as a libertine who had callously deserted his mother. This now appeared to be untrue. Nevertheless, Lord Ashbourne had lived a life of dissipation and he, Michael, had fully expected to be in the position of looking down on him. Yet, within a short time, he had walked into this man's house, behaved like a mannerless boor, and knocked him down in front of his pregnant wife. Then he had come home, drunk himself into a stupor, and insulted the woman he loved, probably beyond all forgiveness. He had received a letter of complaint which would more than likely result in his dismissal. With all his virtuous intentions, he was now the one whose behaviour was in question, yet Rake Ashbourne said that he was not ashamed of him.

Michael sprang to his feet, drew the letter from inside his coat, and threw it at Lord Ashbourne. 'Not ashamed of me? Well, you should be. Believe me my lord, I'm certainly ashamed of myself.'

Ashbourne read the letter. 'Have you any idea who is responsible for this complaint? Whom have you offended?'

Michael looked at his father's face, and realized that here was one man who would never be shocked by the things that he disclosed. He knew an impulse to divulge his suspicions, to tell Ashbourne all about his first meeting with Evangeline, his love for her, and his fears, but something held the words back. He couldn't bear to speak of her betrayal. In the end, he said hesitantly 'I don't know … I'm not sure … I did wonder whether you—' He broke off mid sentence, looking at his father rather self-consciously.

Ashbourne shook his head. 'I would never call upon the bishop to deal with my disputes,' he said. 'Besides, you only knocked me down yesterday, remember? There would hardly have been time for me to compose a letter and for the bishop to write back. Have you no other ideas?'

'I suppose there is Miss Leicester,' said Michael reluctantly. 'I think that perhaps she might have had hopes.'

'Do you indeed?'

'Well, she kept offering to iron my vestments and she wanted us to address one another by Christian names. I had to discourage that and I think perhaps she may have been hurt. But I cannot believe that she would behave in such a way.' He thought for a moment. 'Of course there is Miss Belton. She persuaded her parents to bring her to my services, even though they do not live in this parish.'

'Interesting,' murmured his lordship. 'Anyone else?'

Michael coloured. 'There is Miss Granby, of course. She has been angry with me at times, and … well …'

Lord Ashbourne smiled. It was not an unkind expression. 'Dear dear! For a virtuous clergyman, you do appear to have rather a lot of young ladies running after you, don't you?'

Michael raised his chin. 'What are you implying, my lord?'

'Only that you might be glad of the help and advice of a reformed libertine, my son,' he drawled.

Perhaps fortunately, at that moment Lord and Lady Ilam returned. There followed a discussion concerning what to do about dinner. Lord Ashbourne, quite understandably, was reluctant to leave the cottage, but it did not seem fair to expect Janet to serve all of them in the only room available. It was agreed that Michael, Gabriel and Eustacia would return to Illingham Hall to eat whilst Ashbourne remained at the cottage.

'I have no appetite for a large meal,' the earl declared. 'If Janet can provide me with some bread and cheese then that will be more than sufficient.'

'There is some wine, my lord, if you would like some,' said Michael rather self-consciously.

'You are very kind,' Ashbourne answered, gravely inclining his head.

'Very well,' Gabriel answered. 'One of us will come back later.'

As the three of them were leaving, Ashbourne touched Michael on the arm. 'Tell him,' he said, looking towards Gabriel. 'He is your brother, after all.'

Chapter Eighteen

——⚬〰⚬——

Gabriel had not missed the low-voiced remark that his father had addressed to Michael and, when they got back to Illingham Hall, he encouraged his wife to take a little longer than usual in dressing for dinner, so that he might have a chance of speaking to his half-brother alone.

He was not to be disappointed; Michael was well aware of the fact that Ilam ought to be informed. After a few moments' hesitation, he took the bishop's letter out of his pocket and handed it to the viscount without a word.

Gabriel frowned. 'Do you have any idea of the nature of this complaint?' he asked eventually in an even tone. Michael shook his head. 'This is disgraceful. I have heard nothing but praise for you since I returned. I would like a word with the bishop myself.'

Michael drew his shoulders back. 'I must beg you not to trouble, my lord,' he said a trifle stiffly.

'I don't know who else should trouble himself with this matter, for God's sake. You are the curate resident in my village and you minister to my people. And if you call me "my lord" once more, I might have to deal with you in the same way as you dealt with Raff the other day.'

Michael smiled faintly. 'I wish you wouldn't,' he said. 'Trouble your-self, I mean.'

Gabriel looked at him with narrowed eyes. 'You know who wrote it, don't you? You are doing no good by protecting them.'

Michael turned away to look down into the fire. He hadn't told Lord Ashbourne; he couldn't tell Gabriel either.

Gabriel crossed the room and gripped his shoulder firmly. 'I'm not going to pry. We'll find a way of dealing with this, never fear.' As Michael looked up at the other man, he was conscious of a feeling inside that he could only describe as a kind of glow. It had begun in the cottage when he had told Ashbourne his troubles. He did not want to face this alone. Suddenly, to his relief, he realized that he didn't have to.

When dinner was over, Gabriel returned to the cottage to wait with his father, whilst Michael sat in the drawing-room with his sister-in-law, drinking tea. 'Poor Raff,' she said, in sympathetic tones. 'How he must hate being so close to Jessie and not being able to help her.'

'Do I take it that it was a love match from the beginning?' Michael asked her, remembering what Raff had said about Jessie.

'He snatched her from under the very nose of Henry Lusty,' said Eustacia with a smile.

Michael drew his brows together. 'I knew, but I had forgotten.'

'I must say, I've always wondered why Mr Lusty wanted to be the vicar here after all that had happened.' She stared at Michael. 'Did he know that you were Raff's son?'

'I don't think so,' Michael answered. 'I didn't know myself.'

'If he did, it makes one wonder about his motives in appointing you.'

Michael said nothing in response, but remembered the measuring way in which Lusty had looked at him in the bishop's palace. Why *had* Lusty taken him on as his curate?

Just as they were thinking of retiring, Gabriel returned with the news that Lord and Lady Ashbourne had a baby daughter. 'Mother and baby are both doing well, I understand,' he said, pouring some wine that he had sent for in order to celebrate the occasion. 'I wasn't allowed in.'

'Of course not,' Eustacia replied. 'She will be far too tired to see anyone but her husband for now.'

'I am glad that Lady Ashbourne's baby is safely delivered,' said Michael a little self-consciously. 'Has a name been chosen?'

'If it has, I haven't been told. I've sent a groom to Granby Hall with the news. I've said that we'll go ourselves tomorrow.' Ilam lifted his glass. 'To our little sister,' he said.

Michael shook his head in bewilderment, but he did lift his glass. It was slowly dawning upon him that he had acquired a family.

Michael and Gabriel walked to the cottage the following morning in order to pay their respects. As they reached the top of the stairs they could hear voices behind the half-closed door of Michael's room and, upon entering, they found Lady Ashbourne sitting up in bed, with a rich russet and gold shawl about her shoulders. Lord Ashbourne was in a chair at his wife's side, a book in his hand. He was in his shirt sleeves, his black hair loose and draped about his shoulders. As Michael and Ilam entered the room, the earl and his countess had been laughing at something that his lordship had read. Observing his father as he rose to his feet, the laughter dying out of his eyes, Michael acknowledged for the first time what a very handsome man he was.

'We've come to congratulate you on a safe delivery, ma'am,' said Ilam, smiling as he walked over to the bed to press a kiss on Jessie's cheek.

'Thank you, Gabriel,' said her ladyship.

'You too, sir,' said Ilam, extending a hand to his father.

'Thank you, Ilam,' Ashbourne answered, grasping the hand extended to him. 'It was an arduous experience, but I've come through it pretty well, I think.'

Michael stood in the doorway, watching the scene taking place in front of him. When silence fell, he realized that all the occupants of the room were looking at him. 'My congratulations,' he said a little stiffly.

'Thank you,' Jessie answered, and held her hand out to him. Only a churl could have refused her, and despite his ambivalent feelings towards his father, Michael was not a churl. Gabriel made room for him at the head of the bed. Michael took Jessie's hand and, after a moment, raised it to his lips. There might have followed an awkward moment, but for the entrance of a nursemaid, carrying the earl and countess's new daughter.

'Would you like to hold her, Gabriel?' Jessie asked.

With all the confidence of a father of a child of four months, Ilam took the baby from the nurse. 'One forgets how tiny they are,' he said, smiling reminiscently. 'Look.' He turned to Michael, who touched the baby's hand with one finger. Instantly, the tiny fist closed about the finger with surprising strength.

'Remarkable,' murmured the clergyman. He looked up and instantly his eyes met those of his father.

Soon afterwards Gabriel and Michael set off for Granby Park, mounted on two horses that had been brought to the cottage by one of Gabriel's grooms. When they arrived, they were greeted by Theodora, who explained that Mrs Granby had not yet come downstairs, but that Evangeline had gone shopping with Amelia Belton and Lieutenant Fellowes.

'I'm surprised that she left without waiting to hear about the baby,' said Gabriel, frowning slightly. Michael frowned as well; his disappointment was only equalled by his jealousy.

'She was very sorry, but I think that she wanted to buy her father something,' Theodora replied. 'He is due to return any day.' She and Evangeline had agreed the previous night that they would tell Mrs Granby that Evangeline had gone to visit the new baby. It was clearly impossible to make this excuse to two gentlemen who had just come from the cottage and would know it to be a lie. Theodora judged there to be very little risk. Mrs Granby never appeared before noon, and there would be no chance that they would all meet.

She had judged without the incentive that Mrs Granby had from her husband's imminent arrival. The gentlemen had not been there for more than a quarter of an hour when their hostess appeared in the doorway and greeted her visitors warmly. 'You will be surprised to see me, no doubt, but I am hoping that Granby will be home today,' she said. 'What a shocking thing it would be to be found abed when he arrives. How is the new baby? Is Lady Ashbourne well?'

'The baby is safely delivered, and mother and baby are both well,' Gabriel answered.

'I know that it is no use my asking you what she looks like,' said Mrs Granby, smiling. 'Gentlemen never notice such things, do they? I shall have to rely on Evangeline's description when she returns. Has Theodora offered you wine? We must toast the baby's health.' She turned away to ring the bell, and did not notice the look of puzzlement that passed between the two men, or the frantic signalling from Theodora, indicating that they must not say anything.

The wine came, the health of the baby and her mother was duly drunk, and the four occupants of the room made polite if rather stilted conversation. Michael was just wondering how to manipulate the situation in order to have a private word with his sister so that he could discover the meaning of this confusion, when Mrs Granby excused herself, declaring that there were duties awaiting her.

'I must make sure that cook is ready to prepare Granby's favourite dishes,' she said. 'Theodora will see you out.'

'Now Theodora,' Michael said sternly after the door had closed behind their hostess. 'What is the meaning of this? Where has Evan ... I mean, Miss Granby, gone, and why?'

'Oh dear,' said Theodora anxiously. 'I did promise not to say.' She looked guiltily at the two men.

'Theodora,' Michael said again, 'you must not try to protect her if she is engaged upon some wrong-doing.'

'She is not doing wrong,' Theodora protested hotly. 'She is trying to put things right, and it is all on your account.' She blushed hotly, conscious that she had said too much.

'On my account?' Michael asked, frowning.

Theodora caught hold of Michael's arm and tugged him down so that she could speak to him in an undertone. 'Does he know about the ... you know?' she asked, glancing towards Gabriel.

'The complaint? Yes, he knows,' Michael answered.

'She has gone to Sheffield to see the bishop,' Theodora blurted out. 'She wants to try to persuade him to change his mind. Lieutenant Fellowes and Miss Belton arrived to collect her at nine o'clock.'

'And do they know the nature of her errand?' Michael asked her.

'Well ...' She paused uncertainly.

'You must tell us, Miss Buckleigh,' said Gabriel urgently.

Theodora sighed. 'I might as well tell you the rest. She pretended to Lieutenant Fellowes that she so was angry with you, Michael, about the way that you had interfered in her life, that she wanted to go to the bishop and complain in person.'

'But why rush over there rather than write?' Gabriel asked.

'She told the lieutenant that she wanted to be sure of speaking to the bishop before her father returns. Mr Granby is one of Michael's supporters.'

Michael turned away. 'Perhaps she was telling him the truth,' he said evenly. 'She has threatened to complain about me almost from the first moment that we met. Why change her mind now?'

'No, indeed!' exclaimed Theodora, forgetting about discretion in her anxiety to make things clear. 'She never meant—' She broke off, horror-struck. Evangeline had not said precisely that Michael knew she had written the letter and she did not want to be the one to tell him.

'Oh, enough,' said Michael wearily. 'She tells a different story to everyone. Let her go to Sheffield if that is what she wants. Why should I lift a finger to prevent her? Excuse me.'

He left the room. Theodora stared after him in consternation, before taking a step towards the door. 'I must go after him,' she said urgently to Gabriel. 'He doesn't understand.'

'She really *has* gone to try to save his reputation?' Gabriel asked. Theodora nodded. 'What is Fellowes's motive in this?' he said, half to himself. 'And how is Miss Belton involved?'

'I don't know,' Theodora answered, 'But I do not like him, my lord. I cannot help but wonder whether he intends to take Evangeline to Sheffield at all.'

'He can scarcely harm her with his cousin there to act as chaperon,' Gabriel pointed out.

'From things that I have heard, I think that she may be attracted to Michael,' said Theodora. 'Might she help her cousin in a scheme to abduct Evangeline so that she could have Michael to herself?'

'I suppose people have done rasher things for the sake of love,' Gabriel observed. 'It would do no harm to ride after them, just in case.'

'Before you go, my lord, there is one more thing,' said Theodora, trembling at the thought of what she was about to say. 'It was Evangeline who wrote the letter of complaint.'

'Really?' It was what Gabriel had suspected from the first.

'She did not mean to send it,' Theodora insisted. 'She loves Michael – she told me so. She was angry with him when he tried to censure her conduct, so she wrote it and put it on one side.'

'Then someone picked it up and sent it.'

She nodded eagerly. 'I suppose I should have told him just now, but I couldn't.'

'I think he has guessed,' said Ilam, gripping her shoulder with one hand. 'That's partly why he is so angry, I'll wager. You did right to tell me. Don't worry, I'll look after him.'

When Gabriel got outside, he found Michael waiting with the horses. 'What do you want to do?' he asked.

Michael shrugged. 'Does it matter?'

'Let's go for a ride,' Gabriel replied. They swung into the saddle and, as they left the entrance of the drive, the viscount guided them so that they were heading towards Sheffield. If Michael realized, he made no comment, although he did direct a narrowed gaze at his half-brother. They rode on in silence until after a while, they saw a carriage approaching them. 'That looks like the Belton conveyance,' said Gabriel. 'I wonder why they're returning so soon.'

The coachman recognized Gabriel and Michael, and obediently slowed down. At once, Michael was out of the saddle and at the door of the chaise. Gabriel smiled wryly. The curate might say that he didn't care what Evangeline did. His actions told another story.

At once it was clear that Amelia was the sole occupant of the carriage. When she saw who had brought her journey to a temporary halt, she turned rather pale. 'Where is Miss Granby?' Michael asked peremptorily.

'She is with my cousin,' Amelia answered. She had not reckoned upon having to account for her actions, and was not quick-witted enough to think up another story on the spot.

'He asked you where she was, not with whom she had gone,' said Gabriel, who had joined Michael at the door.

Amelia turned even paler if anything. Both the men confronting her were tall, well built and looked very angry. Her hand went to her throat. 'I ... I ...' she began.

As Michael looked at her, his expression softened. She was a young girl, only a little older than his sister. Shouting at her would get them nowhere. 'Indeed, Miss Belton, you must tell us,' he said, in a much kinder tone.

'She cannot be allowed to go off alone with your cousin,' agreed Gabriel. 'She will ruin her reputation.'

'As if I'd care about that,' answered Amelia, tossing her head with a return of her usual spirit.

'You'd care a good deal if I made sure people knew that you were responsible,' Gabriel warned her.

'I'm not responsible,' Amelia answered indignantly.

'Yes you are,' he retorted. 'You left her without a chaperon. Now where are they, Amelia?'

'At the Cockerel in a village a few miles back; I forget its name,' she answered sulkily. 'I think they were planning to elope all along, even when they told me that they were going shopping in Sheffield. She was certainly dressed in her best.'

'Come on, then,' said Gabriel, after they had sent the carriage on its way. 'Let's be after them.'

'To what purpose?' Michael responded. 'You heard what Amelia said. They were planning to elope all along. Why should I spoil sport?'

'And that's what you're going to tell her parents, is it?' Michael stared at him. 'Listen,' Gabriel went on, 'you have only the word of Amelia Belton that they were eloping and you don't want to trust that. Believe me, I've known her from the cradle.'

Slowly, Michael nodded. However miserable he might feel, however Evangeline might have betrayed him, he could not break the promise he had made to Mr Granby. 'No, damn it,' he said at last. 'You are right. I must look to her welfare, however much she may despise me for it.'

'And, of course, you are still in love with her,' remarked Gabriel.

'I'd have to be a fool to be still in love with her after this,' Michael muttered.

'Love makes fools of all of us,' Gabriel reminded him. 'Shall we go?'

Chapter Nineteen

— ❧ —

Evangeline had known from the very first hatching of the scheme that the journey to Sheffield in Amelia Belton's company would not be pleasant. She had not bargained for the stare of undisguised hostility that greeted her as Lieutenant Fellowes handed her into the chaise. There was not even the pretence of affection which they had assumed in recent years, but which they both knew to be false. Instead, the occupant bade Evangeline a sullen 'good morning' and turned to look out of the window. Evangeline returned her greeting and turned her attention to the scenery on her own side.

Lieutenant Fellowes, who was travelling in the carriage rather than riding, eyed the two young ladies from the backward facing seat with malicious amusement. 'Well, this is very agreeable,' he said, smiling broadly. 'The miles will simply fly by, won't they?'

To tell truth, Evangeline was not sorry to be travelling in silence. She could spend a little more time rehearsing what she wanted to say to the bishop. She must put a clear case to him, but she did not mean to rely upon logic alone. She glanced down at her deep pink travelling gown. She knew that she was looking her best. A little charm would not go at all amiss in her efforts to make him relent.

She was vaguely aware of having passed through some sort of village, when the chaise gave a lurch and came to a stop. Lieutenant Fellowes raised his brows, then said, 'I'll get down and see what's happening,' before opening the door and springing out of the coach.

Evangeline glanced at Amelia who immediately said aggressively, 'Well, don't look at me. It's not *my* fault.'

'I never thought that it was,' Evangeline replied diplomatically, conscious that this delay might mean that they would need to spend even more time in one another's company.

'If you ask me, you've brought it on yourself,' the other young woman said, then coloured.

'What do you mean?' Evangeline asked, frowning.

'Oh, nothing,' Amelia answered hastily. 'I only meant that it was your idea to go to Sheffield, but it wasn't nice of me to say so. I'm sorry, Evangeline.'

She didn't sound very sincere, but Evangeline thought it wise to respond in kind. She was now beginning to feel uneasy, but she couldn't put her finger on why.

Lieutenant Fellowes reappeared in the doorway. He looked a little concerned. 'One of the harnesses has worn through,' he said. 'The coachman has made a temporary repair, but he will have to walk the horses so that it does not snap. I noticed a pleasant-looking inn in the village that we passed just now and the coachman says that there is a blacksmith. I suggest that we go back there and wait while the damage is being repaired. I don't think it will take very long.'

'I hope not,' Evangeline replied, sounding sharper than she intended. 'We want to get to Sheffield and back well before the evening.'

The inn in the village did indeed look welcoming, and the inn-keeper was delighted to have the privilege of serving them. He showed them into a very pretty parlour at the back of the inn, where Evangeline and Amelia sat, while he made arrangements for tea and cakes, and Lieutenant Fellowes saw to the disposal of the chaise. 'It should not take very long,' the lieutenant said reassuringly when he returned. 'The blacksmith told me that he would be able to effect a repair in the time that it takes us to consume the tea and cakes. Perhaps you would both like a little stroll in the garden,' he suggested. 'The day is fine and it will make a change from sitting.'

Amelia excused herself. 'I would prefer to remain inside, I think,' she said with a little sniff. Interpreting this as a wish to be free of her company, Evangeline stood up, for she was indeed a little tired of sitting in one place.

The garden was quite pretty, although rather too small for a stroll, but it was agreeable to be free of Amelia's company, at least for a little while. They talked of trivial matters, until eventually, the lieutenant suggested that tea might now be served.

Amelia was not in the parlour when they went back. The maid who was setting down the tray explained that the young lady had noticed a loose thread on the bottom of her gown and had gone upstairs so that the landlady could stitch it up for her.

'Perhaps I ought to go and help,' Evangeline suggested.

'With Amelia in her present mood?' asked the lieutenant. 'I don't think that would be advisable. Why is she so annoyed with you, by the way?'

The question took Evangeline by surprise, but as she was engaged upon looking in her reticule to see whether she had put in it a needle and thread and scissors for emergencies, her face was fortunately turned away at that point. 'We have never got on particularly well,' she confessed, quite truthfully. 'I suppose we have always been rivals.'

She could have bitten her tongue off the minute the last words were spoken, for they gave him a chance to say, 'Even more so since a certain young curate has come into the district.'

'Don't be so absurd,' she retorted, desperately hoping that she would not blush. 'You know very well how I feel about him.'

'I know how you *say* that you feel about him,' he replied. 'I have to say, though, Miss Granby, that I fear that you have been something less than truthful.'

'How dare you!' she exclaimed.

'Quite easily,' he answered. 'You see, when a young lady is observed exchanging a passionate embrace with a gentleman on one occasion; then on another professes a desire to report him to the ecclesiastical authorities, her sincerity is almost bound to be called into question.'

Evangeline turned away from him, her heart beating rather fast. 'It did not occur to you I suppose that he might have embraced me against my will, and that I might be taking my revenge,' she suggested.

'No, I must say it did not,' replied the lieutenant. 'Had the other party been such as myself, then it might have done. But Buckleigh's one of those fellows possessed of a tiresomely chivalrous nature. It's rather absurd in a clergyman, really.'

'How dare you sneer at him,' Evangeline flashed, turning round. Then she bit her lip, for she knew that she had given herself away.

The lieutenant laughed. 'Truth's out now, isn't it?' he said. 'I suppose that your plan is to speak to the bishop in his favour and not against him.'

'Someone should,' she replied.

'No doubt you think so. I very much regret that this will not be possible. I have other plans for you. How very foolish of you to think that you could manipulate me. In fact I'm the one who's been doing the manipulating.'

'What do you mean?'

'It's just that I'm a little short of cash at present – very short, to tell you the truth. I need some money quite urgently and you will help me to it very nicely.'

'If anyone has told you that my father is wealthy, then they have been spinning stories,' she replied, striving to keep calm.

'I'm well aware that your father is not the richest man in the county, but I've no doubt that he will pay handsomely to have you back – shall we say, intact? Naturally he'll pay a little extra to persuade me to keep my mouth shut. If not, well, you're a tempting creature, there's no doubt about it.' He made as if to seize hold of her, but she stepped nimbly round the other side of the table.

'What a gallant officer!' she exclaimed disdainfully.

'Gallantry doesn't pay my mess bills,' he said frankly.

'What about Amelia?' she asked.

'Gone in the chaise long since. Remember that no one knows where you are, apart from Amelia, and she won't tell. Your mother thinks you've gone to see the new baby. There will be no one to rescue you, my dear.' He made another grab for her. Again she dodged round the table. She had forgotten that he was not aware that Theodora knew the truth. The recollection gave her courage.

'Keep away from me,' she said warningly. 'I must advise you, Lieutenant, that at one time my tantrums were the talk of Illingham. When I lie on the floor and scream and drum my heels, someone will be sure to come to my aid.'

'I do not think so,' he replied. 'I took the liberty of informing the landlord beforehand that you are my errant wife, who had absconded from my side and whom I am escorting back home. As far as he is concerned, Amelia is my sister who has gone on ahead to make sure that our house is ready for us. An extra guinea or two helped to confirm that idea in his mind. In a little while, I shall take you in another conveyance to a place that is a little more off the beaten track, and there you will stay, either until we are found, or until you agree to marry me.'

She stared at him for a long time. Then she turned away, saying, 'It appears that you leave me with little alternative.'

'Not very much, no,' he agreed.

'Then we had better have this tea,' she answered, sitting down gracefully. 'Tell me, Lieutenant, is there any chance of your becoming a major? I have always found a man in uniform attractive, but a higher rank would suit me better.'

He laughed. 'With a father-in-law like Mr Granby, who knows what I may not achieve?'

'Who indeed.' Evangeline had poured some tea. Now she took a sip, and made a face. 'We have been talking for too long and this is cold. Pray, ask for some more.'

He looked at her with narrowed eyes. 'I warn you, if this is some kind of trick, then you will achieve nothing by it.'

'It is not a trick,' Evangeline replied. 'I have been sitting opposite your disagreeable cousin for well over an hour and I have had to endure rather a trying conversation with yourself. I promise you I will not be at all co-operative if I do not have hot tea. It will be as well if you discover that before we are married, for you will find that if I do not choose to be co-operative, I can be very, very unpleasant.'

For a moment, he looked uncertain, then he opened the door and called out for a fresh pot of tea. 'Make sure it is good and hot,' Evangeline put in.

A few minutes later, a servant came in with a fresh pot. 'Is it as you like it?' Fellowes asked, taking his seat as Evangeline took the lid off the pot in order to stir the leaves.

'Oh, yes indeed,' Evangeline replied. 'Is that a dirty mark on your sleeve, Lieutenant?' He turned his head to look and, in a moment, she had thrown the contents of the teapot over him. Then, when he cried out with pain, she smashed the pot over his head, causing him to lose his balance and fall off his chair.

Without waiting to see how badly she might have injured him, she whisked herself out of the room. Gathering up her skirts, she ran along the passage intending to go to the stables, find a mount, any mount, and get away. She was in the yard, looking frantically about her, when the sound of hoofbeats alerted her to a new arrival and a moment later Ilam and Michael rode into the yard.

'Michael, thank goodness,' she exclaimed, holding a hand out towards him as he dismounted. 'He was planning to abduct me and force me to marry him.'

Michael ignored her hand and simply said, 'Did you go with him willingly?'

'No!' she exclaimed. 'Well, yes, but—'

'Oh enough,' he interrupted in a tone of angry cynicism. 'Where is he?'

'He is in the parlour. I've just thrown tea at him and cracked the teapot over his head. Michael, I wasn't running away with him!'

'Of course not,' he answered in the same tone. He turned to Ilam. 'Will you take her home? I'll deal with Fellowes.'

'Michael?' Evangeline said again.

'Later,' he said firmly. 'I'll speak to you later.' He strode into the inn.

'Come along,' said Ilam. 'Let's find a conveyance to take you home.'

'But, Michael,' Evangeline protested, looking towards the inn.

'He's got a lot on his mind,' Ilam replied. 'He'll feel better when he's dealt with Fellowes.'

The gig that the lieutenant had planned to use for Evangeline's abduction was ready to go, and soon Ilam and Evangeline were on their way back home. 'Miss Buckleigh told us that you were going shopping, but when your mother came in and clearly thought that you were in the village, we knew that something was amiss,' Ilam explained, as soon as they were on the road.

'Did she … tell you why I wanted to go to Sheffield?' she asked him.

'She told us that you were going to visit the bishop in order to speak for Michael,' Ilam answered.

'Did she tell you…?'

'About your writing the complaint? She told me, but not when Michael was present. I thought it pretty spiteful, as a matter of fact.'

'Well, so do I,' Evangeline confessed frankly, 'but I never intended to send it.' She paused for a moment. 'Oh dear, if only one could go back in time and put things right!'

'I'm sure you're not the first person to wish that,' Gabriel replied, 'and I doubt if you'll be the last.'

When Michael opened the door of the parlour, Fellowes was just getting to his feet. The officer's uniform was marred by a huge tea stain on the front, and a red mark on his chin where the hot liquid had caught him.

'You're a scoundrel and a coward,' the curate said, 'and a disgrace to the uniform you wear. Do you want to be knocked down here, or shall we go out to the inn yard?'

In response, Fellowes hurled himself at Michael, knocking him against the table. After that, a very clumsy fight ensued, during which each was working out the hostility that he felt for the other, hampered considerably by the furniture and the smallness of the room.

The soldier began the fight with a smirk on his face, but this soon disappeared as he began to realize that he was faced with a formidable opponent. Hearing the noise, the landlord put his head around the door, but soon withdrew it as he could see that to enter would be to put his person at some risk from the violence taking place within.

Eventually, Michael's sheer size and weight prevailed, and he found himself standing over his fallen opponent, his fists clenched, while Lieutenant Fellowes mopped at a bloody nose. As the curate stared down at the other man, he suddenly realized what he had done and, going to the door and opening it, he called out for water, cloth and towel.

'She's not worth it, you know,' the soldier said, from his prone position. Michael took a hasty step towards him, whereupon he added hastily, 'Not when a man's down, surely.'

'I can always drag you to your feet,' Michael responded through his teeth.

'No doubt you can,' Fellowes answered. He ran his tongue around his teeth, then said, 'Thank God,' when he discovered that they were all still firmly in place. 'Before you go rushing back to her side, I think there's something you ought to know about Miss Evangeline Granby.'

'If you wanted to tell me that it was she who wrote a letter of complaint about me to the bishop, then I already know it,' Michael answered, tight-lipped, determined that the other man should not see how hurt he was.

'You surprise me,' Fellowes drawled, his eyes narrowed. So Buckleigh thought that Evangeline wrote the letter, did he? Well he certainly wasn't going to put him right. 'Still, I'll wager there's something else you don't know. Apparently, our Miss Granby enjoys a little game of making what conquests she can, then boasting about it to her friends.'

Michael took a step forward. 'You're a damned liar,' he said. He was conscious of a hollow feeling in his chest.

'It's quite true,' the soldier replied. 'You ought to have a little fellow feeling. You and I are both victims. Those little chatterboxes Barclay and French let the cat out of the bag. You were just another trophy to her. So was I. She makes a habit of it. Ask them if you like.' Judging that it was now safe to rise, Fellowes pulled himself to his feet, but remained prudently on the other side of the table. 'She came with me willingly, you know, despite anything she might say. Did you see how becoming she looked? That was all for my benefit.'

Luckily, since Michael could not think how to answer him, the landlord himself came in with a jug of water and a basin, a towel over his arm.

'Did the gentleman who accompanied me leave the horses behind when he left with the young lady?' Michael asked him.

'Yes, sir,' said the landlord, looking rather warily at Michael, who was clearly the victor in the skirmish that had just taken place. 'He took her in the gig that this gentleman hired.'

'Then I'll take one and go. You,' he went on, turning to Fellowes, 'may take the other back to Lord Ilam's stables. If I were you, I would try to avoid meeting him. Then, if you're wise, you'll discover a pressing need to rejoin your regiment. I don't expect to see you again.'

Michael was walking past the landlord when that worthy, struck by a sudden thought, said, 'One moment sir; would you be a clergyman?'

'Yes, I am,' Michael replied, straightening his cuffs, and wondering how battered his face might be. The landlord looked at Michael's stock, looked at Fellowes with his rapidly reddening jaw, and looked back at Michael again. 'Never knew a clergyman could throw a punch like that,' he said admiringly. 'I'm not a religious man, but I'd try a church that you was parson of, any day.'

'My thanks,' Michael replied, 'and my apologies for the state of the room. I will see that you are reimbursed.'

Chapter Twenty

———⁓∾⊙∾⁓———

Evangeline was dreading facing Theodora when she arrived home. Not only had she failed in her objective of speaking to the bishop, but she had also placed Michael in a situation where he was almost bound to fight Lieutenant Fellowes. She had no idea how such a fight might turn out, but she knew that Fellowes was a soldier and he had revealed himself to be a man with no scruples. What if he were to draw a sword or a knife upon Michael, who would almost certainly be unarmed? She could hardly bear to think about it.

To her great relief, she discovered that Mrs Granby had taken Theodora on a visit to the home farm, so she was spared any questions from either lady, at least for the time being. She took up her post in one of the rooms that faced on to the drive and, in due course, her patience was rewarded when Michael appeared on horseback. She had not realized how relieved she would be to see him unharmed. Now, she knew that she had been feeling almost sick with fear for his safety.

Not wanting to look as though she had been watching out for him, she slipped out into the hall, telling the butler that should anyone call, she would be in the yellow drawing room. Michael was admitted a few minutes later. She could tell immediately from his appearance that he must have been involved in some kind of altercation: his lower lip was split, there was a mark on one cheek that might turn into a bruise; and his knuckles were badly grazed. His clothing was not torn, but looked a little more rumpled than was customary with him.

She rose hastily to her feet. 'You are all right!' She exclaimed. 'Thank God!' She began to hasten to his side, but he held up his hand.

'Please, remain where you are,' he said. 'I merely came to tell you that

Lieutenant Fellowes has been dealt with. I must also thank you for your care of Theodora and assure you that she will be out of your way as soon as possible.'

'But we have been glad to have her. There is no rush,' Evangeline insisted.

'Even so, I would be glad to have her away from here.'

Evangeline flushed with mortification. 'I suppose I may guess why,' she said. 'Michael, I am so sorry.'

'For what?' he asked. 'For writing to the bishop, or for boasting to your friends that you would be able to add me to your list of conquests?'

'Michael, I—'

'I suppose I should not be surprised that you wrote a letter of complaint,' he went on, interrupting her. 'After all, you threatened to do so more than once. Perhaps your purpose in going to Sheffield really was to make another complaint in person.'

'No, no!' she exclaimed, horrified. 'I never meant to send it. It was a mistake.'

'But you did write it.'

'Yes I wrote it, but only after you made me so angry that I could not think straight. I knew immediately that I would not send it.'

'Yet you did send it.'

'No! Well, yes, but ...'

'Even so, it has had the same result, has it not?'

'But I didn't mean it, I tell you. I was going to Sheffield to tell the bishop so.'

'All dressed in your best?' he said nastily. 'Are you sure that you weren't simply planning another little tryst in another inn with yet another man?'

'No!' she declared, horrified. 'No, I wasn't.'

'How can I believe anything you say?' he demanded. 'You give everyone a different story. You tell your mother that you are visiting the new baby; you tell Amelia that you are going shopping; you tell Fellowes that you are going to complain; you tell Theodora that you are going to plead my case. How am I to discern the truth amongst this pack of lies?' He paused. She said nothing but stood looking at him, biting her lip, her complexion pale. 'It doesn't much matter now, anyway. The bishop will have me removed and probably unfrocked. Then I will be gone. No more curate to interfere in your pleasures, eh? You must be delighted.'

'I'm not anything of the sort. Wait, though.' She went on, struck by a sudden idea. 'You are Ashbourne's son and Ilam's brother. The bishop would never unfrock you now!'

He stared at her incredulously. 'You amaze me,' he said, smiling humourlessly. 'You are so spoiled, so used to having your own way that you think that everyone can simply go whining to their rich relatives and have everything put right. Well, it isn't going to happen that way. I cannot and will not go crawling to my mother's lover in order to correct your wrong-doing. You'll just have to live with it.'

'Michael!' she cried, as he walked to the door. 'Michael, I … I love you.'

He turned to look at her. 'I don't think so. You're too spoiled to understand the meaning of the word. The only one you really love is yourself. Dry your tears. Just think, you have the memory of your conquest to sustain you.' She stood staring at the door after he had gone, until, suddenly struck by what she had lost, she ran out of the room and up the stairs, not slowing down until she reached her own bedchamber. Once there, she threw herself face down upon her bed and cried and cried until she felt exhausted.

Much later, hearing the sound of an arrival, she got up and walked to the window to discover that her mother had returned with Theodora. She was very tempted to close the curtains and pretend to be asleep, but she knew that Theodora would be anxious about her brother. She owed her some kind of explanation.

She looked down at the cupboard in front of her, and picked up the copy of *A Vindication of the Rights of Woman*. Then, with an expression of annoyance, she threw it across the room. 'Stupid, stupid book,' she declared. 'Advise me how to get out of this mess if you can!' As it fell to the floor, something came out from between its pages. Evangeline crossed the room to pick it up. It was her letter to the bishop: it had not been sent after all.

She drew a deep breath. Part of her wanted to rush after Michael and show it to him. But he had gone away in anger; even if she had not sent it, it was true that she had written it, and he still thought that she was a liar. She then recalled his other accusation, namely, that she had boasted of being able to bring him to his knees. Where had he got that from? She remembered a silly boast that she had made to Miss French and Miss Barclay when she was infatuated with Ashbourne over two years ago, about being able to ensnare any man that she wanted. She never thought that that piece of foolishness would come back to harm her. She had got herself into a dreadful mess. Whatever could she do now to put it right?

As predicted, Theodora soon came to her room to find out what had happened. Evangeline had intended just to tell Theodora the bare facts of the case, but she was still too overwrought to dissemble. Soon she found herself spilling out the whole tale and shedding a few more tears on Theodora's shoulder.

'Michael will come round, I'm sure,' said the curate's sister. 'He has the sunniest and most forgiving nature of anyone I know. But, Evangeline, has it occurred to you that someone else must have written a letter of complaint if the bishop was not referring to yours?' Evangeline had shown Theodora the lost letter.

'I had not thought about that,' Evangeline confessed. 'I wonder who it might be?'

'Do you suppose that it was Lieutenant Fellowes himself?' Theodora suggested. 'He certainly does not like Michael.'

'He did not speak as though he had written it,' Evangeline replied, 'although he certainly knew about it. I wonder whether it might be one of the Beltons?'

She sighed. So much seemed to have gone wrong between herself and Michael. It was hard to know how it could all be put right. If only she could do something about the complaint. If she could counteract its effects, Michael might begin to see how highly she thought of him. After a lot of thought, she came to a decision. Following a brief conversation with her mother, she called for Elsie to help her into her riding habit.

Almost the last thing that Michael wanted to do was to return to Illingham, but he knew that there was no alternative. All his possessions were scattered between Illingham Hall and his cottage. He could hardly ride off into the sunset on someone else's horse in just the clothes he stood up in. 'What a mess,' he whispered to himself, as he rode along, letting the horse pick its own pace. 'What a damnable mess.' The only thing that could make the day worse in his opinion was if he were to encounter Lieutenant Fellowes on his way to the Hall. Thankfully this did not happen.

Having stabled the horse, he entered Illingham Hall from the back entrance and trudged wearily up the stairs, to be met at the top of the flight by Lord Ilam's valet. 'Allow me to assist you, sir,' he said. 'Your bath is being prepared and should be ready by the time I have helped you with your clothes.'

'My bath?' Michael echoed.

'His lordship gave instructions for one to be filled as soon as you entered the stable yard,' was the reply. 'He said that you would be glad of one after your exertions.'

Michael grunted in response. He could not find the words to say. Ilam is a better man than I am, he thought to himself. Perhaps he should have been the priest after all.

To his surprise, after a soak in the bath he did begin to feel a little better, particularly when the valet brought him a glass of wine to enjoy as he was getting dried. Looking at himself in the mirror, he did not find his appearance to be as bad as he had expected. His swollen lip had gone down already and some soothing ointment on the cut also helped considerably. Once he was dressed, the valet invited him to go downstairs to the small parlour at the back of the house, where bread, cold meat and cheese had been placed on a table.

'I was wondering why I felt so devilish hollow, then realized that somewhere or other we managed to miss a meal today,' said Gabriel, who was waiting by the fireplace with one foot on the fender. The afternoon had turned rather cool and a fire had been lit.

'Have you eaten?' Michael asked him.

'No, I waited for you.'

For a short time, the two men addressed themselves to the food in silence. Then eventually Michael said, 'I must thank you for the bath. It has helped me to feel human again.'

'No doubt,' Gabriel agreed. 'I do hope you have noted my astonishing ability to refrain from questioning you about what happened after I had gone, by the way.'

'You've a right to know,' said Michael, laying down his fork. 'I told Fellowes that he was a disgrace to his uniform and then proved that I was a disgrace to the cloth by hitting him several times. When I had hit him sufficiently to make him stay down, *he* gave *me* a body blow by telling me that Evangeline had written the letter of complaint. So then I went to see her, we had words and, well, suffice it to say that if there was anything between us, it's all over.'

'Indeed?'

'Gabriel, she admitted to writing the letter. I have to confess that I had been hoping against hope that somehow there had been some extraordinary misunderstanding; but it's true. What's more, she actually boasted to some of her friends that she could make me one of her conquests. That's the only reason she showed any interest in me at all.

How could I dream of loving someone who could go against me in such an underhand and spiteful way?' He paused. 'The only trouble is, I do still love her, fool that I am. Well, you'll be pleased to hear that I have thought of a solution to my problems.'

'Which is?'

Michael got up from the table. He had not finished his meal, but his appetite was gone. 'There can be no doubt that the bishop will have me removed. He won't want to find me another curacy now. If I offer to go voluntarily, however, I'm hoping that perhaps he will agree not to have me unfrocked. I have a friend who has some influence at Charterhouse, my old school. If I ask him, I think that he might be prepared to find me a position as a schoolmaster there. Once established, I will be able to have Theodora to stay with me. I was wondering whether, in the meantime...?'

'Of course she may stay with us. Think nothing more of it,' Ilam replied, wisely making no protests about the future that Michael had outlined for himself. He did venture to say, however, 'I thought you wanted to be a clergyman.'

Michael looked at him, a bleak expression on his face. 'Even if I had not destroyed my chances, I am not worthy,' he answered. 'I will go to the bishop as soon as possible and offer my resignation.'

'You can't do anything today,' Ilam pointed out. 'Sleep on the matter tonight, then come with me to see Raff tomorrow.'

'He will not dictate my actions,' Michael said in a carefully controlled voice.

'Naturally not,' Gabriel agreed diplomatically. 'You are a grown man, after all. But the living of Illingham is partly in his gift. He has the right to be consulted about any changes concerning the care of the parish.'

With that Michael was forced to agree.

Michael and Gabriel waited on Lord and Lady Ashbourne at the cottage the following morning. Contrary to his expectations, Michael had slept well after an appetizing dinner which he had shared with Lord and Lady Ilam. Eustacia had exerted herself to please, telling Michael some stories of the time when she had stayed with Lady Agatha at the vicarage. She had even managed to make him laugh with her spirited account of how on one occasion her ladyship had chased Mr Lusty out of the house with an umbrella. She had also told him about how her husband had thrown a punch at his father and she had got in the way so that Gabriel had knocked her to the ground senseless.

'I told you I nearly hit him,' Gabriel reminded Michael.

'But you forgave him,' Michael said to Stacia.

'True love always forgives,' Lady Ilam replied, her gaze softening as she looked at her husband.

'Does it?' Michael replied. That night he dreamed of Evangeline running towards him, her beautiful hair loose and streaming behind her. He woke up to a feeling of bitter disappointment. Yes, he still loved her. He could forgive her everything that she had said and done. But did she really love him? What was more, could she forgive him for his unkind words? He doubted it.

As Michael and Gabriel ascended the stairs, they could hear Lord and Lady Ashbourne arguing. 'I am perfectly fit,' Lady Ashbourne was saying. 'There is absolutely no reason why I should be lying in bed like this.'

'The doctor has said that you should be in bed for a week and that is where you shall stay,' his lordship replied. 'If it is any consolation, I have made myself just as much a prisoner as you.'

'Having you with me is the only thing that makes this in any way tolerable,' his wife replied.

Gabriel smiled at Michael, then knocked at the door and they both went in, to see that Lord Ashbourne was just straightening from having placed a kiss upon his wife's lips. It seemed like such a private moment that Michael wanted to excuse himself.

It was Jessie who spoke first. 'Come in, both of you,' she said. She smiled at Michael. It was an expression of extraordinary sweetness. 'You too, Michael,' she said. Then she turned to her husband. 'Now, Raff, it is high time that this was settled between you.'

'Settled, my love?' the earl echoed.

'Just because I have given birth recently does not mean that my brains have deserted me,' she replied, her tone just a little astringent.

'We have reached an understanding,' said her husband. He turned to Michael. 'Is that not so?'

'Indeed,' Michael answered a little stiffly.

'But how can you reach an *understanding* if Michael does not really *understand*?' she replied. 'Raff, take off your shirt, if you please.' All three men stared at her.

'Jez, my dear, I hardly think …' murmured the earl. As on the previous occasion, he was in his shirt sleeves.

'Ashbourne!' said Jessie peremptorily. Then her tone softened as she said, 'For me?'

Ashbourne sighed. 'When she calls me "Ashbourne" I know I have to obey,' he said. Then to the astonishment of both the other men present, he took off his cravat and began to unfasten his shirt.

'I will bid you farewell then,' said Michael.

'And I,' added Gabriel.

'Nonsense. You have only just arrived,' said Jessie firmly. 'You will both remain here, or I will not answer for the consequences.' By this time, Ashbourne had unfastened his shirt and, after one brief, long-suffering glance at his wife, pulled it over his head. 'Now turn your back,' Jessie told him. Slowly, Raff turned round.

Two years before, Michael had been called upon to attend a dying man who had once served at sea. In order to make his last hours more comfortable, his wife had enlisted Michael's help in changing his night shirt. Whilst performing this task, Michael had noticed the ridged scars criss-crossing the man's back. 'Those are the marks of the lash,' his wife said. 'Flogged within an inch of his life, he was.' To his horror, Michael now saw exactly the same kind of scars marring the contours of his father's back.

'Tell them, Raff,' said Jessie.

He stood facing the window for what seemed like a long time, but what was probably only a minute or two. Finally, he turned to face them. Even his chest, though not marked nearly as badly, had not gone unscathed. 'This was the price I paid for telling my father that I wanted to marry your mother,' he said to Michael. 'My staying away from you was the price I paid to avoid your mother receiving the same treatment. May I put my shirt on again, my dear? I'm not accustomed to being as undressed as this in company.' There was a short pause as he put his appearance to rights. 'As a matter of fact, it took me some little time to recover physically and it was several weeks before I returned to full health. By then, my father had made all the arrangements for Dora to be sent to a distant county and for her family to be housed elsewhere. Despite all my father's warnings, I did attempt secretly to find her, but to no avail.'

'But this was infamous,' Michael whispered.

'I do not expect you to forgive me,' said Ashbourne after another long silence. 'All I ask is that you try to understand.'

Michael stared at his father. Snatches of memory rushed through his mind. Evangeline telling him she loved him and saying that she was sorry, whilst he turned coldly away; his mother whispering Raff's name as she breathed her last; Stacia saying that true love forgives.

None of them ever forgot what happened next. At one moment, Michael and Ashbourne were standing on opposite sides of the bed. At the next, Michael had moved hastily, almost clumsily, around to where his father was standing and caught hold of his hands. 'Of course I forgive you,' he said, his voice full of emotion. 'How could I do any other, especially when I know that my mother had done so?'

'Dora forgave me?' Ashbourne's voice was a little unsteady.

'The very last thing that she said was your name,' Michael replied softly.

Briefly, Ashbourne closed his eyes. When he opened them, his gaze sought out that of his wife. 'Of course she did,' said Jessie, smiling at him. 'If you love someone, then you forgive them.'

There was that phrase again. Suddenly, Michael knew that there was something that he must do. 'My lord,' he said to Ashbourne, 'if you will excuse me, I have an errand that will not wait.'

'Take a horse from my stables,' said Ilam.

It was Michael's intention to do exactly that, but he had only just reached Illingham Hall when Evangeline herself came into view, mounted on her pretty mare and with her groom riding behind. At sight of him, she blushed furiously. He could feel that his own colour was also heightened. 'Evangeline; Miss Granby. I was hoping that I might speak with you.'

'Yes … Oh yes,' she stammered, flustered. 'She wants to tell me to be gone, but is too polite to do so in public,' Michael thought to himself. She turned to her groom, who dismounted, and helped her down. She was about to walk towards Michael, when, with a little exclamation of annoyance, she turned back and took some papers from the bag attached to her saddle. As she did so, she stumbled slightly. Michael thought that she looked tired, as if she had been in the saddle for a long time.

'Let us go into the church porch and talk there,' he suggested.

They walked in silence through the lych gate and up the path. Fortunately, there was no one else about. Once inside the porch, they sat down on one of the benches and turned to face one another, both speaking at once as Michael said, 'Evangeline, I must tell you …' whilst at the same time, Evangeline said, 'Michael, I—' Michael gestured for Evangeline to speak first.

She had been planning what she would say next time she met him; how she would tell him, in the most dignified way possible, that her letter to the bishop had never been sent, that any boasting about conquests was something that she had grown out of long before. Now, in his presence, all of her carefully worded phrases went out of her head. She simply looked up at him, her eyes shining with tears not very far away and whispered his name. Then she was in his arms, and they were holding one another close, as if they would never let go. For a long moment they remained thus, arms around each other, her cheek against his shoulder, his resting against her hair.

Eventually, they moved a little apart. 'Michael, you must let me explain,' she began.

'Ssh,' he responded. 'It doesn't matter. It's all over now.'

'But Michael—'

'I love you.' Then of course she could not say any more, for they were kissing, and their kisses were like a solemn vow of love one for the other.

'Michael, I want you to know that my letter never went to the bishop,' she said, as soon as she was able. 'After you had gone, I went upstairs and found it in the leaves of a book. The letter that Elsie said she had sent for me had been a note to a friend that I had even forgotten I'd written.'

'But although you did not send a letter, someone else did.' He released her gently and stood up. 'My career is still under a cloud and may even be over. Evangeline, I should not be kissing you; holding you.'

She rose to her feet as well. 'But, Michael, you have said that you love me and you know that I love you.'

'Tell me honestly, do you think that your father would look upon me as a good match for you? I am disgraced and as good as penniless; soon I may even be unfrocked. Even if I am not, my career has hardly been characterized by glittering success. It may be years before I get my preferment. How can I ask you to share that with me?'

'It may not be as bad as you say,' she said, after a brief silence. During their embrace, her papers had become scattered on the bench and on the floor. 'You are right in saying that a complaint still exists, but that is only from one person. After you left yesterday, and since early this morning, I have been around the parish asking people what they think of you. Eustacia has been speaking to her staff and Mama has spoken with ours, too. See here' – she fumbled amongst her papers until she had found the right one – 'Mrs Gibbons, our housekeeper said "He was so kind and listened to me and let me well nigh talk his head off and never complained". And old Charlotte, whose husband died, said "He sat by his bedside for hours and such a lovely prayer did he say". And Mama has written a letter …' She fumbled over the pages.

'Evangeline, my dear, no more,' Michael interrupted, taking up her notes to read for himself. 'Have you really been riding all over the parish to collect these notes?' He looked at her tenderly, noting the dark smudges beneath her eyes. She looked exhausted. 'When did you set off this morning?'

'At first light,' she confessed. 'I wanted to catch some of the farmers before they went out into the fields. But that's not important. What matters is that the bishop should see that people here really love you. It would be a wicked crime for you to leave here now and so I shall tell him.'

'It's important to me,' he said. 'You have done all that for me?'

'There's nothing I wouldn't do for you,' she answered simply. After those words he had to kiss her once more. Now, the desire for her that roared through his veins was mingled with protectiveness, adoration and deep respect.

Eventually, she said, 'Michael, I want you to know that I never boasted about being able to … to snare you. I may have done that sort of thing years ago, but—'

He did not allow her to finish what she was saying. 'You are better than I, then,' he said after he had kissed her again, 'for I have always seen you as a prize to be won; a prize that was beyond my reach.'

'Not beyond your reach, but in your arms,' she murmured.

From various incidents that had occurred recently, the whole family had guessed the nature of Michael and Evangeline's feelings for one another. When the two of them turned up at the cottage looking as though there was an understanding between them, no one was particularly surprised.

Jessie was cradling the Honourable Miss Leonora Montgomery, who was awake but looking very contented, and she asked Evangeline whether she would like to hold her. Evangeline had very little experience of holding such a tiny child, but she sat next to Jessie, and took the baby carefully.

'They'll be cooing for ages,' said Ilam. 'Believe me, I know.'

'Shall we…?' Michael began. 'I mean, would you like to come downstairs for a glass of wine? Gabriel? My lord?'

'Thank you,' said Ashbourne. 'But don't call me that.'

'I can't call you—' Michael began, as they descended the stairs.

'I don't expect you to call me father, although you're free to do so if you wish. When Gabriel hated me, he used to call me Ashbourne. Now he calls me Raff. Or call me Raphael if you prefer.'

Michael did not answer, but made himself busy with pouring the wine. That done, he took a glass each to the other two men. 'Gabriel; sir,' he said, as he handed them over.

'"Sir" will do for now,' murmured Raff with a grin. 'Now, Michael – or would you prefer it if I continued to call you Mr Buckleigh?'

Gabriel gave a crack of laughter. The others looked at him. 'It's just the very entertaining notion of Michael calling you Raff whilst you call him Mr Buckleigh,' he explained. After they had all joined in the laughter, they felt much more at ease.

'Michael, we must consider your situation,' said Ashbourne.

Michael straightened his shoulders. 'When I was a boy, James Warrener told me that nobody owed me anything. I have always tried to live by that maxim. You owe me nothing and I have no wish to be beholden to you.'

Raff stared down into his wine for a long moment. Then he looked up at his first-born son. 'The other day, before you left this cottage, you told me that you were going to walk away just as I did. Well, perhaps I didn't exactly do that, but I was not there to help you. The reason I was not there, was because *my* own father would not help *me*. I want to be a better father than he was. I don't ask to fight your battles for you; just to be allowed to stand alongside you. May I do that?'

Michael stared at him, then slowly nodded. He was surprised at how moved he felt.

Chapter Twenty-one

———⁘———

The day following Michael and Evangeline's reconciliation brought good news. A note from Sir Lyle Belton arrived for the curate later in the day. In that note, he expressed his regret for his wife's hasty actions. Her foolishness had been encouraged by their scapegrace nephew, Lieutenant Fellowes, whose presence would not be welcome again at the Cedars. He considered her reasons for complaining to be quite inappropriate and had insisted that she write a letter to the bishop withdrawing her complaint.

'I find it hard to believe that Lady Belton would do such a thing,' said Lady Ashbourne. She had made such an excellent recovery that the doctor had given permission for her to be conveyed the short distance to Illingham Hall. There she would remain for the time being. This meant that Michael now had his cottage to himself.

'I suppose it is quite logical when one thinks about it,' Eustacia answered. 'Apparently Amelia had been determined that she should have Michael for herself. When she discovered that his affections were already given to Evangeline, she made such a fuss that her mother wrote to the bishop.'

'It seems very unfair that a man's career should be put in jeopardy all because of the infatuation of one silly woman,' Jessie replied.

'I hope it will not come to that, my love,' murmured Lord Ashbourne. His visit to Sir Lyle the previous evening had been private, brief and to the point. In it, he had reminded the baronet that it had been Sir Lyle's own nephew who had plotted against Evangeline whilst staying under his roof, using his conveyance to further his schemes. When Sir Lyle had complained that Michael and Evangeline had kissed in the vestry,

Ashbourne, much amused but not betraying the fact, had intimated that they had been as good as engaged at the time. Amelia's hopes of snaring the curate could never have been more than wishful thinking.

The first effect of Lord Ashbourne's offer to stand alongside Michael was felt when a letter arrived from the bishop a few days later, saying that he would wait upon the earl at Illingham Hall and that he would see Mr Buckleigh at the same time. The complaint had been withdrawn, but the bishop still felt that a discussion about the curate's career would be advisable.

Michael walked into the village to visit his father at Illingham Hall as soon as he had received the letter telling him of the change of plan. He found the earl sitting in the back parlour with his wife and daughter-in-law. The two youngest members of the Montgomery family had lately been attracting their fair share of attention, but they had both been taken upstairs by their respective nursemaids. Gabriel was out dealing with some estate business.

Michael was a little inclined to accuse the earl of manipulating the whole situation, but with a great air of innocence, Ashbourne denied this accusation. 'I informed the bishop that my wife had only just given birth to our child,' he explained. He was, as always, immaculately dressed, his every garment fitting him to perfection, his movements easy and graceful. 'I am not surprised that he offered to come here so that I would not have to leave Jez's side.'

Michael had spent many anxious hours wondering how to tell Theodora about his parentage. To his great surprise, in a quiet moment, Lord Ashbourne had offered to do so whilst Michael talked with Lady Ashbourne about the baby's Baptism. A little later, Michael had asked his sister very tentatively how she felt about the matter. The maturity of her reaction had surprised him.

'You were born when he was too young to be able to take responsibility for you,' she reasoned. 'Just think, Michael, he was less than my age!'

'He was much too young,' Michael agreed. He was thinking about how protective he felt towards his sister. Who had been there to protect and advise Ashbourne when he had most needed it? No one.

'He said that he would have liked to get to know you when you were younger, but that it had not been possible,' Theodora went on. 'Then when you got older, he did not want to interfere in your life.'

'Yes.' Ashbourne had obviously not told her about the beating he had received. Michael found himself admiring the man for his reticence.

Quite clearly it was something that he only shared if compelled to do so.

'Just think, I am in the same position as you, now,' said Theodora happily. 'You have a father and a stepfather, and so do I.' She paused. 'Of course, he isn't really my stepfather, but he says that I can think of him as one if I want to. You're so lucky, Michael. You haven't just found your father, you have a stepmother, and a brother and sister-in-law and a niece, and now you have a new baby sister as well. I only have you and Papa.'

'You can share any family I have,' he replied warmly, putting his arm around her.

Every day, Michael went to Granby Park and each time he was greeted with the news that Mr Granby had not yet returned. He did not know whether to be glad or sorry. He could not in all conscience offer for Evangeline until the threat of dismissal was gone, yet he longed to claim the privileges of an engaged man. Perversely, Mrs Granby seemed to have gained new resources of energy. Guessing what might be in the wind, she had developed strict notions of chaperonage and did not leave them alone for a single moment. The best thing that happened was when Evangeline brought him a glass of wine and fleetingly he touched her fingers with his own. How sweet it was, yet how tantalizing!

The meeting with the bishop took place in the library at Illingham Hall. It was a handsome yet welcoming room, with high, mullioned windows, dark panelling, and oak furniture set upon a dark-red carpet, whose predominant tone matched the curtains which hung at the windows. The bishop and Henry Lusty were shown into the room, where they were joined by Lord Ashbourne. On this occasion, he had chosen to dress in a coat of dull gold brocade with a matching waistcoat. His bow of greeting was perfection. 'Welcome to Illingham Hall, Bishop, Lusty,' he said. 'May I offer you a glass of wine?'

Both clergymen accepted, the bishop rather abstractedly. This was the first time that he had met Ashbourne. The earl's reputation together with Lusty's rather jaundiced view had led him to expect a drunken debauchee. This immaculate, smoothly courteous gentleman was very far removed from his imaginings. 'I trust that Lady Ashbourne is in good health,' said the bishop. 'I understand that she has come safely through her confinement.'

'That is correct,' replied the earl. 'She is well, as is my daughter. You may see them before you go, if you wish.'

'My congratulations,' said Lusty stiffly. Ashbourne acknowledged his words with a grave inclination of the head.

'Now, to Mr Buckleigh,' began the bishop.

Ashbourne held up his hand. 'Forgive me, but I did promise my son that I would not discuss this matter in his absence,' he said.

'Of course,' said the bishop, beaming. 'I shall be pleased to meet Lord Ilam again. I understand that he, too, has recently become a father.'

Ashbourne smiled, but said nothing. Moments later, the door of the library opened and Michael and Gabriel walked in and made their bows. Quite deliberately, Ashbourne walked over to them and stood next to Michael.

'Ah!' exclaimed the bishop, speaking before he had considered the wisdom of doing so. 'The likeness is not strong, but now that I see you side by side, I can detect it. Lusty thought that you might be related and I can see that it is so.'

Ashbourne raised those famous brows. 'Did he?' He glanced at Henry Lusty, who was looking very embarrassed, as well he might. 'He is right, of course. Mr Buckleigh is my son; a fact that I am delighted to acknowledge. One wonders, however, about Mr Lusty's reasons for sending him to Illingham. I would be interested to hear your thoughts upon the matter, Bishop.'

The bishop spluttered for a moment or two, his face turning a similar shade to his bishop's purple. 'I ... I ... I ... think that Mr Lusty's only motive was to allow the young man to prove himself,' he said.

'Without informing me or Lord Ilam?' Ashbourne continued. 'Anyone who did not have the highest regard for you might suspect a desire to embarrass me. Mr Lusty ought to have informed you that I am a shameless rake who is utterly beyond embarrassment.'

'A trait that you appear to have passed on to your son,' said Mr Lusty impetuously, unable to keep silent any longer. 'Part of the complaint says—'

'You mean the complaint that has been withdrawn?' enquired Ilam, a hint of menace in his voice.

'I would like the opportunity to speak,' said Michael, his voice firm and dignified. He turned to the bishop. 'I am grateful to you, my lord, for coming all this way to talk about my present situation. I am also grateful to you for three other reasons. The first is that in sending me here, whatever your reasoning might have been, you have enabled me to meet members of my family for the first time. I had thought myself to be virtually alone in the world. Now, I have a brother, a sister, relatives by marriage …' He paused, then looked at Ashbourne. 'And I have a father. You have also made it possible for me to meet the lady whom I hope very much to marry. Finally, though, you have given me another chance to exercise my ministry as a clergyman; a ministry that with your permission I would like to continue.'

The bishop nodded seriously. 'No doubt you would find it hard to support a wife on a curate's money.'

Michael drew back his shoulders. 'Her family is not poor, but I have no desire to live off my wife; or my father,' he added, looking at Ashbourne.

'A commendable sentiment,' agreed the bishop. 'There is much to discuss.' He turned to Ashbourne. 'My lord, with your permission, I would like to have a little private conversation with my chaplain.'

'Of course,' Ashbourne answered. He rang the bell. 'Conduct the bishop and Mr Lusty to the small drawing room,' he said to the servant who came at his summons. After the two clergymen had left the room, Ashbourne turned to Ilam. 'Give me a few minutes alone with Michael, if you please.' There was silence for a short time after Ilam had gone. Eventually, Ashbourne said, 'This is rather difficult for me to say. I'm only too aware that had I been permitted to marry your mother, you would be my heir and Ilam would not exist.'

'That had occurred to me,' Michael replied. 'I shouldn't like that. I … like Ilam.'

'It relieves me to hear you say so,' Ashbourne answered. 'Did I have two legitimate sons, however, I would expect to provide for the second as well as the first.'

Michael straightened his shoulders. 'You *have* provided for me,' he said stiffly. 'You paid for my education and care until I gained my majority.'

'You forget that for the early years of your life, that provision was made by my father,' Ashbourne replied. 'I consider that I have done less than my duty by you.'

'I don't want your duty,' Michael stormed. 'I want—' He broke off abruptly.

'Yes?'

Michael shook his head. 'I don't know what I want.'

After a long silence, Ashbourne said, 'You told the bishop that you would like to continue to be a clergyman. Is that really your desire?'

Michael explained how he had begun reading for the priesthood to please his stepfather, but had continued on this journey for its own sake.

'I would be deeply grieved if my journey on this route was to end now,' he confessed.

'Is that likely?' Ashbourne asked him. He poured them each a glass of wine. 'It does not seem to me that your sins have been so great.'

'You do not know the whole story,' said Michael heavily. He told Ashbourne about his two previous curacies and about the way in which each had ended. 'This was my last chance,' he concluded. 'I have thrown it away.'

'But it seems to me that most of this was not your fault anyway,' the earl responded. 'These women who have thrown themselves at you, for instance.' Michael lifted his head and stared straight into his father's eyes before looking away. 'I see,' Ashbourne responded. 'You lay that at my door.' Again, there was a long silence. Eventually, the earl said, 'My son, I am very far from contradicting you. You have an inheritance from me which is nothing to do with any money or goods that you may or may not choose to accept. For good or ill, you have found that you are attractive to women. It's something I discovered about myself in my youth. I have not always used that gift honourably. You have been much wiser and more restrained in the feeding of your appetites.

'There are great similarities between our natures and our abilities. There are also vast differences between the paths we have taken. But I believe that the solution for both of us is the same: a good marriage.'

'Sir?'

'Marry Evangeline Granby. Do you doubt her ability to keep any others who may pursue you at bay?'

Michael smiled wryly. He thought about her courage during the hold-up, her spirited defence of her virtue at the Cockerel, and of how she had ridden all over the parish on his behalf. 'I think her equal to anything.'

'And do you love her?'

'With all my heart.'

'Then let us see what transpires.'

It was not long after this that the bishop returned accompanied by Ilam. 'Mr Lusty is awaiting me in the carriage,' the bishop said. 'Lord Ashbourne, I would be grateful for a little private conversation with you.'

'Come with me,' said Ilam to Michael. Then, when they had got outside the door, he said, 'There is a lady here who is very anxious to see you. She's waiting in the garden.' Ilam led him to a side door, opened it and pointed to where Evangeline was pacing up and down on one of the gravel paths that went to make up the parterre.

When she saw Michael, she gathered up the skirts of her riding habit and ran to him. He caught hold of her and held her close. 'I couldn't wait,' she said. 'I had to know what was happening.'

Michael shook his head. 'I have no idea. At least I have had the chance to be very frank and open with the bishop,' he said.

'Was he angry?' Evangeline asked.

Michael shook his head. 'He seemed willing to hear me. Now he is speaking with my father.'

They both paused, taking in what he had just said. Neither of them commented upon it. 'I am determined to see him,' said Evangeline. 'The bishop, I mean. He must be made to understand that if there has been any impropriety, I am just as guilty as you are.'

'No, you are not,' he protested.

'I kissed you just as much as you kissed me,' Evangeline pointed out.

He had to draw her close, then, and kiss her lightly upon her lips. 'You are very gallant to say so, but a clergyman is supposed to set a better example.'

'Yes, but you are only a human being,' she reminded him, 'and not the archangel after whom you are named. Human beings make mistakes, so surely clergymen who make mistakes are more under-standing of their parishioners' failings because of it.'

'Then let us hope that the bishop himself has made plenty of mistakes in his time,' Michael said with wry humour. They walked through the parterre and down one of the avenues of over-arching roses, not yet in bloom, but promising to be a delightful sight in a month or two. 'Will you mind being married to a clergyman, if I am forgiven, and your father gives his consent?' Michael asked her.

'Will I mind?'

'It's not a very exciting calling in many people's eyes.'

'You can't really be yourself unless you are doing what seems right to you; so if you want to be a clergyman, then that's what I want as well.'

'Evangeline, dearest,' he murmured, pulling her into his arms, and kissing her. He paused. 'I must tell you that my father has offered to support me with an allowance. I told him that I did not want it. No doubt he would also purchase a commission for me, if I asked. I don't want that either.'

'Then neither do I,' Evangeline responded. She hesitated, then said, 'We will have my money after all.'

'I will not live off your money,' he said firmly.

'We have to live off something,' she pointed out reasonably. 'What does it matter where it comes from, after all? Once we are married, it will be ours, not mine.' When he was still silent, she said urgently, 'Michael, I love you because you're you, not because of any money that you have or haven't got.'

He smiled at her words, but there was a hint of anxiety behind his eyes. In an effort to dispel it, Evangeline said, 'I have to tell you, my darling, that I think you would look very fetching in purple. How old is the bishop, do you suppose? Might he be stepping down soon? Would you like me to suggest it?'

Michael had to laugh then, despite the continued uncertainty of his position.

They heard the sound of footsteps and saw Lord Ashbourne and the bishop walking towards them. Michael released Evangeline, flushing, but the bishop did not appear to be annoyed.

Evangeline stepped forward, despite Michael's attempts to prevent her. 'My lord Bishop,' she said curtsying, 'I am Evangeline Granby, and I am one of Michael's – I mean, Mr Buckleigh's parishioners.'

'I am pleased to meet you, Miss Granby,' said the bishop, beaming as older gentlemen generally did when confronted with Evangeline's remarkable beauty.

'I must tell you something about him before you make a decision,' she went on.

'Miss Granby,' the bishop began, whilst at the same time, Michael said, 'Evangeline,' and Lord Ashbourne looked on with an expression of wry amusement on his face.

'No, please let me speak,' said Evangeline, holding up one hand. 'Mr Buckleigh is a good man and a fine clergyman, and he is liked by all his congregation. I have here comments from many of the parishioners to say how much they value his work.' She handed him a notebook into which she had copied everything that anyone had said to her about Michael. 'If he has been guilty of impropriety' – here she coloured a little – 'it has been entirely my fault for leading him astray.'

'No, really, Evangeline,' Michael protested, as much because her words made him sound a little pathetic as for any other reason.

'Indeed,' murmured the bishop.

'You must not think that I make a habit of this,' Evangeline went on, her face still flushed. 'I must tell you, my lord Bishop, that I ... I love Mr Buckleigh, and ... and ...'

'Thank you, my dear, you have been very brave,' said the bishop, taking her hand and patting it benevolently. 'If you will forgive me for speaking now, I have some news which I think will please you both. Lord Ashbourne and I have been discussing your future, Buckleigh. Lusty's duties as my chaplain do not permit him to attend to the needs of Illingham as he would wish. The solution would be for him to have a parish nearer to Sheffield. Such has now become available. This means that the living of Illingham will shortly become vacant. Lord Ashbourne and I would both be pleased if you would be prepared to be installed as its vicar without delay.'

Michael's face was suffused with delight. 'Prepared?' he echoed. 'My lord, I should be delighted.' He wrung the bishop's hand, after which Evangeline surprised that clergyman by throwing herself into his arms and kissing him on the cheek. But it was Lord Ashbourne who was the nearest to being confounded when Michael turned to him and said quietly, 'Thank you ... Father.'

Chapter Twenty-two

———⚬◦⊙◦⚬———

'I cannot believe how good she was,' said Lady Ashbourne, looking fondly down at her daughter.

'She was much better behaved than Claire,' Eustacia replied frankly. Both babies had been baptized at the same ceremony, but whereas Jessie's baby had cooed contentedly throughout, Miss Claire Montgomery, perhaps more aware because she was older, did not settle, and assaulted everyone's ears with a piercing scream the moment that Michael had poured water over her head. The children were still clad in their christening dresses, following the ceremony which had been conducted by Michael in the family chapel at Ashbourne Abbey. Now, the family was gathered together in the drawing room, waiting for dinner to be announced.

There were a few additional guests. Mr and Mrs Granby were present, together with Evangeline, who was looking absolutely ravishing in a delectable shade of cream. Doctor Littlejohn was also there, as was Theodora Buckleigh. As Michael's sister, she was already accepted as a member of the family and had called Lord Ashbourne 'Steppapa' almost from the first, an appellation which clearly delighted him, for all his sang-froid.

The general conversation was interrupted as Michael appeared, having taken off his vestments and tidied his things away in the chapel. As he entered, there was a spontaneous round of applause, which made his colour rise a little.

'It was a wonderful ceremony,' said Lady Ashbourne, smiling. 'Thank you, Michael.'

Lady Ilam readily concurred with this sentiment, adding, 'No doubt

I will eventually persuade her not to scream the place down every time she sees you.'

'It was a pleasure,' he replied.

'You did appear to know one end of a baby from the other,' declared Lady Agatha. 'At least it won't be a punishment to see you occupy the vicarage.' She was still quite unabashed at the scene she had caused and, unsurprisingly, had never apologized.

Michael looked round at the other occupants of the room; his new relatives, friends, and his wife-to-be and her family. Following the news that he was to be installed as vicar, he had spoken to Mr Granby at the earliest possible moment. Mr Granby had been impressed with the young clergyman from the very first. He had always indulged himself with a dream that one day, Evangeline might seek to unite herself with as worthy a man. It was not a brilliant match, but any doubts that Mr and Mrs Granby might have felt were laid to rest in one moment, when the young couple had disagreed about some matter and, after a brief discussion, Evangeline had been heard to say, 'Of course it will be as you wish, Michael.'

Sir Lyle and Lady Belton and Amelia were among the guests at the baptism. A second and more public visit from Lord Ashbourne had had a great effect upon them. He had pointed out with all his customary suavity that the whole problem of Amelia's infatuation with Michael had been because there were so few single young men in the vicinity. He and Lady Ashbourne were intending to bring his stepdaughter out the following year. They were prepared to introduce Amelia to the *ton* at the same time. Recent events had made Lady Belton realize that this would be a wise course of action. Amelia was so delighted that she was even prepared to consult Evangeline about London manners. Evangeline was less than ecstatic about meeting Amelia who had behaved so traitorously. She was able to see the wisdom of being on good terms with close neighbours, however, and remembering the deviousness of Lieutenant Fellowes, could accept that Amelia was probably more deceived than deceiving.

Miss Leicester was also among the guests. There, too, Lord Ashbourne had worked his magic. A new school for girls was due to open in the town of Ashbourne shortly and the earl had persuaded the schoolmistress to help with advice and expertise. She was so delighted that she was very willing to forget her interest in the curate.

Michael's prospects had been improved considerably by some news that had been brought to Ashbourne Abbey by the earl's man of business. He had travelled to the village where Michael had lived and had discovered that James Warrener had indeed left the whole of his collection of antiquities to Michael in his will. The family, who had descended like vultures, although they had had nothing to do with their relative in his lifetime, had attempted to defraud Michael by just giving him one item, pretending that that had been the sum total of his inheritance. Michael, who had had no idea of Warrener's intentions, had simply accepted the bowl gratefully, with no idea that there was a good deal more owing to him. Lord Ashbourne's man of business had put an end to these fraudulent games and ensured that Michael's property was packed securely and taken to London, where it would remain awaiting Michael's instructions.

'It will at one and the same time give you an income and ensure that you will not be obliged to ask me for a damn thing,' Ashbourne had told him carelessly.

'I'm well aware that I owe this to you,' Michael had responded. Ashbourne had waved his hand dismissively. Then the clergyman had added, 'I'm happy that it should be so.'

The day when Michael had actually been installed as vicar had been an occasion for celebration involving the whole village. It had coincided with the beginning of the week when the wells were dressed with greenery and blessed, and Michael had thoroughly enjoyed taking part in this ceremony which was at the heart of the village community. His whole family had walked round with him too, as had Evangeline and her parents. I'm no longer alone, he thought to himself. It was a thought that had continued to warm him long after the tea party that Ilam had given for the village was at an end.

Before dinner was announced, Ashbourne, Michael and Gabriel had gone upstairs to the long gallery. Briefly, they had stood beneath the portrait of Raff's father. 'If I'm honest, part of the reason that I stayed away from this place for so long was because of that,' the earl had said. 'I always felt as if I lived in his shadow. I even felt that way after he was dead. I don't think I really shook it off completely until I married Jessie.'

'That's funny,' Gabriel had said, passing on to the portrait of the present earl, 'I always felt as if I lived in yours.'

'Good God,' Raff had exclaimed blankly.

Michael had smiled to himself. He had never felt as if he had lived in anyone's shadow; yet there had been a part of his life that had been unknown to him, rather like a forbidden room concealed behind a locked door. Quite unexpectedly, the door had been opened and his life had acquired a new dimension. He was still exploring what it all meant, but now he did not feel threatened or afraid.

They had walked on to a section of the wall on which hung a painting of an unknown Elizabethan gentleman. 'I would like a painting of my sons to hang here,' the earl had said. '*Both* my sons.'

'But, my lord,' Michael had protested.

'Damn it, which of us is he speaking to now?' Gabriel had asked his father.

'I don't know, but I fancy we can account for him between us,' Ashbourne had replied. 'Two pairs of coal heavers' shoulders are better than one, after all.'

In no time at all, Michael had found himself pinned firmly to the wall. 'Now, *Michael*, who am I?' Ilam had asked, grinning.

'You're Gabriel,' Michael had answered, his expression mirroring that of his half-brother.

'And who am I?' Ashbourne had asked.

There was a moment's stillness. 'You're my father,' Michael had replied.

'What about a portrait of yourself with your whole family, sir?' Gabriel had suggested, after they had released him and they began to make their way downstairs.

'Excellent idea,' Raff had agreed. 'This has been a splendid day altogether. Much though it pains me to do so, I have to admit that I am very proud of both of my sons.'

'You will unman us with this praise,' Ilam had replied.

'Such is not my intention; but you do amaze me, both of you. Not for you the years of dissipation and senseless behaviour that were my path in life. You have both done much better than I.'

Suddenly, Michael had known exactly the right thing to say. 'But we had the advantage over you, for we had a much better father.'

After the two babies had been baptized, Michael and Evangeline found the chance to wander off and lose themselves in each other's arms.

'How does it feel to be part of a family?' Evangeline asked him, as they strolled amongst the trees behind the parterre.

'A short time ago I wouldn't have known how to answer that,' he said. 'Now, I can say that it feels very good. You guessed, didn't you?'

'I suspected that you must be Lord Ashbourne's son, but I had no way of knowing how much you knew. That was why I went to see him instead of you. When Lady Agatha said, in that wicked way that she has, that she was taking you to meet the earl, I knew that she was hoping to witness some sort of scene. I thought that the best thing that I could do would be to get there first so that I could warn him.'

'Then I arrived and made a scene anyway,' Michael answered, leading her to one of the stone seats that was set in an arbour amongst the trees. 'For how long did you suspect?'

'To be honest, I had an inkling from the very first,' Evangeline confessed. 'When I saw you in Sheffield and you looked at me in that rakish way, you sort of reminded me of him.'

'There was a time when I would have fought against that,' he replied. 'I can't deny that I feel the seeds of … of rakishness within myself; but I don't need to act upon that tendency. I can make a choice. Nevertheless, my darling, when I look at you, desire comes roaring through my veins like a fire.' He groaned, and pulled her closer. Then he kissed her, holding her tight, plundering her mouth with his passion. When at last he released her, her hair was somewhat disarranged and her lips were rosy from his kisses.

'Michael, do you suppose that you are the only one to feel this fire?' she said, as soon as she was able. 'You are not a rake: you are a principled man with strong passions, and my hope is that from now on all of them will be directed towards me.'

For some little time after this, his every effort was exerted to assure her that this would indeed be the case.

Epilogue

—⚬⚬⚬⚬—

After Michael and Evangeline had gone off on their honeymoon, Theodora went to stay with Lord and Lady Ashbourne at Ashbourne Abbey. Eventually, she would make her home with her brother and new sister-in-law at Illingham Vicarage. She also spent some time with Lord and Lady Ilam, and frequently visited Mr and Mrs Granby, who were finding the house a little empty and quiet with their only daughter gone.

The first time that she stayed overnight at Granby Park, she was invited to sleep in Evangeline's old room. 'You will find some of her things are still here,' Mrs Granby said.

Theodora walked over to the window, remembering some of the conversations that she and Evangeline had had on that very window seat. Lying on the chest of drawers was a book and, picking it up, she saw that it was Mary Wollstonecraft's *A Vindication of the Rights of Woman*.

'Borrow it if you like,' said Mrs Granby. 'I think Evangeline has finished with it.'

'Do you know, I think I just might,' Theodora replied with a smile.